FATHER
SWEET

FATHER SWEET

j.j. martin

DUNDURN
TORONTO

Cover image: istock.com/SlothAstronaut
Printer: Mi5 Print, Toronto

Library and Archives Canada Cataloguing in Publication

Martin, J. J., 1970-, author
　　Father Sweet / J.J. Martin.

Issued in print and electronic formats.
ISBN 978-1-4597-4396-0 (softcover).--ISBN 978-1-4597-4397-7 (PDF).--
ISBN 978-1-4597-4398-4 (EPUB)

　　I. Title.

PS8626.A76954F38 2019　　　　C813'.6　　　　C2018-906504-4
　　　　　　　　　　　　　　　　　　　　　　　　　　C2018-906505-2

  Conseil des Arts du Canada / Canada Council for the Arts  Canada ONTARIO ARTS COUNCIL / CONSEIL DES ARTS DE L'ONTARIO / an Ontario government agency / un organisme du gouvernement de l'Ontario

1　2　3　4　5　　23　22　21　20　19

We acknowledge the support of the **Canada Council for the Arts**, which last year invested $153 million to bring the arts to Canadians throughout the country, and the **Ontario Arts Council** for our publishing program. We also acknowledge the financial support of the Government of Ontario, through **Ontario Creates** and **Ontario Creates**, and the **Government of Canada**.

Nous remercions le **Conseil des arts du Canada** de son soutien. L'an dernier, le Conseil a investi 153 millions de dollars pour mettre de l'art dans la vie des Canadiennes et des Canadiens de tout le pays.

Care has been taken to trace the ownership of copyright material used in this book. The author and the publisher welcome any information enabling them to rectify any references or credits in subsequent editions.

The publisher is not responsible for websites or their content unless they are owned by the publisher.

Printed and bound in Canada.

VISIT US AT

 dundurn.com | @dundurnpress | dundurnpress |  dundurnpress

Dundurn
3 Church Street, Suite 500
Toronto, Ontario, Canada
M5E 1M2

author's note

I am asked often if this story is true.

This is a work of fiction. It is not a *Million Little Pieces* memoir. It is a personal story inspired by unfortunate, all-too-real circumstances.

Some readers, especially those familiar with the Hollywood film industry or my former fellow parishioners at Good Shepherd Parish in Blackburn Hamlet, may believe they recognize certain persons. I have not lifted anyone whole cloth from reality and plunked him or her into this story, though they may have influenced particular characters. So, I encourage you to resist the urge to cast living or dead real-life persons in the roles of the fictional people in the novel.

What I have tried to do, however, is capture certain places and times, and maybe some shadows of truth. Hopefully nothing that matters has been lost.

It is important to note that clerical abuse of authority, which has resulted too often in physical and sexual abuse, is real and ongoing. It is impossible to talk about clerical sexual abuse in Canada without mentioning the Church and state's exploitation of Indigenous communities, and the settler community's failure to acknowledge and stop that abuse. The Canadian government colluded with Christian churches to abuse thousands of Indigenous children for generations. The last residential school was shut only in the 1990s.

The connection between governments and church-run schools did not end there, however. To this day, Canadian governments continue to subsidize and administer Catholic schools in state-sponsored religious favouritism unique to Canada among similar countries. Although I attended these schools, a debate is long overdue regarding whether or not they should exist as taxpayer-supported institutions.

Cases of abuse continue to be revealed around the globe. As I was editing one portion of this book, I deliberately toned down the pedophilic overtones of the fictional Mexican apostolic society. However, taking a break one evening, I was shocked to read new details of the Peruvian Sodalitium Christianae Vitae of Father Luis Figari. This society can best be described as a priest-and-child BDSM cult. Truth is so often worse than fiction.

If you wish to do service against the very real atrocities of clerical abuse, state-sanctioned or otherwise, I advise you to donate money or time to the Survivors Network of those Abused by Priests (SNAP) and/or to the National Centre for Truth and Reconciliation. Both are real institutions seeking justice. The former offers help to individual survivors, and the latter focuses on large-scale reconciliation and restitution issues, involving the tens of thousands of Indigenous children in Canada who suffered as a result of systematic exploitation and oppression by the state and Christian churches.

For additional reading, there are excellent academic and non-fiction resources available for your review. I recommend the very powerful *A Knock at the Door*, edited by Aimée Craft, or the

Final Report of the Truth and Reconciliation Commission, available from the Truth and Reconciliation Commission; and of course, A.W. Richard Sipe's seminal *Sex, Priests, and Power: Anatomy of a Crisis*. Finally, there are endless heartbreaking personal stories available through the SNAP and TRC websites.

J.J. Martin
Autumn 2018

Caught in a mess of evil and good.

— Alex Janvier

part one

1

One time, my younger brother Jamie and I found a robin's nest with only one egg in it. It reminded me of our suburban town. Like an egg in a nest, Blackburn Hamlet was snuggled into a forest on all three of its sides. If I could have had my way, I would have chosen to live in those woods, where I felt free, instead of the house I shared with my parents and Jamie on Woodwalk Crescent. Of course, twelve-year-old boys are not given such choices.

Although the town was one hundred and fifty years old when we moved there in the early seventies, a big rush of development had refashioned Blackburn, changing it from a dingy old farming village to a suburb of Ottawa with new houses strung out along roads that echoed with the sounds of road hockey, bikes, and balls.

You could bicycle every street in an hour, easy. Whenever we did, we traced all of Jamie's and my regimented world. School. Home. Scouts. Church.

One bright morning, we passed the rectory where Father Sweet lived. The door opened, and I was startled to see Danny Lemieux, another altar boy I knew, emerge with a backpack, as if he had slept over. His eyes met mine as I rode past him as if in slow-mo, and we stared at each other without greeting.

It was so much better spending time outside town. To the south was an ancient marsh. To the east, farms and scrub led to the original wilds. And to the north and west, past a municipal nursery and bound only by rivers, was unspoiled land that we kids turned into a playground, outside the reach or rules of adults. We could be ourselves there.

It was a place of woodland, farms, and muskratty bogs, full of fox and beaver, too close to the city for bears, I believed. We did whatever we pleased on the well-packed mud trails we said were made by Indians. Often Jamie and I would collide with friends, hiding and then hollering amid the trees and ravines. We built forts, shot at raccoons with BB guns, caught frogs, and slid naked in the clay at Green's Creek, the local trickle.

We knew that Nature held death and danger. Our parents were always telling us that. But to boys, danger sounds like adventure. Except for bears, of course. I did not like to think of bears. Nature was the first place I discovered beauty and peace. You just relaxed and there it was. Truth. As much as you arrived in Nature, it entered you. It was obvious how to act and what to do. Everything made great sense. Not like at home.

The 1970s were a time of transformation. Traditions were changing, confusing the adults. And confusing us. At home, I kept myself organized at all times and thought of myself as a Scout, even when the troop was not in session. It was my defence. Exactly as Baden-Powell advised. I made my bed each day and slept at night with the windows open as late into each season I could. Each morning, the dawn chorus would wake me, and I could be the first to rise. My first cool breaths could be the wet air of the forest around Blackburn. If I was careful and didn't make any noise, I could enjoy the quiet of the house. I could even slip outside, and to the garden shed.

There, we protected that lone robin's egg in the nest we found, and we kept it warm with a box and a light bulb.

I probably gave it a name, the unhatched chick. But I don't trust my memory to recall, not entirely.

When you name something, you give it a soul. We can't give names to the things we don't know, and nameless things aren't familiar to most of us.

What I do remember is that the egg never hatched, despite the waiting and my hopeful midnight visits. Weeks went by. Eventually we cracked it open. And there, inside, we found the shrivelled ball of a dead monster.

This was the summer Jamie and I, both of us devoted Boy Scouts, were building a platform tree fort a fifteen-minute jog from our home into the bush. Finishing our outpost far from adults, before school started in September, was the most important thing in the world to me.

This was the last summer I slept with the window open.

Every person has one summer in their life that claims him, and this was mine.

2

"Come here," I said to Jamie. "I'll teach you how to know if rain's coming."

We stood at the edge of a small clay escarpment, above the Green's Creek ravine, observing treetops and the birds scattering and socializing. Behind us stood a big, old chestnut tree, whose trunk branched at ten feet into a giant hand, as if to catch a huge chestnut ball dropped from God.

It was in this tree where we were building the fort. My mind had it kitted out like a multi-level Japanese forest temple from a Samurai book I'd seen in the library, but it had become modest in the building. A mostly level platform lashed and nailed into the crook of the "hand," and some half-dreamed plans to construct a roof.

It was loud with swishing trees as the wind turned.

"You know, the bush communicates," I said. "Know what I mean?'

"Sort of," Jamie said, but he didn't really look like he did.

"First, listen," I said. "The birds sound different. Hear it? They're all chirping at once? Means 'take shelter.' Right before the rain starts, they'll go silent. You listen for that. Now, smell."

We both inhaled, enjoying the gorgeous smell of the air, drenching our lungs with oxygen.

"That wet-plant smell? You get it?"

"Yah."

"Like when you crush weeds. Plants give off that scent before it rains. About a half hour." I stretched out my hand at the poplars. "Now, lookit. See, the leaves show their undersides. They do that when a front comes in, the wind will blow. The leaves twist."

"Hmm," he said.

"I bet you five dollars Mum is having a migraine."

"Nah. We haven't been home since morning."

"Huh?"

"She said *we* give her migraines."

"Wanna bet?" I said. I smacked his shoulder. "Mum gets migraines when the air pressure drops. And it drops before it rains.

"I'll take that bet, sucker."

"Good. You'll pay me tonight."

I laughed. I planned to give him plenty of grief later, making it look like I was profiting off him.

"Now, you wanna know the last way to tell if it's gonna rain? For real?"

"K, how?"

"Check the newspaper night before."

He grimaced. "Aw, you bugger."

I felt proud of my skills, which I'd learned from other Scouts, the Scout leaders, guys like Mike Racine, reading, and, most of all, listening to the bush. There's nothing fake about a woodland. It's not pretending to be anything it's not. And there was more there than we could see or hear. Butterflies see colours we can't. The flowers have colours and patterns invisible to us. Animals hear sounds our ears are unable to catch. When you are in the forest, you may have your opinions, but you need to assume it knows more than you do. That's being natural. I remembered what Mike had told us: "Within Nature, there's vast freedom."

I loved Nature and I hated school. I hated it because it was everything opposite to the bush. But, of course, Jamie and I were not in control of our own lives. We were just kids. We had to endure the rules, do our chores, to satisfy our teachers, priests, and parents so that they would leave us in peace.

"Well, well, if it isn't the gaylord brothers," said a pubescent, cracking voice.

Coming up the trail were Rob and Squirm, two bullies, each a year older than me.

"Two little queers, running through the trees, k-i-s-s-i-n-g," said Rob, who was tall and smarter than troll-like Squirm.

"That doesn't make any sense, kid," I said to Rob, keeping my cool.

"Don't call me kid, you kid."

We moved to leave. I didn't want them to get any sense there was a tree fort behind us. Fortunately, the lumber we stole from palettes behind Joe's Variety was stacked and hidden in the bushes. You couldn't spot the actual structure unless you looked up the tree.

"Whoa, whoa! Where you off to in such a hurry?" asked Squirm.

"Nowhere," I said, trying to sound nonchalant. "You sucks want to talk?"

"How about you, shorty? You scared?"

"Don't call him that," I said.

"Fuck you guys!" My brother's voice was downright squeaky whenever he shouted, and it didn't help him appear any more threatening.

"Shorty's feisty today!" They laughed at us.

"Sticks and stones," I said, and then pulled out a rumour that had been circulating behind Rob's back for ages. "Lookit, I don't give a care. But I'm not the one who showed his dink to the hobo."

Rob and Squirm exchanged surprised glances and my little brother's jaw dropped.

"You shut up," said Rob, jabbing his finger at me.

Squirm searched for a comeback. "He made good money off that."

"Yah! I got ten bucks, you fag." Rob was sneering down at my little brother.

"You like that word. Takes one, I guess."

Rob gritted his teeth. "We got something for youse. Squirm, bring the bag over."

Squirm came to the front lugging a black garbage bag. I started breathing hard when I saw by the sag of the plastic that something big and dead was in there.

"We got a little present. Since our paths crossed. Hey, you still shitless over bears, Fonzarelli?"

Now would be a good time to take off, but I couldn't catch Jamie's eye. He was staring at the garbage bag.

"This loser was in Cubs with me," said Rob to Squirm.

"Yah, before you got kicked out of the pack," I said.

"I couldn't stand hanging out with you babies anymore."

"Right," I said. "Is that why they sent you home? Like a baby?"

"I wasn't the one who cried when we went to that stupid little zoo in the country. All over some old bear."

I shrugged and tried to appear that this wasn't a big deal, but it was true. I nearly fainted on a field trip to an animal reserve in Kanehsatake, a Mohawk community in Quebec. We were at the fence for the bear enclosure. I drifted to the back of the pack, next to Akela, and even found myself clutching at his elbow. The cedar bush shook, and a big male bear lumbered toward us. To my eyes, the scrawny chain-link fence seemed useless as chicken wire against those claws and a good shove from those legs. I gasped and cried and the whole pack laughed. The ruckus drew the attention of the bear, which — curious, and maybe hungry — stood up to get a look at the kid in the back trying to climb up Akela's arm, and meanwhile my heart choked me.

Squirm, who was a big dumb kid, probably held back a grade but so brawny he might one day have a career in football or security, manoeuvred behind us.

"Why don't you leave us alone?" Jamie said. "Mind your own business."

Rob seemed delighted by these questions. He took a deep, malicious breath like he'd been given the perfect opportunity to teach us something important. "'Cause," he said, with a hunter's smile, "you're here, and we're here. So here we are."

My brother and I looked at one another.

"And now we found you and shorty running around like queer squirrels doing God knows what."

My blood went hot. "You're full of shit."

He laughed. "You don't get it, kid. It's okay, I'm here to show you but good."

Squirm reached into the bag and pulled out by the tail, with his bare hands, a dead animal covered in mud.

"Got a bear cub here," he said. "Once the mama bear smells the cub on you, well, you know what she'll do to you. Unless you get down on your knees and kiss my boots. And call me master."

My brother sniffled and I could see his eyes filling up. Dead things made him nauseous.

"You guys are just brutal," Jamie whispered.

"Squirm," I said, in a calm tone. "You touching that thing with your bare hands is pretty stupid."

He laughed and blinked at me. "Chicken?"

"Course not. It's only a dead raccoon."

"No, bonehead. It's a bear cub."

"Bears haven't got tails."

Squirm looked down at the tail in his hand.

"You know what roundworm is?" I asked.

"Shut up, you faggot!"

"Better go to the clinic for your shots. Probably you both have roundworm now. They'll eat up your brain. You especially, Squirm. You're not playing with a full deck."

Squirm dropped the raccoon.

"Just being helpful, guys," I said. "Never touch a dead raccoon."

Their faces shifted with worry. "I barely touched it. It was mostly Squirm!"

I felt the first drops of rain hit my forehead and cheek.

"Aw, shit," Rob said. "We're gonna get soaked."

"I want to go see the doctor. Like, right now," said Squirm.

They turned and ran off, quick and demented.

"Simple as that," I said to Jamie, who was wiping snot on his sleeve.

New raindrops dappled the mud on the raccoon. It looked pitiful. I wanted to apologize to this unfortunate, dignified animal dragged into our stupid middle-school drama.

My brother grabbed my elbow and I felt him shaking. We stood like that for a bit so they could get ahead of us and home, over by the rundown old houses near the original public school on the East side of Blackburn.

I used a thick branch to move the raccoon carcass off the trail, so it could rot in peace. Jamie's face was pale.

"Hey. Listen to the rain falling on the leaves," I said quietly to him, touching his back. "There's nothing like that sound."

"I really thought they'd kick the crap out of us."

"Nah. They're just giving us the gears. They're goons. Retards. They figure they own the bush. Nobody owns the bush. The Queen, maybe."

"Is that true what you said about roundworm?"

I looked at him. "I said what I said to keep us safe. It was the right thing at the time."

My brother gazed sourly at the carcass.

"But never touch a dead animal with your bare hand," I said. "I didn't lie. Not really. A white lie, maybe."

The clouds stopped hesitating and let us have it in sheets.

When we got home, drenched and dank, we heard Mum sigh from her bedroom. We kicked off our shoes, I sucked air through my teeth and we crept toward her, lying in the dim like a vampire.

"I assume you beggars want dinner," she said, massaging her eyebrows. "You boys will be the death of me."

The hall light cast a beam across her face. She looked ghastly, with the dry, pancake-batter bags under her eyes so dark they looked green. Half her head was in rollers, and the other half bed-mussed. She'd been trying to sleep off the migraine.

I tried blocking her exit at the hallway door. "Mum, don't worry. We'll eat Shreddies or open a can of soup."

"Don't be ridiculous," she replied, reaching for the wall blindly.

"We're sorry, Mum. We gave you a headache," said Jamie.

She stood swaying in the half-light before leaving her room.

"I'll offer my suffering to the souls in purgatory," she said in a faraway voice. "Lordy, use my sacrifice for something."

She went to the kitchen and burned two chicken breasts in the pan and singed her thumb. After she collapsed on her bed, we had Shreddies in front of the TV. Dad came home and we listened to him growl at her while he ate the burnt chicken.

My brother tried to pay me five dollars to close off our bet, but I told him to forget it and just put his faith in me, next time.

3

I hated going back to school; I wished summer would go on forever. I found the school year a tough slog and was not looking forward to the return, only a few short weeks away. Every day during the school year, Jamie and I walked to the local English Catholic school.

The schoolyard was always raucous with swearing. It was weird: we were punished for swearing in English, but there wasn't a problem if we swore in French. Maybe speaking French was a sign that we were absorbing our education, so we could curse with abandon in the other language because it didn't count. Teachers knew what we said was vile, but took no action. Of course, we did not learn those words in French class, but from *joual*, the sloppy, blasphemous street French of teenaged neighbours and drunk uncles. Ours was a Catholic school, so it was made all the more bizarre that the swears we used out loud were sacrilegious. Whereas English cursing is based on filth and sex, French insults the Catholic Church, God, and the dignities of our rite.

And for all the Christly decency and love the school advertised, to the kids and given the way we all treated each other it remained — mostly — *l'enfer tout décâlicé. Ostie.* Fucking hell. Goddamnit. Jamie certainly understood this.

Jamie was born one year after me. He has epilepsy. From time to time he suffered a "flash" (his word). A grand mal seizure. I had grown up witnessing them and found them no more than an unwelcome intrusion, but my parents were enormously embarrassed by these episodes. Afterward, he always needed a nap, and my parents harassed him for laziness because they believed he was malingering or being weak. They had difficulty accepting that the epilepsy wasn't just a ploy to stay home from school. As he grew older, seizures were happening more often.

Finally, when Jamie began grade three, they took him to the doctor and he was formally diagnosed.

This was a really heavy blow to our parents. The label. After hearing the diagnosis, my mother went completely silent, waited until home, then dropped to her knees and hugged Jamie while bawling into his neck. She sobbed so loudly I was certain that there was more to it. My father stood nearby, fists clenched. They said no words. Over Mum's shoulder, Jamie looked at me with wide, confused eyes. What in hell was happening? I shrugged at him. There was nothing to say. I didn't see what had changed, except that now Jamie had medicine to take each day, and it would reduce the seizures. It all seemed like good news. To me, anyway.

The next day, for some reason, my mother marched into the principal's office to tell him about my brother's diagnosis and to say that teachers should not expect much from him.

Of course, by afternoon recess, the whole school knew. My little brother became a great subject of ridicule in the schoolyard.

I found Jamie being passed around like a toy by a group of laughing kids who were calling him "spaz" while they tried picking him up. I saw his face try to be game with the teasing.

"Come on, guys," he said. No one acknowledged him. He had become an object. A doll.

He clammed up and lowered his eyes in defeat, in a way that made my heart hurt.

And that was it. Rage blasted out of me, like fire from a coal furnace.

I selected the biggest kid in the group — an arrogant boy named Sacha Tusk — and charged at him like a ram. I could not talk or shout if I wanted to, my throat was choked off. Before I knew it, I had landed a strong, hard punch into his right eye and he staggered backward, falling onto his ass, holding his face. All laughing stopped. I took a moment to wipe away my tears. Then I straddled Sacha, clobbering him while he cried and covered his head and the group of kids grew huge around us, chanting.

It was the first time I ever punched anyone.

When Mr. Plante arrived and broke up the mob, no one would admit what had happened, including me. When I got in trouble that night at home, neither I nor Jamie told our parents anything. We were put to bed without supper.

But I felt great.

After brushing my teeth, I stood at the door of Jamie's room and smiled at him with great satisfaction. He looked up from his *Fantastic Four* and smiled back.

4

All I looked forward to, with the end of summer drawing near, was going back to Scouts. A new leader joined the troop over a year ago.

It was last spring, when we were given our special badges in celebration of seventy years of Scouting in Canada. Right after the flag-raising ceremony, a big, dark-haired man wearing a lumber jacket hovered near the exit, keeping one hand wrapped on the push bar.

Our Scout leader, whom we called "Blanter," waved this guest to his side, then introduced him.

"I want you kids to treat this fellow with respect, you hear me?" said Blanter. "I don't want any laughing or name calling. You're here to learn from this, uh, this gentleman. So keep quiet. Right?"

Blanter stood with a raised finger while our guest stood silently and blankly at his side. "Right? Okay then. Let's give a warm Scouts welcome to Mike Racine, a real, live Algonquin Indian who drove in from Maniwaki to visit us."

Mike Racine kept his head bowed and said nothing. We clapped, politely.

After a pause, Mike opened his mouth to speak. "Anyways. Let's go outside." His voice was quiet, reedy and gentle.

Mike came to teach campfire hygiene, but he also led us on a springtime walk in the woods by the Legion hall. As we went along, he pointed out trees and birds, naming them in a low voice that drew us close to hear it better.

"Sometimes if I get lazy I'll think of the cardinal as only a red blue jay, but they are very different. There is a deep lesson there, if you pay attention. Let's listen, if we can hear. The cardinal has a beautiful, complex song. The blue jay screeches," said Mike. "They have completely different batting styles, too."

Amid the troop laughter, I'm sure I saw Blanter sulk.

We found a bare patch of earth and Mike showed us how to build a sandwich of logs to store a fire overnight.

"Watch," he said. Mike took his hands out of his pockets and we saw that he had no tools, no equipment other than a folding knife. He built a few hip-high posts using sticks and cracked logs out of deadwood with his boot, loading them into the posts with moss sandwiched in between. "Got it?"

It made sense. It was logical. All his lessons, taught with barely three words, got into us fast. The words would be useless. He took out a Bic lighter and touched off a blaze at the cardinal points of the structure that he had built. It was beautiful and simple.

He showed us how to store fire and move fire, alternating smoke levels.

Blanter seemed so average by comparison.

While demonstrating how to clear embers, Mike described a forest fire he and his local band fought off using only controlled burns and shovels. Not a single house was lost, though it burned all around his town. We were slack-jawed.

Here was a big, silent country man who hunted and knew the land in a way we could only dream of. Unlike Blanter, who was okay overall, but always seemed keen to sell us on something he read in the Scout book, Mike didn't have to get his knowledge from a book. He was a guy who saw things as they were and operated with confidence.

"This guy's my hero," I whispered to Jamie.

5

It was our final Scout meeting before the summer. Blanter had lost his voice but for a hoarse whisper, and he could not command the troop. Mike Racine stepped in as temporary Troop Leader.

He seemed to get along easily with all the Scout Leaders, bantering with them and telling them quiet jokes, and we loved Mike's approach, leaving the Legion hall and going straight into the woods to talk about Scoutcraft until sundown.

"The earth is your mother," said Mike. "You know what mothers are like. You love them. You help them. They are wise. And they love you and feed you." His eyes twinkled conspiratorially. "But you misbehave, and they smack your ass, like real hard."

While the Scouts laughed, the other troop leaders there growled at us, "Boys, boys."

"You might think Nature is yours. It's not. You belong to Nature. It's not yours to use. The earth has let you be here."

By the time his session with us ended and we marched back to the Legion hall, the entire troop had slowed, trying to copy his quiet manner.

On the walk, I plucked a long grass and chewed the stem.

"Sweetgrass, eh? Good for you," he said.

"Yah?" I said.

"You angry?" he asked. "Stressed?"

"Why do you ask that?"

"When you're angry, chew some. Or throw a bit on the fire and let the smoke touch you. It's a medicine."

At that he walked on ahead, but somehow left me feeling ten feet tall.

"Good tip," I said. "Thanks, Mike."

Cautiously, Jamie asked Mike why he was here visiting our troop.

"Doing my part," Mike said. "You doing your part?"

Two Patrol Leaders approached Blanter to ask if Mike could return.

"Why not? The price is right," whispered Blanter, holding his throat. "He looks like Jesse from *Beachcombers*, eh?"

I rolled my eyes and wished Mike was our Scout Leader.

6

When Scouts was over for the season, Jamie and I started spending more time in the bush. Still a week or so of school to go. The excitement for the summer was building for both of us. He rode ahead of me. Racing on his bicycle, leaning to the speed.

As soon as we entered the greenbelt's leafy shade, we relaxed and took deep breaths of the cool, woody air.

"Everything makes sense in a forest," I said to Jamie. "It's simple, you know?"

We kept riding and soon came to our tree fort. It was immediately obvious that someone else had been there. Rob and Squirm, probably. It sickened me to think of them invading our tree fort. I was glad they hadn't destroyed it, at least. They'd carved their names in the trunk along with a few others, but that was all. Somehow, it had become a little community centre and escaped destruction. Someone had left a soggy *Playboy* there, which we flipped through and laughed at and then got boners from all the pictures of the plump boobies and long, shining legs. Mostly we just lay on our backs and talked, manning an outpost away from the adults.

"Today, Miss Cross got sick," Jamie said, as we lay on our backs in the treehouse. "They had no time to get a supply teacher. After recess, she was gone and Mrs. Byle was there instead."

"The librarian?"

"She brought a projector and showed us two movies. The first was, like, don't let strangers give you candy. This fat guy in an ugly green car gives this girl a peppermint and then grabs her. Why?"

"I don't know. Kill her, I guess."

"Yah, but what for?" My brother opened his arms toward the sky. "Maybe he just wanted to give her more candy."

"Come off it. At Halloween those mental cases put razor blades in the apples or poison the toffee."

"So, why would someone do that?"

"You really don't get it," I said. "You're too young to see how the world works."

I said this often to Jamie, taking advantage of my additional months of life.

"What do you mean?"

"Does anything adults do make sense to you?"

He was thoughtful for a few moments.

"Next, Mrs. Byle shows us this cartoon," he said, ignoring the slight and continuing on. "An old guy keeps turning away people who come to his door looking for help. There's, like, a beggar, and a leper, and a kid. The old guy slams the door. Right? Then he's sick, and he's dying. Now the beggar, the leper, and the kid reappear to him, but now it turns out they're Jesus, like, they magically transform into Jesus — and Jesus asks why he slammed the door on him three times. So this old guy cries and Jesus forgives him and he goes to heaven."

Since we attended the Catholic school, we had to suffer through a lot of movies like this. We were always watching films that were supposed to teach us moral lessons, or warn us about something dark that surrounded us.

I waited for Jamie to say more, but nothing came. "So what?" I asked. "What are you getting at?"

"Which is it? Do you help strangers or do you run? Right? Why did she show us these movies?"

"Oh, who knows?" I took a breath. "Better just steer clear of the whole mess. Just say nothing. It's not like there's anything you can do about it," I said. "Sometimes you can tell when adults are getting themselves … into trouble, sort of."

I told Jamie about the only time we had sex education in school.

One day, my grade six teacher, Mrs. Cattleford, tried to teach a lesson she nervously called "health class." It was about babies — before they're born — how they grow inside a mother. It wasn't about sex or having a baby. Just about how a little baby grows inside a mother. She never explained how it got there. She stammered and fumbled her way through it, showing us cartoons on an overhead projector.

Brian Birk, who was the class clown, kept interrupting. "How did the baby get there?"

She just stared at him and didn't say anything. Then, finally, she said, "We'll learn that later."

"Yah, but just tell us. I don't get it," he said.

She sort of chuckled, without smiling. "When you're older, Brian."

He was so good at playing innocent and dumb.

"It involves something … biological," she said.

"Oh. Like a disease?"

"Of course not, Brian. It requires … an exchange of … material."

"My word!" Brian went into a pantomime act, appealing to us in confusion at something he pretended was shocking. "I don't understand what she's getting at."

Someone whispered to him and he clutched his neck like a society lady grabbing at her pearls. The class exploded in laughter.

"That's enough!" Mrs. Cattleford said, her face red as her dyed hair.

While we laughed, Brian made exaggerated shrugs and expressed mock horror at the whispering he pretended to be too delicate to understand.

"Stop it!" she said. "Everyone quiet right now!"

Every sentence Mrs. Cattleford uttered was in the same tone. The words she used were different, but what she said — repeatedly — was "Stop talking. Stop asking. Stop."

Our teacher may have dressed like a backup singer for Linda Ronstadt — she wore flared pants, macramé jewellery, and an enormous blouse patterned splotchy-blotchy in orange, black, and red, but like the rest of the teachers, Mrs. Cattleford was pretty straight. She was not cool, though she believed otherwise.

This lesson was a great example of her limits.

She tried to be cool, though, tried to be fun and friendly — most of the time, anyway. One morning her mood was sunny. "You children don't realize how good you've got it," she said, patrolling between the desks and sipping coffee from her mug while we worked quietly on a heads-down exercise. "School is like holiday camp now. And believe me, teachers are different than they were. We're fun! Why, back when I went to school it was like being in the army. An army run by nuns. But ever since the sixties, everything is free! Your generation doesn't appreciate what we did for you. Nowadays, you're free to do what you want."

"Recess all day!" shouted Meena Thomas, one of the girls.

"Now, now," said Mrs. Cattleford, taken aback as the class became riled up. "Raise your hand if you wish to speak."

It was too late. Everyone spoke at once.

"Brian, where are you going?" she asked. Brian Birk had suddenly risen from his chair and was sauntering toward the door.

"Well, I'm going outside."

Mrs. Cattleford gritted her teeth. "Excuse me, but sit down this moment."

"No, thanks. I'm doing what I want."

Laughter nearly drowned her out.

She waddled over to him, hunched like a vulture. By his ear, she dragged him back to his seat. I could see his eyes water from the strain of her grip or humiliation.

"Why would you do this to me?" Mrs. Cattleford said, genuinely. "I'm your friend."

Our school was new in the 1960s. There were no real classrooms. We had "learning forms" arrayed in a daisy wheel around a sunken amphitheatre holding a library. A single, large skylight illuminated the atrium. Each learning form was lit by a single thin window, which was blocked from having a view of the schoolyard by brick fins that extended outward. Students were meant to focus on their lessons, and not to be hypnotized by sunlight. Teachers were meant to collaborate and co-teach across the learning forms.

Of course, it did not work, and the teachers complained to us every day about how much they hated the architects of our school and hated the layout and just wanted a normal classroom. It was how I even learned that architecture was a job.

All the teachers used bulletin boards, shelving, and mobile blackboards to barricade themselves into a makeshift classroom. The teachers complained about noise and rubbed their temples. Instead of a door, you would enter our class by moving aside a wheeled divider.

If a class got rowdy, it was infectious because the other forms could hear it and everyone would go bananas. So now, as Mrs. Cattleford's class openly rebelled against her, we could hear other kids in the school beginning to rile.

"Everyone stop at once! The noise!"

One of the dividers rattled and Mr. Plante, the teacher next door, leaned into our form like a monster emerging from a wall. He was a towering blond man with Farrah Fawcett hair and a big moustache. His satin cowboy shirt was open to his chest and a gold cross shone through his chest hair.

"Mrs. Cattleford," he said, in a threatening growl. "Is everything all right here?"

The entire class fell silent, in awe of Mr. Plante looming into our space.

"Yes, of course, Mr. Plante," said our teacher quietly. I suddenly pitied her. "Everything is under control."

He surveyed us at our desks. "Listen to Mrs. Cattleford. If I come back …" He raised a finger, and then curled it into his fist. Then he hammered it against the divider, making everyone jump, including Mrs. Cattleford.

He left and we did not dare breathe. Mrs. Cattleford stood near the front blackboard with her fingers on her chest.

"And that," she said in a whisper, her eyes moist, "is why we need to have rules. And to follow the rules. And you need to follow the rules."

Her throat pulsed and she assigned us all to stay in that recess and write lines: *I must not disrupt the class.*

We never did receive the sex and childbirth lesson Brian Birk was promised. The explanation stayed in that same, shame-filled adult darkness I sensed throughout our little society in Blackburn. Keeping kids innocent of the truth was part of the "normal" way of things. Like with many things, adults assumed someone else would take care of it, somehow. *Just, for God's sake, don't talk about it with me.*

7

S couts I loved. School I hated. And then there was church.

On Saturday afternoon, we went as a family to church for confession from four until five. I wished we'd stay for Saturday evening Mass and just get it all over with, but our family were Sunday morning Mass–goers. The Saturday-goers were the laziest of Catholics, the guiltiest. The ones who slept in on Sundays and didn't care if you knew, like our neighbours across the street, the Samskys.

Mr. Samsky used to time his Sunday-morning visit to the front porch so he could wave at us in his dressing gown as we left for Mass and he shuffled back inside with a mug of coffee and the *Ottawa Journal* tucked in his armpit.

Protestants on our street were invisible on Sunday mornings. I assumed they were at church, but Blackburn Hamlet had no other chapels except for the French and English Catholic ones. They would have to go elsewhere in the township, I figured.

"They don't go to church," my father corrected me, speaking from the front seat. School was now over. Scouts was over. But our church routine just carried on. Endless.

"Seriously?"

"What a silly question! They're barking up the wrong tree, those ninnies," my mother said, cutting me off. I stopped talking.

For good measure, she added a last word. "Protestants. Ha! Are you so conceited that you believe you know better than anyone? Lord, love a duck."

My father sighed and called my name. Blood left my head and went to my feet at the tone of his voice.

"I noticed my saw is missing from my workshop," he said. My father kept a small workshop in the basement with a pegboard, outlining all his tools. It was easy to see when something went missing, such as the saw Jamie and I used earlier that day in the woods.

"Which of you boys took it?"

"Me," I said immediately, worried Jamie might take the heat. "I did."

He grunted. "And so, you are a thief. A thief obsessed with sharp tools."

"It's hard to cut wood without a saw."

Thank God he was unaware of my Scout knife, which I had won during last year's bottle drive.

"When you do an examination of conscience, remember you stole from your own father. Confess it."

"I will," I said cheerfully.

Our parish was raising money for its own church building. In the meantime, we held Masses at Église Saint-Claude, the local French church.

People of the two parishes did not intermingle except during the transit between alternating Masses. On Saturday afternoons, both priests heard confessions at the same time. French in the left confessional, English in the right.

My father walked ahead of us, while Mum held our wrists. I broke free and caught up with Dad.

"Dad," I said. "I'm sorry I took it. Without asking. But we're building a tree fort. Can I please borrow your saw?"

"Sounds reckless."

"Nothing too big. Just a few nails and ropes. Some lumber from a palette we found."

"No." He stared straight ahead.

"But why? We're careful."

"You don't know what you're doing."

"I've got my carpentry badge. I've helped you — watched you — a million times."

"No."

"But why?"

"Because I'm your father, that's why."

We stopped at the entrance of the church. He lowered his eyebrows at me. "Listen up. We're going in for confession. After the week I've had at work, it's time for me to get clean. You should take this seriously for yourself."

He dipped his right hand into the stoup and crossed himself so violently drops of holy water splashed my cheek.

We took to the right side of the church and knelt. Dad's kneel was heavy, as though his knees gave way and collapsed.

My father never talked about work, but it clearly ruined his happiness. I knew little about what he did, but I assumed he was very important. Whenever I asked him a simple question, like "How was work?" he would stare into the distance and — if he answered at all — say something like "Everyone's got their place" or "There is nothing I can do, it is my cross to bear."

I assumed he was something cool and frightening like a secret agent, because he worked at Indian Affairs, which was exotic and mysterious and — judging by his mood — unpleasant.

My father was a proud man, and he usually stood straight and tall, but I could see that when we went to church, his private sins, whatever they were, bore down on him like a load of logs and humbled him into a slouch.

His stern and righteous face rose up from his slumped neck to take the full brunt of whatever guilt Jesus reminded him of while he examined his conscience. All four of us knelt in the pew, as a family. Though I simply daydreamed about hockey or building the tree fort, I imagined God berated my father. Yelled, even, straight into his mind, silent to the rest of us but a cacophony inside Dad's head.

As we moved forward in the confessional line, he looked steadily smaller, until the light turned green and he went in to tell Father Sweet his deepest, darkest shame. My proud father, guilty, ashamed, and small, shuffling to hear from Father Sweet his penance or absolution.

To me and Jamie, Dad was our judge, our commander. The final authority.

Father Sweet was the only man with the power to correct him, and to make him stand straight again.

One Sunday after Mass, Danny Lemieux and I were clearing the altar. While snuffing out the candles, Danny showed me an old altar server trick. He told me to dip my fingertips in the hot beeswax so that it would make a shell. It stung at first, but cooled into soft, honey-scented enamel, like white chocolate.

By accident, I knocked over the big liturgical candle, and it shattered into blocky shards on the ground. Mrs. Gain — the mean, cylindrical volunteer who coordinated the Eucharistic ministers of the parish — unexpectedly appeared.

She sank her talons into us immediately. Although Danny kept silent, my lies shot out fast as gunfire.

And then Father Sweet arrived, calmed her down with comments about her dress, winked at us, soothed her. She sauntered off and Father Sweet led Danny to the sacristy with his arm around him. I saw him touch Danny's blond hair. Meanwhile I swept up and skulked away, never to mention to anyone it was entirely my fault.

Father Sweet had a knack for appearing at the right moment and saving misbehaving kids from the wrath of adults.

Naturally, typical boy-stuff myths developed.

Father Sweet — who was short, flabby, and had the skin tone of mayonnaise — climbed Everest. He fought as a commando in The War. He was a race-car driver in Monaco. Although he came from a wealthy family, he gave up everything to be a monk in the Egyptian desert, but then fell in love with a sheikh's beautiful daughter, who subsequently died. He became a parish priest because he could never ever be with her. I don't know where we got these stories, but there were many.

These schoolyard legends about Father Sweet — especially among altar boys — were so embellished that it would not have surprised us to hear he had performed miracles. In our imaginations, a legend lived among us. It got so bad that adults repeated a few. Father Sweet was in a class above.

There's probably a simple explanation. Whereas our families watched TV, drove our kids to hockey, ate ketchup meatloaf, and loped off to bed at a decent hour, he lived alone, ate Friday fish every day, communed with arcana, composed symphonies at night, and wrote homilies that tracked a life of the mind no bourgeois parishioner could fathom.

He could have been descended from some lower heaven, or New York, and not the pudgy, bald, frizzy-bearded gnome he otherwise appeared. How can you explain this unusual figure dropped into our midst?

And right here in dull old Blackburn Hamlet.

Our parish was very lucky to have Father Sweet, people said.

After he confessed, my father pulled himself back to the pew and did his penance, often with a rosary.

My turn.

I went in and knelt. The screen slid open and Father Sweet's profile appeared in shadow against the linen.

"Bless me, Father, for I have sinned. It's been one week since my last confession."

Father Sweet asked my age, but — of course — never my name.

My sins were always the same: lying, not listening to my parents, and, although I still considered it defending myself, arguing or fighting with others. I admitted to swearing at or fighting with others, such as Rob and Squirm or any other dickheads who crossed me. I mentioned Jamie and I had stolen a stack palette from behind Joe's Variety, but I suggested it was probably garbage, anyway.

I could not see Father Sweet through the fabric screen, but he was itching again. He often fidgeted during my whispers.

"We are all sinners," he said. "We inherit sin. Did you know that?"

"Yes," I whispered.

"How can one atone?"

"Uh. Do a good turn for someone? Every day?"

"Well, that is always good. But it is only through deeper engagement with the Church that one atones. Remember Jesus's words about the way and the truth and the life. We must come to God with humility, ready to atone. Penance brings us to reconciliation."

"Okay."

He prescribed one decade of the rosary and three Glory Be's, bookended with an Act of Contrition at the beginning and end.

I headed out to the pew to pray, joining my dad, whose back was already starting to straighten.

8

Summer was nearly over, and as Jamie and I were skidding our bikes toward the treehouse build site, we passed a culvert that drained the town's high streets into the stream. From time to time, a homeless man was said to camp there. The consensus at school was this guy was a dangerous creep. I had never seen him, but I knew that this was the guy from whom Rob earned some fast cash.

I spied a shaggy bearded man wearing an unseasonably warm collection of jackets, wool and heavy cotton, all soiled into the same oily brown. He looked like a wizard.

The hobo was surprised and glad to see us. He waved and spoke to us in a thick Ottawa Valley accent: "Hallo, lads! More of yas! Busy day today."

"Ignore him," I said to Jamie. "Don't look at him. Let's go."

"You know, your pals come through here were selling a quality show. How 'bout you lads? Youse in show business?"

My brother tilted his bike to the ground and swiped a sharp stone to throw at the man. I kept a pedal up, prepared for a rapid getaway. My instincts were keen, but I didn't sense real danger. I knew we could outrun him easy.

"Hey. Don't," I said, nodding at the rock in Jamie's hand. "Come on."

"You wanna make a quick ten?" called the hobo. "Ten whole dollars!"

"They talk about you at school, you know."

"Who? Teachers?" said the hobo, suddenly alarmed.

"No, kids," I said. "Everyone says you're a sick pervert."

"I'm a man of the world! Could teach you lads sump'n. Besides, I just wanna have a look."

"Look at what?" Jamie asked. He was tossing the rock up and down in his hand.

"Yer pecker, shorty!"

My brother laughed but I didn't. I grabbed the rock from Jamie and flung it hard at the hobo's face. The rock missed him, but my attack clearly had an effect.

The hobo waved his arms like a windmill, trying to regain his balance, He struggled to climb out of the culvert, but we were already on the move down the path and away from him.

"*Sanctifié!*" cursed Jamie as we cycled beneath the arching trees.

"Don't slow down. Keep up." My brother's legs pumped furiously, but he lagged behind.

Fast as we rode, the howl of the hobo echoed after us like the bay of a wolf. "Fuck ooooooooooooffffff," he cried.

We arrived at the build site, where we had stashed the palettes, ropes, and a Beaver Nuts tin filled with nails and screws stolen from Dad's workbench.

"Man. You are good at hiding things," I said to Jamie. "I could not see any of our stuff from the trail. Let alone the fort."

"That's the advantage of being low to the ground," Jamie said.

"You're not that short," I said.

He shrugged.

"Ah," I said, waving a dismissive hand. "Who cares?"

"Yah. Who cares."

Whistling the Sol the Clown theme song, I hoisted a plank on my shoulder and turned around so I narrowly missed the top of Jamie's head.

"Hey, watch it!" he yelled.

"It's just a joke … I wasn't really trying to hit you."

"You're still a dick." He paused. "I don't see what's so funny about hobos, anyway."

"They're harmless," I said. "Just boozers."

"What about the bum? Shouldn't we have helped him instead of throwing rocks?"

"That guy is up to no good."

"How can you tell?"

"He's dirty and weird and drunk."

"He looks gross," Jamie said, "that's for sure."

We sorted nails. He looked upset.

"What's wrong?" I asked.

"I just don't get it," said Jamie. "Paying Rob to see his wiener."

9

The next morning, we attended a religious ceremony. Larry Lozinski, my dad's friend from work, and his son, my friend David, had invited us. David was Jewish — he and his family were the only Jews we knew. So, we really didn't know what to expect when we arrived. What we saw wound up deeply offending my parents, and we made an abrupt exit immediately after it was over. My father drove us home, angry as hell. He drove so madly around cars and buses on Innes Road's narrow two lanes that cars honked at us — a very rare occurrence.

Usually, my dad was silent and lockjawed. As he never seemed to speak about himself, it was hard for me to be certain exactly what he was feeling or what was going on in his head. Each morning, he awoke after a short night's sleep with his mouth set in the same day-long clench from the evening before.

Periodically, he would blow up. Like right now, as we drove home from my friend David's house. Dad's jaw gyrated furiously as if he was chewing his teeth out.

"Larry told me it would be like a baptism," Dad said. I watched him eat the corners of his mouth. "And I don't want to hear anything from you two back there." He jerked his thumb at Jamie and me. We undid our little clip-on ties and exchanged frightened glances as we fastened our seat belts.

I think I knew what my parents were upset about, but I tried to understand to be sure. Was it what the *mohel* had said? He said, "Now I'm going to say a blessing Aaron would say every morning to the people as they wandered in the wilderness. Today let it serve to remind us our lives are a wilderness, and we, too, wander it. May this child find meaning and peace in his life." Was that it?

We had entered their bright house in Beacon Hill, which smelled of dinnertime and was loud with laughter and full of jostling, happy people. Well, not entirely, David's mother had eyes brimming with tears and eyebrows twitching upward to the centre of her forehead. Women rubbed her back and hugged her, which I thought was nice and I found myself staring. My own mother stood leaning against the wall, arms crossed, and one brow arched into her hairline. In a way, David's mother was the opposite of our mother, all soft curves and care. When the crying baby emerged at last, passed from aunt to aunt, uncle to uncle, David's mother reached out to the infant like he was precious gold. The baby was finally carried in ceremony to the *mohel*, and to the knife.

Dad's knuckles were shiny as marbles at the top of the steering wheel.

"I can't believe what that disgusting old man did with his … his lips," Mum said.

"And Larry told me not to worry, it would be like a baptism. What kind of religion —"

The car lurched right without stopping at the light.

Yes, I saw it, too. It looked like the *mohel* put the baby's penis in his mouth. Did he? He certainly bent over. My parents gasped out loud. I said nothing, but, yes, I found it weird, especially with the knife and everything. But, then again, it all seemed weird. My brother missed the whole thing because he was attacking a bowl of chips. David, who was my age and played hockey with me, seemed royally bored. I took my cue from him, and assumed this was normal. Apparently my parents did not think so.

As soon as it was over, our parents grabbed us by the scruff and we left.

In the car, they spoke as if we could not understand them.

"That horrible godfather character, what did they call him? The Quacker?"

"The Kvatter."

"Well, that joke — if you can even call it a joke — was plain sick."

"What are you supposed to do when you're faced with something like that?" my father said.

"You leave, that's what you do. You just leave." Mum pressed her lips together in a thin line.

We pulled up our driveway. Without a word or a glance, Dad kept the car running while we staggered out, nauseous. He squealed off to work before I even shut my door. Mum marched to the kitchen and made angry clatter with pots and pans.

My brother and I tore off our good clothes like escaped convicts, and donned our grubbies. We were headed back to the woods.

"Don't be late, boys. Home by five," Mum shouted as we mounted our bikes. "Father Sweet is coming tonight."

There it was. We groaned. She meant we had to wear nice clothes — again — and endure a long, tedious meal with adults. There were precious few days left of summer holiday. And Father Sweet himself was coming to our house. An excruciating "best behaviour" evening.

10

Later, after we returned home to clean up for dinner with Father Sweet, I overheard Mum on the phone.

"What has happened to us, Trixie?" she said. "When I was growing up, nobody ever got divorced. I didn't even think it was possible for Catholics to get divorced! I know. I know."

Oh my god, I thought. *Is she talking about her and Dad?* I was on the second floor and crept thief-like toward the stairs, just out of view.

"So what? When my dad came back from the war he drank all the time.... Sure.... Yes, I think he did, but Mother stuck by him.... Yes, even after what's-her-name ... no, that's for sure. They never change, you're right.... Boys will be boys."

My brother joined me and we both sat on the hallway floor in silence, breathing as little as possible.

"Marriage until death. Father-knows-best. Church on Sundays. On and on.... Exactly — me, too."

My brother mouthed words at me, *I don't get it.* I gestured for him to shush, and I shrugged. *If she hears us eavesdropping*, I thought, *we'll get spanked.* It felt like hiding from a wild animal.

"Well, we're the 'me' generation, after all. Or maybe this is the Pepsi Generation, ha-ha-ha.... Yes. That's true."

Now came a long pause where she listened to Trixie's tinny voice in the receiver.

"Just a minute, Trix," she said. My brother and I locked eyes and held our breath. Was she checking to see if we were stealing a listen?

Then, I heard her strike a lighter. Mum lit up a cigarette.

"Clearly something's supposed to be different, I agree. I don't understand how a family is supposed to *be*," she said quietly. "We got liberated in the sixties…. So here we are! I guess…. She was such a hippie. Me, too! But, my god, you've got to come back to earth. I mean how are you supposed to raise, well, *respectful* children? How are you supposed to be good? Society will come apart at the seams…. You remember those bombs in Montreal wasn't that long ago…. No, of course I'm not saying that. I'm only saying — you know — people can't just do whatever they want. We're all sinners. That's what they say. No rest for the wicked. Exactly. You gotta do what you gotta do."

She took a long, thoughtful drag on her smoke. "She swans about like Princess Margaret. You know, I suspected something when they stopped going to Mass. She should have dragged him to church, eh." She exhaled smoke. "Yep. Dragged him. Temptations out there just too strong. Well yes, that's true, too, eh…. Men. Tsk."

Mum listened to Trixie for a while, humming agreement.

"Makes me think, you remember Father Sweet's homily last week? No? Hm. He said suspicion of good men says more about you than them."

She laughed.

Mum's voice got low. "Will she still go by 'Birk'? Mmm-hmm. Do you know if she gets full custody of Brian and Briar?"

Brian Birk's parents were getting divorced. Unbelievable. In grade five I remember Brian insisting that divorces only happened because the wife was a slut. He got in a few fights over this one.

My brother and I sighed in chorus.

"Poor Brian," I whispered. My brother nodded.

"Well, Trixie, none of this is really any of my business, either," my mother said. "But you let me know if you hear anything new. Bye, love."

We tiptoed away from our listening perch.

I secretly worried it could happen to us, as well. Back in my room, Jamie asked me why I figured divorces happened. I told him I had no idea. But Mum's words stayed with me the rest of that evening, even though they made no sense to me — that somehow if Brian's parents had kept going to church their family would have survived.

11

Father Sweet himself made quite a regal picture at the head of our dining-room table. But I couldn't quite reconcile the Father Sweet eating my mother's peas with the Father Sweet at school and Mass.

When Father Sweet appeared at school, teachers straightened their backs and enunciated like bad actors who needed to poo, or as if in the presence of the Royal family. No adults who knew him seemed immune. I was dragged to an ordination at the Notre Dame basilica once and I heard two old ladies whisper in the pew behind me they hoped to hear Father Sweet sing, in his famous, quavering voice. They did not know him, but they knew his legend.

I admit I felt a tinge of parish pride.

During Mass, the other altar boys and I got a good view of him up close in his element, the weekly service.

These were his masterpieces.

Many of his sermons were dramatic historical lectures on the lives of the saints and the ancient traditions of the Catholic Church. By contrast, most priests I can remember would shake off their hangovers and deliver weekly homilies about everyday things like neighbourliness, peace of mind, charity, or forgiveness. They might even throw in the odd TV show reference or a joke. I remember one homily at the Notre Dame basilica, delivered by a funny celebrant whose name I forget. He was talking about sin, of which you didn't need first-hand experience to know was wrong. This was like many things in life, he suggested. "For example," this priest said, "it burns with a blue flame, but I don't encourage you to try it." That was a real crowd-pleaser. Especially among boys.

On the other hand, if Father Sweet uttered jokes, you needed a university degree to understand them. If he ever said "TV," it would probably be an abbreviated Latin expression; he often slipped Latin into Mass, causing my father and a few others to nod solemnly.

I remember in one homily about the daughter of Jairus, he spoke ecstatically of Saint Martina, a ten-year-old martyr for the early Church. Milk spurted from Martina's neck when she was beheaded, moving many witnesses to join in Christ. At the time the story sent shivers through my spine. Thinking back now, I mostly remember his face turning red when he described her long, swanlike throat in orgasmic detail.

These lectures acted like anaesthetic on the kids in the congregation, but they obviously made grown-ups behave like our religion was important, righteous, and Father Sweet a genius.

And he was a musical genius, too. Lesser celebrants may have mumbled their way through the liturgy, but Father Sweet usually sang it. When he crooned that Christ has died, Christ is risen, and Christ will come again, he hit such a pitch you'd imagine Jesus roaring in on a 50cc dirt bike like Evel Knievel, accompanied by a horn section, a dance troupe, and fireworks.

From our up-front vantage, altar servers like me observed the audience effect. The congregation was a field of stick-straight men and women with wide eyes, unmoving, blank-faced, with slumping or fiddly kids mixed in. And there were the ones in between — teens or preteens — who shifted from the stare-eyed stillness to fidgety, and back again.

Every grown-up wanted him as a prop for their dinner party, as I learned by overhearing my parents' jealous talk about our neighbours, the Lemieux family, who were very close to Father Sweet.

If you could get him, and if you had a piano, he would lead the party in a sing-along of ancient show tunes. Everyone was proud if they could host a party with him as a guest.

By dessert, the summertime sunset blasted into our dining room. Father Sweet was praising the benefit to the spine of a nap on a hardwood floor while Mum set out bread pudding and a boat of hot maple syrup.

Of course, Dad had asked him to say grace when we first sat down. Father Sweet replied that he would sing for his supper, chanting a Benedictine grace that Mum said was truly beautiful. Now, while we passed the syrup, he said there was a second part of the blessing to sing.

He moaned a Latin dirge. It was evocative and mournful, and I found myself smiling at him.

A surprised twinkle flashed in his eye. That's when he zeroed in.

"Here now," he said to me, pointing his chubby little finger. "Tell me what mischief you got up to during the summer, my lad."

The spotlight startled me. My parents shot me warning looks.

"Just ball hockey. Bike rides. Stuff like that."

"He's going back to Scouts in a couple weeks," my father announced with pride. "His Patrol elected him Patrol Leader for this year."

"Ah, Scouts!" Father Sweet cried. "The happy few! Enjoying the call of God's Nature. Brother love! The mentorship of hale youth by hearty men!"

"Yes," my dad said, after a confused pause.

"I imagine he's quite a woodsman! Look at him. Lean as a jackrabbit. Fit as a wolf."

My dad cleared his throat to speak in his most pious tone. "Father, we've taken to praying the rosary once a week. Usually it's Sunday evenings, but we would love to have you lead us tonight. How special is that, eh, boys?"

My mother nodded and smacked my shoulder. "Yah, yah," we said.

Father Sweet mopped his beard with a napkin — the beard that did not hide the fact his face looked like a baby's — and he clapped his hands so we would rise.

Everyone retreated to the living room. This was the most sacred room in the house, despite its nauseating orange shag broadloom (which came with the house) and collection of fussy, dusty Victorian furniture. We were never allowed in here to sit on the uncomfortable sofa or wingbacks, and certainly never to place drinks on the high-polish tables. I got jammed between the hard armrest and Father Sweet on the loveseat. As he reached into his pocket and withdrew a linty rosary, Mum fetched ours from their casket in the china cabinet.

Father Sweet led us through the whole performance, all business. Across from the loveseat was a mirror, and I stared at Father Sweet in a sort of half-sleep. His cheeks and eyes and pouty lips. His shiny bald head. And those gorilla arms. It was such a mismatch. As if some of his body had long ceased growing and others had regressed into animal parts.

Twenty minutes later, Dad checked his watch. "Gosh, look at the time."

Father Sweet took his cue.

"Thank you for a truly, truly outstanding meal," he said, taking my parents' hands. "Things are so sleepy at the church this season, with parishioners off at the cottage. It does make one lonely. Your kindness and generosity have touched me greatly."

In a surprise move, Father Sweet dodged right up to my side, yanking me close against his hip. "You know, handsome young Scout, what do you say we go camping? Just the two of us?"

My mother's eyes lit up and she clasped her palms together at her breasts. "Oh, he'd love to!" she said.

I sputtered. "Well, school is starting soon."

"Oh, it's not for two weeks, son!"

"But Father, surely you've got duties," said Dad. "We don't want to cause you any trouble."

"As long as I'm back for Saturday evening Mass," he replied, scrutinizing my hair and face. "Say we leave Thursday? Ten a.m."

"He'll be ready," said Mum.

"And we'll hand the little varlet over," Dad said, being funny.

He blessed us, we crossed ourselves, and he drove off.

"Well now! How about *that!*" Mum said, breaking the silence and beaming with pride.

My brother and I gaped at the front door.

"Dad," I said, grabbing his wrist. "Please don't make me go camping with Father Sweet. Please."

"You're spoiled." Mum frowned. "You'd just be lolling around here otherwise."

"Please, Dad. It's going to be so weird."

"Tough titty," said Mum. "This'll be a great experience. Who knows what effect this might have on you?"

"Nonsense," Dad said, pulling his arms up and disengaging from me. "Your mother's right. This will be a good opportunity for you."

"I wonder if I ought to pack your rosary," she said to the ceiling.

12

I laid out my gear on our bedroom rug. My brother stretched out on my bed, grumpy.

I ignored him and arranged my stuff on the floor. Bedroll, flashlight, knife, magnetic chess, some utensils, first aid kit, and the other usual things, like Muskol, matches, and a tin canteen. An extra pair of long-pocket camping trousers and a single set of shorts. A couple of wool layers. My K-Way windbreaker. I tried to be as prepared as possible. Be prepared — a Scout's motto. If I didn't know what was to come, I could at least know my equipment.

"Sorry. I borrowed this without telling you," Jamie said.

He handed me a red-painted Sucrets tin filled with tiny emergency gear — a Scout project from last year. I scowled at him.

"Give it."

"I put fresh matches in. You're lucky, going camping."

"Bull-roar. I should get a badge for this," I muttered.

I was not bringing the great, brand-new International Orange nylon tent he and I bought that summer with paper route money. Father Sweet told Mum he would bring a tent, and plenty of food, as well.

"So," Jamie said, "what's the *bear* situation?"

"Shut up."

"Yah, I heard last week that a grizzly ripped two campers to shreds near Pembroke."

My breathing was hard, but I managed to deflect him. "There are no grizzlies anywhere near here and you know it."

"Well, maybe it was a black bear. Common as raccoons this time of year."

"Shut *up*," I grunted. And punched his shoulder.

It was enough. My goat was got and the game ended. "Guess I'll use the time to get ahead of you in Hardy Boys," he said. "You're not taking a book, eh?"

"No," I said, not yet knowing the value of burying your nose in a book on a long trip.

"Wish I got invited," Jamie said.

I looked at him. "Me, too," I said.

Our parents had made clear over the course of our young lives that I was the golden son, and he was the spare. The lesser spare.

With care, I holstered Dad's sharp hatchet, protected by a leather guard, into the side of my pack.

"Wow, you're taking the hatchet. Does Dad know?" Jamie said.

"Dad's a pot with the lid on too tight," I said, very quietly.

For twenty minutes I waited on the floor by the front door, slumped on my backpack. If I was going off to war — I imagined — I would be smoking.

Dad came to peer out the front door window. I hoisted myself vertical.

"What's this?" he said, pulling the hatchet out of its holster.

"For firewood."

"You know I don't like you using this without my supervision."

"I'll be careful. I promise."

"If it's important, Father will have one." He placed it on the sideboard next to the mail basket, laying it down like a grenade that might explode if mishandled.

I frowned at it.

Dad checked his watch. He was meant to be at work in Ottawa, but was waiting to see us off.

"I need to make a call," he said, and left me alone at the front door, giving me opportunity to fiddle with my pack and provisions a bit more.

Finally, Father Sweet's navy Beetle of pre-Beatle vintage pulled up, fifteen minutes late. The windows were wound down and he flapped his hand at us, flashing a grin as wide as the windshield.

"Look here, this is important," Mum said, grabbing my shoulders. "Say your prayers."

"I don't want to hear when you get back you were difficult," Dad said, raising an eyebrow and a finger at me. "Just listen to Father. Do what he says. Don't cause problems."

No one clutched at my sleeve as I marched out and the screen door slammed. I put my pack under the Beetle's hood and climbed in.

"Be good!" my mother called.

"We will," Father Sweet replied, backing out.

"I was talking to him!" She laughed. "Don't let him give you any guff."

13

"What is the message of Christ?" Father Sweet asked me, keeping his gaze on the road ahead. We weren't even on the highway yet, having just driven past the penitentiary outside Blackburn.

I regarded him from the side of my eyes. I expected he would ask me these sorts of things during our entire trip, and then report back the results to my parents.

"Like, be good?" I replied. "And share and stuff."

"There can be only one answer." He laughed, shaking his head. "It is love. Simply love!"

"Yah, well, of course. Yes."

What made my parents — actually, all the Catholic parents in Blackburn — hold Father Sweet in such esteem?

I was twelve, and the world was an incomprehensible morass of mystical, adult secrets. Somewhere shadowy, I sensed, the many things adults didn't discuss freely were being whispered about away from my ears.

So-and-so did something unspeakable. Did you hear what she is doing now? I heard that he's a mm-hm. I wouldn't be surprised if she had a problem with you-know-what.

This wasn't true, of course. Whenever children like me asked questions or asked for clarity, I saw evidence of this secret world, written on the irritated faces adults displayed as you were told to never mind. The truth was, no one talked to us, so we had to figure it out by eavesdropping, smiling stupidly and trying to suss out what they wanted us to say so they could leave us alone.

If there was one thing I did understand, though, it was that we were Christians. And to be a Christian is to believe that the world you see is not the true world. Even as a twelve-year-old, I knew there was what you could figure out from what you saw, and the interpretation the adults wanted. I was immersed in a big charade. The true world thrived invisibly all around me, foaming with terrific power. Agents of evil posed in friendly guises. Ghosts floated behind my back. My thoughts were broadcast to angels and demons. I was never alone, I was observed at all times, and my thoughts notated and reported up to Jesus or the Heavenly Father. Although I might not see any consequence of any action or thought, it was there nonetheless. Like an oil stain on a dress shirt. Fortunately, it can be taken out when laundry's done for your soul during the sacrament of reconciliation, which we did weekly as a family.

Here's how I viewed the world. A flock of spirits followed me like birds scavenging, waiting for me to drop a crumb of sin. In the dark, in my bedroom late at night, I might even speak to one of them, and perhaps might chance to glimpse something if I was truly unlucky. So I'd pull up the covers and shut my eyes so that I couldn't see the forms swarming over me.

Occult spirits and universal evil were real fears. That, and bears. So, ghosts and bears. In religion class or Father Sweet's homilies, how to conquer fear was a very real skill I figured the Church could teach me.

In such times as you are afraid, Father Sweet would tell us, one only need pray and ask for intercession and the hand of God

— a huge, ghostly hand, I imagined — would intercede. If you deserved it. The whole thing gave me little comfort.

Father Sweet's baritone voice and weird enunciation was hypnotizing. Imagine a Victorian time traveller forever befuddled and amazed by the wondrous modernity of the twentieth century; that's how he spoke. He pronounced "thermometer" as two hyphenated words sounding like "thermal-meter." He carefully spoke all three letters "S" in "issues." He used words like "forfend" in sentences, and would angrily correct you on the difference between further and farther. Boys were nervous to open their mouths.

In a way no one else did, he formalized our names. If you were Tony, Doug, or Chris, you became Anthony, Douglas, and Christopher to him; pronounced with great elocution. Sometimes you might even become French or Italian. I remember Chris Becker turned into "Christophe" that way. He let Christophe's name luxuriate on his tongue, but he disliked the boy himself, considering him a brute. I can't recall, however, him ever calling any of the girls by name. He just nodded at them, or pointed.

Often, you could spot a mess of boys' bikes piled in front of the rectory, a red townhouse close to the school where he lived alone. They came because he always had plenty of candy and pop.

My own initial visit to the rectory occurred when my mother dropped me there for an altar boy pizza party. One car after the next, parents drove their sons to the rectory and left them.

The pizza was cold, but it was from Wong's, the best pizza in Blackburn, and its doughy, cheesy skin was worth eating, even hours old. I kept to the back of the dozen other acolytes. Danny Lemieux was the lead altar server and got pride of place for everything. Father Sweet's hand never seemed to leave his neck.

In the rectory, you saw how different Father Sweet was from the rest of Blackburn Hamlet's folks. In addition to his parish duties, he was a composer, with pieces in the latest *Catholic Book of Worship*. A harp, a flute, a piano, an organ, an oboe — he had them all in his music room. The whole house smelled of the tobacco that he smoked in his cherrywood pipe; it was cluttered with musty books, published in a variety of languages, stacked in every room and overflowing shelves. The dim rooms were decorated with Renaissance prints, Orthodox icons, rococo lamps, and pictures of Greek pottery. It felt like a cross between a dusty flea market and a fancy salon.

His upstairs bedroom itself was austere as a monastic cell, with a cot, wooden chair, and cross. Down the hall was the guest room. Its walls were papered in red velvet and the queen-sized bed was covered with an expensive-looking quilt. He lay down on the bed next to a big teddy bear he introduced as "Aloysius."

I was told by Rocky Robicheau that these sorts of tours of his lair were frequent. "Anytime you want to come here," said Rocky, "he'll give you donuts. At any hour."

After we had pizza, he read aloud stories from a writer named Chaucer that he claimed was English, although we didn't understand. But we laughed anyway because — clearly — he meant them to be funny, and maybe even a little naughty. Surrounded by altar servers at his feet, Father laughed himself silly.

"So, did he talk to you?" Mum asked me when I finally came home after walking in the dark.

"No," I said. "I ate three slices of Wong's pepperoni."

"So, he didn't talk to you." Her voice had a sting of disappointment in it. "But you liked the pizza."

"Okay, I guess."

She rolled her eyes. "Boys."

14

The car stank of oil. Father Sweet was unable to shift it smoothly, so the ride lurched forward and back, side to side. Nauseating. For him, driving appeared to be a chaotic, random effort. Again, he appeared to be a time traveller befuddled by modern technology. He maniacally pulled levers, steered and pumped pedals, like Wile E. Coyote operating a contraption. Moreover, without his Roman collar he looked like a kook. Instead of his suit jacket he wore a frayed woollen duffel coat in yellow-and-brown plaid. And — incredibly — jeans.

"Aren't they 'cool'?" he asked, pointing at the stovepipe, handmade denims he wore. They had patches. Deliberately. As if part of the style. "The nuns made them for me!"

"Where are we going?" I asked.

"I know a place up the Gatineau near Moose Lake," said Father Sweet. I'd never seen him so excited.

"Is that near Maniwaki?"

"Never heard of it."

"I know a cool guy from Maniwaki."

He handed me a paper bag of foiled chocolate eggs left over from last Easter. "Eat as many as you like," he said. "It's just us boys!"

He was taking me out of our province and into Quebec. The nearest bridge was in downtown Ottawa, and we had to drive through the massive construction projects under way in the city. Everywhere you looked, old buildings were being demolished in favour of big, new concrete offices and apartment blocks.

Now, as Father Sweet and I drove, the city looked like a war zone. The construction was impossible to ignore, and Father Sweet brought it up.

"I am learning about modern things. I love the purity of the modern ethos," he said.

The word *modern* made me think of sci-fi, and I tried to conceive a way to talk about *Space: 1999*.

"Do you know you are the first generation born since Vatican II?"

I actually did know this, because our teachers reminded us on a regular basis. We were, they told us, the first generation of our renewed religion. Not just renewed; it was a new religion, practically.

"Yah, for sure."

"Vatican II was a modernist conference."

Again, I pictured Moonbase Alpha. Priests wandering around on Moonbase Alpha. In school and church, although Vatican II was mentioned often, no one had ever explained to me what it actually was, and it felt too late to ask now.

"Now with our pastoral flock married to the liberties of today, just think of the flood of new Catholics who will enter the Church. It is extraordinary."

I leaned over to get a better look. Yes, his own words seemed to be moving him to tears.

"Consider Lower Town," he said.

"Lower Town?"

"Yes! That Catholic, French neighbourhood right over there." He gestured. "All those terrible old homes, destroyed and replaced with straight lines of modern townhouses. Simple and egalitarian. Like a monastery! Families now live in a modern, clean religious community and look to the Church for guidance."

Amidst the new townhouse terraces, a lonely spire from the original French church remained in a no man's land of construction pits and dirt.

"See?" said Father. "So orderly. And there is the church, anchoring tradition."

"Blackburn Hamlet is modern," I said, not quite knowing what the point was, but assuming our house was not much older than me, and we were talking about houses.

Father Sweet waved his hand in dismissal. "Blackburn still has too much of an old-town style with curved roads. No, the strong, parish community of Lower Town with a priest as head of a regimented community gives us the best glimpse of a Vatican II future."

"Okay."

"The Church will even regain ground in Quebec. You'll see!" He took a deep breath. "Yes, my boy, these are good days. The Church has found a way to bring all our glorious traditions to a wider contemporary sphere. And you are at the vanguard! A modern man!"

"You bet."

We crossed into Quebec at the Alexandra Bridge, passing Samuel de Champlain's monument, with the Native guide squatting under his boots.

"Ah, Champlain," cooed Father Sweet. "Bringing the light of God's civilization to the savages. His voyage not unlike our own. But for the canoe. I should've thought of that. You'll be the bare-skinned Indian scout!" He laughed.

"Okay," I said.

"How are the chocolates? Here, let me have one. Are you thirsty?"

He handed me a big bottle of Coke.

"I'm not allowed Coke."

"Heaven forfend! Have you had it before?"

"Of course."

"Well, between us boys, I won't tell," he whispered.

The Coke was warm. Lips quivering and puckering, he slurped the bottle without wiping after I'd had a sip. He tooted the horn for no other clear reason than he wanted to make noise and let out a cheer.

"Hooray!" he cried.

We hit the country roads. He clicked on the radio.

"We can listen to whatever you want! What music do you enjoy? I bet it's rock-and-roll."

He found a station.

"How about this? Do you like this?"

He tried to groove to the song, but its rhythm was plainly alien to him. He listened to the lyrics — hard to hear — but something about sliding through life, a sink, and people needing time to think.

"Hm. Is this a song about Protestants?"

"Protestants?" I replied. I had never considered that pop songs could be *about* anything.

"Silly, isn't it?" he said. "People needing a minute or two to think. That's the difference between us and Protestants. And Jews, frankly. They reserve private judgment, but not us."

"What's that mean?" Did my Jewish friend, David Lozinski, have private appointments with a court judge?

"Admonish the sinner and instruct the ignorant. The thread of the Christ God weaving through the line of Peter to today's

Church. Take comfort, judgments have been made for you! You can have faith in God without judgment yourself. You know how to stop sin. You need only relax and act, to follow God. Simple trust in the Church. Such a gift. Oh, such a mercy. Something you have, that they have not. It is to pity."

"Are you talking about Protestants? Or Jewish people?"

"Yes. These are people with a broken outlook on life. It is because of the source, you see. Sin becomes instant and chronic because they stop to think *ad excogitandum relativismi*. Not for us the 'slip and slide through life.' We walk confidently with God. If you place the Sacred Heart of Jesus as the font of life, then all is correct on your path."

I sat for a bit trying to gain my bearings in this bizarre discussion, searching for something to add to the conversation. It was exhausting.

"What exactly is a font?" I asked finally, feigning interest.

"A spring, a source. A fountain."

I envisioned a heart as a grotesquely messy fountain and nodded grimly.

"Indeed. It is in baptism that one's new life begins. The infant is a shadow, polluted and unrighteous. But full of potential. Even its senses are dulled. Imagine a man enshrouded like Lazarus. He cannot truly hear the birdsong, cannot truly, truly feel the touch of his brother, or his words of love. The paschal sacrifice gave us the gift of everlasting life, enabling the flesh of the body. It starts at the baptismal font. That is why we baptize the young, you see? Why wait for new life to begin? The Lord teaches us to love this potential. Love the sinner."

He grew excited and kicked his feet a little.

"Oh! That blessed, perfect age of innocence, between infancy and the brutish rout of manhood! These other people are merely shadows, but they have potential," he said, raising a finger. "It is not us, as people, but God himself passing through us, like blood. Lust, covetousness, the usual thought-infectious demons are our greatest enemies. It was so in the Garden, when the first of God's people were children, pure in their intercourse. They had no lust. With lust we become venial. If veniality is averted, well, it is holy, holy, holy. All pure love is good. You wouldn't want to be a shadow, eh?"

"No," I replied confidently, as if I had followed anything he said.

He smiled widely and nodded. He took a deep breath and sighed.

"I thought not. I knew it. Meditate on how lucky we are to be citizens of the City of God. The world is becoming darker, with the Soviet Union and its iron drapery. The frivolousness of television comedies. The sexual flagrancy of Women's Lib. But it is not real, it is not this." He seized my hand. "And there is God, and our glorious traditions, their sublime mélange of the Hebrew and the Hellenic. Perfect love, in the highest form of our brotherhood. When we fail, and become artless and lustful, where is God?" He moaned, letting go my hand. "Well, thank God for sacramental reconciliation, and mercy. The body can fight the soul, or be a vessel of love for union with another, under the ancient methods of the Church. It is then that the flesh becomes perfectly sanctified. Lust is the enemy. The body's perversion. We must tame the temple of the soul — our bodies — so two souls can become one. You see? Only we know we walk in righteousness, the brotherhood of man. Very simple. The roots of our tradition, where all is correct, only man and his missteps, riddled with sin."

"Okay."

"You understand, of course?"

"Oh, sure." I nodded.

He seemed relieved, as if he'd been waiting to get it out. "Do you know, I could tell you were different — special — the moment we met?"

I bit the side of my cheek. The song finished.

"What musical band was that?" he asked.

"Journey, I think. Sounds like it."

"The Journey," he cooed. "How appropriate. I must learn more about contemporary things. The Journey. The Pilgrim Church. Why, you've just given me my next homily, my boy!"

"Oh, okay."

"All our efforts are vanity. Except the effort to be the pilgrim, to resume the walk with God in concert with the Church. The sacred journey. The Good Shepherd is such a merciful king. We must only follow. It is only by the grace of God, by the sacraments of His Church that the soul is saved, reconciled with Him. One is unable to save oneself, you know."

"You can't save yourself?" I tried my best to sound intellectual, despite feeling exhausted by the conversation.

"No. Of course not. Yet through baptism, reconciliation, Eucharist, *you* are saved," he said, slapping my leg.

"Well, that's good."

The hilly farmland gave way to black pine and beech forest.

"You know, this reminds me of the landscapes of Fra Angelico. Are you familiar with his works?"

"Who?" I said. "What?"

"Oh, my dear boy!" He threw his head back and laughed at my lack of knowledge.

This time his hand didn't so much slap my leg as gently land on it, and rest there.

15

Leaving the car unlocked a kilometre back and sweating under the packs and bags, Father Sweet led me past a bend of the Picanoc River onto a shady bluff, ten feet above the water.

On the only patch with enough sun to sustain healthy grass, he flopped down to catch his breath while I surveyed a few steps into the bush. It was dark and carpeted with needles. There was a firepit, bits of plastic and beer cans, obviously a popular spot for teen campers. The forest curled around the grassy patch, providing a fair shelter from the wind. I decided where to pitch the tent.

"Good flat spot," I said, heading down to fill my canteen from the river. I looked across. The opposite bank was dark with sloped rock that would break your neck in a slip.

"How lush. How Arcadian," Father Sweet said, inhaling a squeaky sniff though his nostrils. "We are as far westerly as one can be east of Eden, my lad. Whereby Eden itself must be Pembroke, eh!" The next major town two hours west was Pembroke.

"Guess so."

I stepped several paces toward the bush to pee on some ivy, and was startled when he crept up silently, to stand shoulder to shoulder with me.

"Time to unbung the ale, eh? Good idea." He pulled out his hairy plug and peed right into my stream.

I looked away.

Nestled in the shady grass, I spotted something dead. Was it the flattened and baked-out carcass of a deer mouse or chipmunk, drained and mummified in the sun? Impossible to tell. Only a wart of fur and a stub of tail remained. And what I took for a little face and little head — its mouth — were actually some kind of deformation on its back. Like seeing a face in the clouds or the moon.

"Did you bring a hatchet, Father?" I asked.

"No, my boy, why?"

I chewed my cheek.

Plenty of dead trees, so maybe it won't be such a big deal, I thought. *A few good kicks.*

I knocked down a deadwood six-footer with a hard punt, and it broke into two uneven logs. Piece of cake.

Father Sweet's eyes widened. He perched his fingers over his breastbone. "Oh my," he said. "Straight out of Kipling! You are a wild boy."

"Let's see that tent," I said.

He fumbled with a grey canvas sleeve, dumping the poorly stored innards.

It was an army-surplus two-man pup tent, mottled as an oyster and smelling like a hospital laundry bin. That brand-new, orange acrylic one I left at home was a plush Cadillac compared to this.

"Look, there's a rip here." I took a deep, dissatisfied breath. "Oh, man. And it hasn't got a floor."

He rummaged in another bag and, with a shrug, presented me two rumpled oilskins that appeared not to have been oiled since the Korean War. Floor and rain tarp.

"This is your tent?"

"Mmm!"

To earn my camping badge I had learned to make shelter from less, I reminded myself. The air smelled like wheat. There would be no rain. Nevertheless, I used my heel to cut a drain around the tent edge. My Scout knife made short work of paring some younger juniper boughs I cross-laid for a cushion under the oilskin. The trick is to get them thin before they've grown too woody. Usually just a hand-length of tip. You put them in a cross-hatch pattern and it feels a lot softer than ground. Soon the tent was going up.

"Look at you! What a marvel," Father said, admiring my productivity, and sighing at me. He hovered close and smacked his lips searching for a topic. "What are you now? Lead altar server?"

"Just Acolyte Two," I said, hoping he'd stop talking when he realized my low, half-hearted rank as an altar boy.

"That's right," he said slowly, frowning. He looked at his boots. "It's Daniel Lemieux, isn't it, who's lead. How could I forget?"

Father Sweet plonked himself down, appearing troubled.

Fortunately, the tent poles were all there, but three spikes were gone. I needed something else, so I replaced them with hand-whittled hardwood stakes and rocks. There was plenty of rope for the tarp.

He lowered his voice to ask whether I had a close relationship with Danny Lemieux. "Do you talk?"

"Not really," I said, picturing quiet Danny, two years older than me. He played Bantam hockey, I played Peewee. "Other than us both being altar servers, I don't know him well."

"So, you haven't talked with him. Not recently."

"Nope."

At this, Father Sweet smiled wide and folded his arms proudly.

"Do you know the history of the altar boy?" He stroked his whiskers. "No? It's one of the most imperative relationships in

Christendom, you know. More important, really, than husband and wife. Why? Because it breeds the ministries of Christ himself."

"Okay."

"It emerged from the tradition of Hellenistic apprentice-ships, you see. A family would give their son into the propriety of a master. That was a more enlightened day. It is a relationship closer than that of a father to a son, or husband and wife. The master has the responsibility to lovingly nurture vocation and bring the boy into the priesthood. *Adelphopoiesis* for our unique bonds. My own initiation came from my mentor — and later, first parish priest — the Monsignor Aloysius Gast." He sighed dreamily. "Oh! The highs. Oh! The lows. How little I appreciated him then. But how I miss him now."

I nodded and kept to my whittling. He stared.

"The *closest* a man and a boy could become," he said slowly, leaning toward me. "Entwined souls. Flesh, sanctified by vow."

My breathing accelerated.

"You hear me?" he asked.

I decided it must be a test of some kind, like in religion class when he asks abstract questions for which none of us are stupid enough to raise our hands. So, he randomly picks someone. It's always the wrong answer, and then he illustrates the catechism in a completely baffling way. What to say? What did he mean?

Father Sweet looked through his eyebrows at me. "You know, there is a difference between useful information and useless," he said. "The useful allows man to see his place in the universe. To fit right with the plan of God. For example, Christ's understanding of human need. Christ became man, knowing all our torturous desires. And our pleasures. Now Christ's passions are inside good Christians. All other information has little productive value."

I surveyed my work; the campsite's soft grass and sweet-smelling trees, where his stained tent poked above the earth like a cancerous cyst. Without my knowledge of Scoutcraft, we wouldn't have a chance of shelter.

"Tent's done," I announced in a drab voice, hoping he would be satisfied and shift the subject.

"Our home!" he cried.

He jumped in eagerly and patted the oilskin next to him. "Let's test it out."

I had a thumbnail I bit too close, and I wedged another fingernail under it. After a good, nervous pinch, I cautiously crawled alongside.

Father Sweet's breath smelled like eggs and wet ash. It was intimate and quiet under the tent.

"You know," he said leaning close to me and meeting my eyes with his, "for boys who show their grit, Acolyte One is in the offing."

He waited for that to sink in.

"Where is the food?" I asked.

"I've got a full sack."

I backed out. "Let's inventory."

His brow knotted and he followed me, silently handing over a bag.

The "full sack" previously held Cavendish potatoes. I reached in to pull out a box of Red Rose tea, pipe tobacco, a box of Kraft Dinner, two cans of Heinz beans, some cracked hard-boiled eggs in a paper bag, three hot dog wieners in an open wrapper, and a sticky, half-full bottle of Camp Coffee. At the bottom was an aluminum pot.

"This is it?"

"Of course! And where we lack, we shall eat off the land, like *coureurs de bois* fed by God's natural bounty! Or, we can see it as a fast. Which only increases our righteousness."

"I'll start a fire. We can eat the hot dogs and eggs now before they smell up and attract a bear."

"Pshaw. We'd hear such a beast coming. Besides, it would make for some good fun chasing it away!"

"Bears don't make noise when they're foraging. You can't fight them off without a gun if they plan to eat you. We haven't even got a hatchet. Have you got a gun?"

"Of course not!"

"Well, then."

"You seem to know your bears."

I wanted to change the subject. "Any good Scout would."

"Your face changes when that word is spoken." He nodded. "Bear."

I rustled in my own pack and found only emergency rations: two granola bars, a squashed Dairy Milk, four raisin boxes, three pepperettes, and a can of water so old it was in Imperial measure.

"I didn't bring a rod and reel. You?" I asked.

He stared blankly.

"I'll make a couple rods after lunch," I said. Scoutcraft would help us extend this lousy supply of food.

While he said his midday prayers, I examined the logs I kicked over. There was no easy way to split them into decent firewood without a hatchet.

Father Sweet removed and kissed his prayer shawl.

I looked him in the eye. "No hatchet, right?"

He shook his head and I took a deep breath.

From deep in my pack, I pulled out the smuggled hatchet I had taken from home. The very one Dad had forbidden me to bring.

"But you've got one," Father said. "How confusing!"

I chipped into the first dry log and said nothing. Brandishing the hatchet out in the open made the hairs on my neck stick up.

"I will help," said Father Sweet. He strode over and hefted the new log. "I imagine you wish to divide it longitudinally."

"Yep."

He propped it up. As I fumbled to get him to hold it properly so I could nick it, the head of the hatchet grazed his bare forearm. He startled. Suddenly, he pulled back his hand, and the bit edge made a long shallow cut in his skin.

He collapsed like I'd punched him in the head and fell back on his ass. "Blood!" he cried. "Blood! Blood!"

"Oh shit!" I cried, and dropped the hatchet, barely missing my own foot.

I seized his arm on the wound and pressured it shut. "Hold this," I said. "I need to get a bandage."

"Oh, my dear boy. I can't, I can't," he whimpered.

"Look away," I said, then guided his hand over the cut and got him to squeeze it. It was not deep — more of a scrape — but it was wet and he shivered and moaned at the feel.

I fetched some gauze from my St. John's kit. After a rinse from the canteen and a few minutes of pressure, it was clotted. Not bad at all.

However, I started to shake.

In a wimpy voice, I reasoned with him while I wrapped his arm in gauze. "Not so bad, is it? Doesn't look so bad to me. Just a scrape."

He wouldn't look at me.

"Listen, no need to tell my dad about this," I said finally. "I mean, don't tell my dad."

"Your father?" he whispered, turning to face me, a minor smile emerging. "Why is that?"

"Well, it's the hatchet. See, I'm not supposed to have it."

There was a pause that felt like an hour. Whenever I imagined my father, I saw heavy black eyebrows that converged like two knives pointing in my face. I believed the sharp hatchet, about which I already felt guilty, would cut the rope at my lynching.

"You naughty little boy," Father said in a sensual, quiet growl. He pulled my chin up with his other hand and gazed deeply into my eyes. "Secrets, eh?"

"Guess so," I replied, looking away.

"Secrets." He nodded. "We've got a little secret, haven't we?" I mumbled.

"We'll have to make sure our adventure here remains sacrosanct."

"Yes."

"We wouldn't want to get in trouble," he whispered. He released my chin. "I swear secrecy, if you do."

"Okay."

"But you must swear that this trip is ours alone. Our secret. All of it."

"I swear."

In silence, I assembled a tripod fire and we ate wieners and eggs skewered on green sticks, without talking.

16

After lunch, I cut some larger switches with my Scout knife. I suggested Father Sweet go into the woods and find me old acorns and a tin can. I threaded the string and twisted some tin into little hooks while he propped himself on one shoulder, smoked his pipe, and watched me. The sun got hot. I changed my shirt. He paused to squint at my body, whispering, "Sublime as Elgin marble."

"Tonight I'll try making a rabbit trap," I said. "I've never done it, but it's worth a shot."

"Truly, an amazing lad."

"It's just Scoutcraft."

"Be prepared," he said deeply, saluting me with his fingers in the trefoil.

I chuckled.

"Ahhh," he sighed. "*There* it is. Oh, you have such a lovely smile, boy. Do you know that?"

"Mm."

"Let me ask you, do your parents know that? Do they appreciate what a truly, truly extraordinary boy you are? I sense not."

"Hand me that acorn."

"*Sicut malum inter silvarum sic dilectus meum.* As the apple among the trees of the wood, so is my beloved."

"Okay."

"*Et fructus sit dulcis.* And his fruit is sweet. What a fine fruit of the woods you are."

"Thanks."

Something whistled in his nose. I saw him trowel a salamander-sized bogie out of his nose with his fingernail and wipe it on a rock.

After a few hours, I had assembled a good campsite, with a circle of rocks around the fire, a well-stacked sixth-of-a-cord of wood, and provisions hanging high off a tree branch. It might be a worthwhile project to lash a latrine, as well, but this was a short trip. I felt productive. I surveyed my work. I had built us a fortress of comfort against the wild.

"I am a man of Nature," Father Sweet announced, smacking mosquitoes off his arms. "In Nature, man is nurtured by the Lord. Air. Water. The food of the earth. Spirit-warmth and soft grass on which to bed. For us, it is impossible to sin. As in the Garden. Once the Woman gave rise to avarice and lust — that is when the worst of civilization arose. The best of civilization takes us back to the naked, pre-lapsarian beauty of God's Nature. The worst leads to lust. And the Enemy. One need never worry in Nature. It is simple. We are all innocent children. God takes care of us."

"I like camping, too," I said, assuming that was his point.

"Ignorant savages, such as those poor Hurons first discovered by the good men of the Catholic mission, foolishly tried to interpret the cosmos without the light of Jesus. How senseless it must have been for them, bumbling in the wilds, not knowing what the world meant. What incredible mercy came from God, sending the Word of God here, eliminating their chaos. Their relief total. Singing of him wherever they went."

I shook my head silently, and thought of what Mike had conveyed about observing the natural world. A deep lesson I was continuing to work on.

Movement caught my eye.

A falcon circled overhead. I assumed there must be something worthwhile in our vicinity, like a mouse warren or bunnies. Father Sweet observed me and sidled along.

"Falcon," I said, noting the wings. "Incredible animal. Look at that."

"How glorious," he said. "Do you know why birds fly, my lad?"

"Definitely hunting, that one."

"The birds fly in praise of God."

"Right," I said.

"Who lords over the forest?"

"Isn't it the Queen?"

"The Queen." He scoffed. "A few hundred years of law. The sovereignty of the Christ God, though, has been here and will be here forever. You understand?"

"Right. Of course."

"These insects are vexatious!"

Flies swarmed our heads like electrons. They'd find some shit or a carcass eventually and leave us alone. Mike Racine said that bugs, birds, and trees make life from every little thing we take for granted. Everything connected to everything else.

"They're just living their lives," I said, regarding the flies. "They don't mean to bug us."

Father Sweet hung his paw on my shoulder.

"Here we are, foot-stuck by sin on this mundane institute, Earth. How sweet to slip that bond and soar higher, higher, higher. Nearer to God."

Here was another of his spiritual lessons. Train the mind to observe what was around us, but then make a correct interpretation. Describe the true, invisible world. Sensible enough for him.

Father Sweet knit some new idea in his mind. I could tell because he asked me, "Have you read Rousseau?"

"I know a kid named Chris Rousseau."

"Oh, my dear, dear boy! You are a delightful hoot!"

I wondered why he found it delightful to make me feel like an idiot.

"Nature is evidence of the Lord, but it is also opposed to us. It is a land where our least civilized impulses can take hold. Consider Eden. We two must be an ark within Nature. That is what the Church gives us — a vessel where we can be right with the Lord while adrift in a sinful world. We can be in the world but not of it. This is what a Catholic education provides you. Do you understand?"

"You betcha," I said, turning my attention to something practical. "I'm going down to the creek."

"Before you go," he said, "tell me a bit about your mother."

Odd question, I thought, *but he's the boss.*

"She and my dad have been married a long time," I said. "My dad works at Indian Affairs."

"I know that. But tell me about her."

I pictured my mother, thin and scrawny, her chin jutting out and her steel hair dry and dropping cigarette ashes. Her neck as long as my forearm as she waves my brother and I away so she can light up a smoke and talk on the phone without our hearing.

"Like what?"

"For example, let's say, what is she most afraid of. I ask as her parish priest, you understand."

"I don't know," I said. She never seemed afraid to me. But I had seen her angry plenty of times, usually when Jamie or I had done something wrong. She got a run in her nylons once because of the zipper from my parka. She told me she'd never been more humiliated in her life. "Being embarrassed, I guess."

He seemed pleased with this answer and began humming to himself.

17

Later, we fished in the river. Father Sweet sang and carried on, unable to keep quiet.

"Sing with me. Surely you know the refrain?"

"I don't."

"It's Handel! What the devil are they teaching you in that infernal school?"

I tried to think. "Like Handel and Gretel?" I asked. He laughed, but I meant it. When I thought of school, I thought of math. Learning geography. Learning French.

In my pocket I had a pack of Thrills gum and I gave him two pieces, hoping it would silence the singing.

It reduced him to humming while he chewed.

"Mm! Delicious," he said.

I shushed him.

He tried to reset his hook, but cringed and fussed.

"I will weep!" he said.

"What?"

He held a worm in his palm. He'd lost the last one I put on without catching a fish. Father Sweet, I learned, could not bear to hook worms. "They are skin! Too fleshy." He shivered.

I baited his hook, but he caught nothing, anyway.

Eventually the fish nibbled and I landed three small crappies for dinner.

"Do you want to clean them?" I asked, knowing the answer.

He shook his head and shuffled away.

"Father, make a basket of your shirt like an apron," I said. "Could you go out and collect sumac leaves? Like those there. A big bunch."

I picked at my thumbnail as I watched him go off, singing his Handel and Gretel and ripping sumac from branches.

He returned with some twiggy sumac in his "apron." While handing it over he came close and breathed through his nostrils onto my face. I pruned the sumac to only the tender bits.

"The fruit of the vine is worthless without the work of human hands," he said.

I cleaned the fish into filets for the pot — two for him, one for me. I seasoned them with a bit of garlic mustard weed. Meanwhile, using some wild raspberries and the sumac, I steeped a lemonade in the Coke bottle. Then I got him to find and wash bulrush roots to roast in the fire.

My stomach groaned.

"It's funny what hunger does, eh?" I said.

"How so?"

"It's a pretty lousy dinner, but it smells to me like Thanksgiving."

"In the priesthood we fast often. Prepare yourself!"

I nodded, noting that — somehow — he was suggesting a career direction. My vocation. *Is this the reason my parents wanted me out here with him? Is that what I'm meant to become?*

"This filet looks delicious!" he said. "We are fishermen. And fishers of men!"

I had poached the fish. As I was about to put it onto some birchbark, a small amount of saliva squirted out his mouth onto my arm.

I wiped it off.

Before sunset, I set the rabbit trap. My Sucrets tin had just enough twine for a tiny noose.

"We'll see if this works."

Silently, I wondered what I would do. Cleaning a fish is one thing, snapping a rabbit's neck is quite another.

"This will catch a hare?" he said, puffing an incredulous scoff. "It appears too simple. Doesn't one need more cunning and trickery?"

"It comes in here and it's snared there. That's it."

"I would have assumed more of a labyrinth was required to set a trap." He contemplated me. "Something clever. This is … snatching a running rabbit straight from the twigs!"

"Pretty much."

I walked back to the campsite.

He invited me to say vespers with him, but I told him I couldn't, saying I needed to prep the campsite for nighttime.

As dusk turned purple, and with the coals still red, I made a sandwich of the fire logs, hoping to keep the fire going overnight. Good old Scoutcraft and something Mike Racine showed us on one of his visits. I put two thigh-thick, long logs in the pit and used green sticks thick as Scout staves to brace the sandwich from falling sideways. The filling was twigs. Jamming three embers into the sandwich, it smoldered and started soon after he finished his prayers.

The bulrushes were fibrous, and I picked threads out of my teeth while I puttered around.

He washed the fish smell out of the pot, filled it with water, and put it on the fire.

"Something for you," he said.

At the boil, he added Camp Coffee syrup from his sticky bottle, poured the mixture in my canteen cup, and prodded me to drink.

"I don't like it," I said.

"Pish. You haven't tried it!"

"I have. My granddad drinks that."

"Drink it, please."

If he loves it so much, why no cup for him? Was this another test? I hated Camp Coffee. Why drink it now, anyway?

"You drink it," I said. "I'm not thirsty."

"It's for you. A special drink for you."

I poked the fire. "I like Postum," I said.

This appeared surprising to him and he was lost for words. His mouth opened and closed.

"Postum again," he finally muttered.

I listened to him breathing and whispering to himself under his breath. The cup cooled, undrunk. Frustrated, he splashed it out, then spent minutes contemplating the bottle, tilting it and shaking it, giving it a whiff, muttering. We watched the fire.

After full dark, the air chilled significantly. With a long sigh, he pulled out his *Hours Liturgy* to recite compline, so I took this as my cue.

"Been a long day. I'm ready for bed," I said.

On hearing this, he finished his compline prayers in a rush with his eyes wide and peering at me obviously as I puttered around.

He clapped and rubbed his hands. "Yes! Let's hit the hay!"

I was exhausted, but I was not keen to be alone in the tent, again, with Father. I hoped he'd be quiet.

He wriggled into the tent and tied its ribbons shut, wheezing urgently. By flashlight, I watched him squeeze out of his clothes in acts of excited gymnastics. He stripped down to peculiar grey underwear resembling a girdle.

"I shall zip our sleeping bags together!" he said.

"No, thanks," I said, and turned out the flashlight.

The dark became visible through my remaining senses. Sounds of fabric on skin, muffled under canvas. Gross smells of sweat and soil, spiked with juniper. The heavy manoeuvring I felt against my leg.

"Let us caucus for warmth!" he said.

"It's plenty warm in here."

He groaned.

I turned my back to him. I remained fully clothed. I burrowed deeper into my down bag and set my face deep into the base angles of the tent. A canvas pocket of air was all I had, stinky with earth and oilskin.

He breathed through his mouth, and the only sound was his shivering breath and dry swallowing. The sound of panting and licking lips filled the tent.

His fingertips stroked my back, awkward with the angle. I felt his quivering hand trace the outline of my neck, and I flinched. His fingers dipped into the bag and onto my shoulder blades. Every hair on my body prickled up in gooseflesh. Low in his throat, he mewled.

"Hey," I said. "Quit it."

He grunted. After a moment he withdrew his hand.

In a whisper, face close to my head, he talked about the sleeping porch at his family's house, growing up in Cape Breton. He returned from boarding school for summer. Cousins and uncles would all share beds, sleepless in the summer heat. And they would play games under the covers.

"Would you like to play a game?" he whispered.

"No. I want to sleep." My eyes were wide, staring at the black. I breathed the tiny amount of cool air draughting in from the tent edge.

He continued to mouth-breathe and move his sticky tongue around.

Outside, there was a hoot.

"Ooh! Now what's that?" he said.

"Owl."

He snuggled up to my back.

"Are you sure? My word! It sounds beastly!"

I tried worming away, close as I could scrunch under the tent. Any farther and pegs might pull up, sending me to roll right into the open air.

"Definitely."

"Perhaps the owl sees a predator."

"You mean like a fox? Or," I said in a different voice, "you mean like a bear?"

"Yes, that's it," he said. "Heavens. It could be a bear."

This wasn't true, of course. I was rational enough to know. I knew what a bear sounded and smelled like since the day I was born. It was as much in my bones as it was in my occasional nightmares — where it never appeared but snuffed and snorted in the darkness just out of my sight.

But the way Father Sweet said the word — in a slow, hypnotic drawl — pulled it right from my bad dreams and into the tent; the breath on my neck and warmth of the monster right at my back.

Ghosts, and bears.

I froze as he pulled in close. He writhed in a kind of slow dance, giving off heat, breathing on me.

This went on for a while, but I stayed flinched and crunched up while he mouth-breathed and writhed.

He became restless. Flopping on his back, his side, his back again, and sighing, as if something was on his mind, but I ignored him. He whispered my name. I still ignored him, pretending to sleep. He stroked my back again, hand trembling.

He moaned and then held his breath.

Finally, there was a torrent of activity. He thrashed about, as if beset by itching. He hiccupped. He sounded as though he might sneeze. I thought maybe he was having a seizure or was being stung by fire ants. Before I could ask if he was all right, the behaviour stopped abruptly and he sighed loudly. He settled down and began snoring loud as a bear.

I remained awake, rolling over in my mind the dozens of unusual sentences he'd spoken to me that day.

18

In the black of night, I forgot where I was.

I awoke with a start. My face was pressed to the ground, smelling grass and cold mud. Behind me droned the grizzly snore of my tentmate. As he snorkeled the air, I recalled my situation with urgent dread. I was in a tent. I was far from home. I was a twelve-year-old boy. I was alone with Father Sweet.

In silence, I crawled to the flap and undid its ribbons. This old pup tent had no zippers, which was good. I kept it quiet.

In our little clearing, the semicircle treeline appeared by starlight to be a wall. A black palisade. It stood on guard against my leaving. But the summer night smelled good and fresh. A few deep breaths and I felt a bit better. The cold air fought off the hard lump in my throat.

Only me, and the forest, which in those days I considered a friend.

Deep in the sky and spread into the Milky Way was the unpolluted light of our stars, a heavenly river of petrified fireworks. Majestic, kindly, long and uncomplicated as a gravel road.

One troop meeting last year, Blanter, the Scout leader, brought in an antique navy sextant to show what it could do. He encouraged us to borrow it and learn celestial navigation if we wanted and earn a badge. Imagine that. I looked up to those pinpoints, imagining I could read where I was and where I could go. Incredible. Magical. Instructions from God, truly.

I looked down. There was Father Sweet's stained tent, dull and sickening under the starlight.

Could I just leave? If I were serious, I suppose I *could*. Simply follow that brook downstream until I came to a town. I could phone home. Maybe Dad would pick me up. But what would they say, my parents? What kind of trouble would I be in? What would Father Sweet tell them? I can't imagine.

Dad's face loomed before me, fist-like, and I shuddered.

The campfire was down to embers, but I was using one of Mike's techniques to keep it alive overnight. It seemed to be going okay.

A gorgeous night-quiet filled the forest. The only sounds came from the Picanoc River burbling away, and the brush of leaves in an overnight breeze.

My eyes got droopy. I tiptoed back to the tent and into the buzzing of his breath. I might fall asleep again. Maybe.

I lay on my back, feeling every lump of the hard mud beneath the tarp. The regular tick of a clock did not apply now. Night was an interlude. Somehow, I had placed myself outside my own life. There was what I knew from the past, and now this purgatory. Camping with Father Sweet forever here. I had no sense of a future.

Father Sweet called this Eden. Or rather, the farthest west, East of Eden, whatever that meant.

I missed my family. *We're tough,* I thought. *Serious people. I can do this.*

I thought of the *bris* we attended last week, and my dad's anger. Why was he so angry? *Like a baptism,* Dad said. Something to fix original sin. Except it involved knives, rather than water. And dinks. And blood.

Inherited sin. Your gift for being born.

19

With a heavy arm around me, pinning me, I woke up feeling the various crooks, lumps, and angles of his body poking against my back and bum. He must have farted, because the tent stunk. And it wasn't the frivolous, amusing fart smell of a kid at a sleepover. This was a serious, deeply unfunny stench.

The canvas glowed brown in the sunlight. My eyes were dry, like I'd been up all night, instead of awake for my one moment of escape for some fresh air. But I must have slept at some point.

He groaned.

I didn't respond. He groaned louder.

"What's wrong?" I said, finally.

"It's my infernal back, dear boy. I do not have the lissome spine of youth, as you do." His eyes glinted at me. "It is stiff. Will you rub it?"

It was then I realized the fart smell was coming from his mouth. The more he talked, the worse it got.

"Okay."

With great energy and no sign of a stiff back, he unbuttoned his skivvy, peeling it like a banana to his waist, and laid himself out flat. His skin, flabby and tufted with hairs, was cold and damp. I knelt to his side and prodded at his clammy, rubbery back.

"Lower," he said, so I moved down. His torso wriggled like a maggot. "Lower."

I got up. "I'm going to start the fire."

I unzipped the flap, feeling nauseous. The fresh morning air was a cool relief on my face. I shivered in the cold as I went pee.

Overnight, the campsite itself had remained untouched by critters. Not one ember from the fire was left alive. My log sandwich had burned, snuffed, and failed. So much for the expertise my camping badge had earned me. In the sunlight I collected dry grass and twigs to start again.

I yawned and it brought no refreshment; my teeth chattered together.

I checked in on the little rodent carcass. It had been picked apart further by bugs. Or scavengers. Maybe even by its own kind. The body now looked like the head of something larger. It was an illusion, but I perceived now a hollow-eyed face, a ghoul bent on frightening me.

Father Sweet crawled out slowly, his face crumpled with frustration. He silently pissed into the forest and ripped a big fart.

He sat on a stump, picking crumbs from his beard and eating them while I lit a new fire.

"Do you want me to show you how to light a fire?" I asked, feeling that he was grumpy and volatile. "It's a good practical skill."

Shaking his head, he sighed loudly, as he had done last night, the way someone does when they are spoiling for a fight.

"We had a Native guy come and talk to the troop a few months ago about fire tending. He was awesome."

"We must dislodge this," he said, scowling, waving his hand at me like a magician. "Between us."

I stacked logs into a small criss-cross rack. *Dislodge what?*

"Did you hear me?"

I mumbled, shivering again. Avoiding his gaze, I gave the thumbnail a good solid bite that shot a pain deep into my arm.

"A queer seducer you are indeed, boy."

A what? A queer sorcerer? As in witchcraft? Why would he think of me as a sorcerer?

"You led me to sin last night," he said darkly.

I remained silent.

"It was your sudden frigidity and declension."

"My what?" I said. "I didn't clench anything."

"You forced my soul to be craven. You know that to spill seed is a sin. This results from thwarted natural love, which is God's way. Don't play dumb."

I stared at him, trying my best. Trying my best to understand and keep him happy.

"I'm sorry," I said.

He chortled without smiling, then made the sign of the cross in the air. "I forgive you."

Automatically, I blessed myself in response.

"Don't cook anything," he said, gruffly. "We'll celebrate Mass first."

"Okay," I replied. "Don't know what I'd cook, anyway."

He ambled to his pack and removed a black lacquered case the size of a small shoebox.

"What's that?" I asked.

My question pleased him, and he relaxed. "I'll show you."

Off came the finely crafted lid. Inside was a series of neat compartments holding miniaturized implements of the Roman rite: candles, chalice, linens, cruets, even a tiny censer.

"Wow. It's really cool," I said. It reminded me of the miniature Sucrets kit I had made. I loved kits and tools of any kind. "Can I touch?"

"More than that, my boy. Set up for Mass," he chirped. "We'll use that log there as an altar. Sincere as Abraham and Isaac's."

I pulled out the first thing, a bronze disc like a woman's makeup compact. I recognized it as a pyx, a pocket container for consecrated Eucharist. It was engraved: *AG ad BS*.

"This set was a final gift from my mentor and first senior parish priest, the Monsignor Aloysius Gast. See the *AG*?"

"What's *BS*?"

"My name. Benjamin Sweet. This pyx is dear to me. The miracle of communion is the heart of our faith. A wafer made by human hands, in fact, becomes the body — the actual body — of the Son of Man. Amazing."

I set up our altar.

Celebrating Mass outdoors felt weird. To me, Mass was an indoor activity. And I had never considered the little paper-thin communion wafer we ate became skin or something. I thought it was like Santa. A fib you're meant to play along with.

A crow perched on a nearby branch. Probably hoping this was a picnic. While I set up, it watched me with a wary bead of eye.

"We'll use the Vulgate liturgy," Father Sweet declared. "For fun!"

"Sounds fun," I muttered.

This made Mass challenging for an altar boy like me who didn't know Latin and couldn't do the responses, but the order of the game stayed the same. The ewer still gets poured. The chalice is raised. I managed to keep up, after all. It was a long Mass considering it was just the two of us. He added all his morning prayers and singing, as well. At the Eucharist, I was compelled by him to do it on my knees and *in lingua*, which at our parish was only fashionable for elderly people.

"*Corpus Christi.*"

"Amen."

Afterward, I was happy to restock the playset into its lacquered kit-box.

"Although the Holy Father has proscribed it, I still have great fondness for Constantinian tradition," said Father Sweet. "Catholicism is a precision science. You know it more here in Nature, away from any civic distractions. The Eucharist holds the immensity of God in it."

"Sure."

At his request, I put on the pot for some tea. Meanwhile he babbled on about this and that. His commentary was lengthy and impossible to follow.

"The single most important achievement of the human race, that's what the liturgy is. Oh, the sacraments are perfect. Hundreds of years of revelation have made them. Even if the men who perform them are not perfect they are a perfect good …"

The fire was stoked back up. I planned a breakfast of pepperettes, granola bars, and tea.

He talked on and on, in his droning blather.

"… very useful. What mercy. What grace. What love. And only in his greeting us …"

"I wonder if we snared a rabbit last night," I said, speaking over him. It did not stop his monologue.

"… through the Church, and as a man-God in Jesus can the Church militant …"

He carried on over my shoulder as I checked the rabbit trap. "Trap's empty," I announced.

"… engulf us, understand us and meliorate us. Don't you agree?"

"Yep."

We ate our breakfast, washing it down with tea from the shared cup. Afterward, I whittled him a rudimentary spoon.

"I'm going to hack down firewood," I told him, handing him the new utensil. "You can help."

I smiled when he said he planned to rest his back and smoke, and I wandered off in search of good dry logs.

Often when camping, time accelerates and simple tasks like preparing a fire, foraging, fishing, or cooking speed the passage of hours. By contrast, this trip's tedium ran counter-clockwise. I checked my watch, expecting lunchtime and found it had barely passed nine.

20

On my return, arms full of logs and kindling, I discovered he'd gone into my pack and set up my chess kit.

I stacked the firewood, then sat down to play.

"I'll be white."

"Imagine God becomes man. Why?" he said. "To know what it is to be man. That's why. The needs of the flesh. But oh, also its pains! And its *pleasures*. Then, the Good News. By his own sacrifice of blood and body, we — his people — are marked and saved. Only by becoming man could he give this gift."

"Your bishop," I said, pulling it off.

"Aha! Sacrifice."

It cost me a rook, while putting me a move away from losing either a knight or my own bishop.

"You know," he said, "I was thinking of something special we could do. We could become blood brothers."

It struck me as odd that Father Sweet knew this boyhood tradition, common amongst Scouts.

"What for?"

"Well, we can share secrets."

"Like confession?"

"No, outside confession. Such as … special secrets."

"Let's finish the game."

"If I win, then we do it. If not, it is your choice. Have we got a deal?"

We made the deal, though I'm not sure how I agreed or what happened next, but it was a quick finish, and in a few short moves I was mated. Bewildered, soon enough I was bleeding and repeating words of fidelity to him in a daze.

"We're different from others, you know. Those of us in this special order — you the acolyte, me the priest. It is a secret society, apart from the world."

Our eyes were level with one another.

I found myself nodding slowly.

I was standing and staring into the fire, holding shut the bleeding pinprick on my palm. The blood he offered came from a bit of crust under his gauze. The axe nick I'd made by accident.

"Is there anything you wish to ask me, lad?" His arm was around my waist. He was not much taller than me.

"No. I'm okay."

"Anything at all? Questions about God? Maybe you want to talk about your family? Or your body. Your body is about to go through changes, and perhaps you'd like to talk about your body and some new feelings you may experience?"

"No."

"No, what?"

"No, Father."

His hand moved to my head.

"I see how special you are. I haven't quite figured you out yet, however. A marvel, I think, wise beyond your years. Steely of gaze. Fit of breast. Capable of spirit. You entranced me the moment our eyes met over dinner.

"You are Alexander, beautiful and vital. And I, well — I am Aristotle." He sighed. "I have travelled many roads, you know. It's a hard life I've lived. From my earliest days in boarding school, to the seminary. Never settling. Ever nomadic. Such is the lot of the pilgrim. We must take succor, love, and friendship wherever we find it. I perceive we are the same, you and I." He seized my hand. "This. *This* — what we have — is precious. I am so glad you chose me."

I bit my thumb. Lunch was Heinz beans, with a dandelion salad of crumbled chocolate, raisins, and fresh raspberries.

21

While foraging for dinner near the campsite, something unexpected happened to me.

I got the feeling that I was about to die, though everything seemed fine on the surface. I stopped to catch my wind, finding myself hungry for air, unable to take a satisfying breath. Immediately I felt sick, as if I were in an elevator, descending quickly. I felt a huge weight pressing on my chest. Although my eyes were wide open, the sunlight seemed hazy. Every sound came sharp as a buzz saw. The forest seemed mean-spirited, haunted with evil-sounding squirrel chatter and squawking blue jays. The crows seemed angry.

Where were we?

We're a million miles from anywhere. We have always been here, alone. Him and me. There are no other people. Anywhere. There is no end to this. Ever. We made the firepit, we packed the earth, we made the land flat. We always caught the fish. We always ate the sumac.

Usually I loved the feeling of isolation, but not this time. Something felt wrong, as if everything I did was wrong. God watched me and was starting to hate me the way I figured he hated my dad.

Colours went bright as fingerpaints. My chest tensed in pain. I couldn't breathe.

It was as if the air lacked oxygen.

I felt like I might die.

"Look! Wild carrot!" Father Sweet cried. He sounded faint, distant. As if on a cliff a mile away. Each word slowly came to me. "We can eat this!" he said.

It took enormous energy to focus, to keep my words steady. They came out quavering, afraid to frighten their owner. "It might be hemlock," I said.

"Hemlock!" he replied, reverently.

"I think they look a lot alike. Not sure." Now that I was talking about something I could pretend to know about, I made an effort to sound normal and calm, breathe steadily, and to blink away the tears that unexpectedly filled my eyes. "Which is which? I dunno and I haven't got a guidebook with me to check. Better just steer clear."

It was a heavy task, speaking and keeping my cool. I was trying desperately to save myself. I believed I was losing my mind in a panic. I was convinced that if I didn't concentrate I would forget how to breathe, keel over any moment and die. I couldn't explain why.

"Hemlock! Socrates's vehicle!" Father Sweet talked for several minutes about Socrates.

I tried to slow my breathing, which was rapid and irregular. I needed to do something to calm myself.

Beside me swayed tall grasses. I sat cross-legged and pulled at them.

I weaved a rudimentary basket from the grasses. It took time, and was distracting, though the basket looked more like a floppy hat or broken-down bag. It was tied off at the ends and could carry a handful of something light.

"Could you find raspberries, please?" I asked him, feeling more controlled now. "Raspberries only. Don't pick any other berry." I handed him the basket and pointed him at the bush.

He was off, and I took advantage of the gap.

With my knife and knee, I snapped six sticks, each a half foot long.

In fast, nervous movements — praying he didn't come back too soon — I frantically pulled up the corner pins of the tent. I carefully unfurled the oilskin floor, revealing the juniper boughs of our bed.

Sowbugs and millipedes scurried as I carefully plotted an invisible line, bisecting the tent into my half and his. I staked the sticks into the ground, leaving only an inch poking up. Finally, I replaced the oilskin floor and pinned the tent down.

Panting, I finished just in time to see Father Sweet returning with his basket, a proud look around his mouth.

"I found no raspberries," he said. "But I have collected these red berries here."

"Those are poison."

22

We fished again, as the day ended.

Rather, I fished again.

He made no effort to help. Instead, he watched me, smiling, smoking his pipe on the shore, propped up on an elbow. I caught seven crayfish and two sunfish. Enough for a fish stew.

He prayed as the air cooled and the sun set, while I cooked.

I quietly served dinner. A cup for me, the pot for him. It tasted dank, watery, and unsatisfying. More like a sandy broth of bad water. With fish chunks.

No matter. He was in a good mood.

"Here, have a good long drink of this," he said cheerfully.

It was a full flask of rye whisky. *A real man's drink*, I thought. I wiped the top with my sleeve and gulped a slug. It burned, and rose up sharp in my throat. I spat and coughed while he chuckled.

"Let the warmth reach your bones. I should have brought this out last night instead of that infernal Camp Coffee. Drink more!"

I handed it back.

He took a sip, and tried passing it again. I shook my head and he gave me a look similar to the look my father shoots me when

I've forgotten to do something like sweep the porch or take out the garbage. Father Sweet sighed and rattled his head.

He pulled out his liturgy and mumbled through evening prayers.

It was warm and bright around the fire. At our backs whispered the cold dark of the bush and a few things rustled among the leaves and twigs. Anything might crouch there. On past camping trips, I'd be curious about the raccoon or fox. Now it seemed more likely to me to be a predator. Madman. Killer. We squatted on opposite logs while the fire stung my eyes and embers popped up. I could see Father Sweet's face changing in the firelight, one look replacing another in quick succession. It grew dark.

He hummed in tenor an eerie chant.

"A ghost story?" he asked.

"I guess," I replied after a pause.

He thought a moment.

"There is a road not far from here that leads from Gracefield," he began. "It is the road we drove on yesterday, in fact. In parts, it is no more than a gravel trail through the pine forest. At night, this road is cursed. Evil spirits of the Devil frolic and lurk there.

"One night, many years ago, a young man drove alone. By the side of the road suddenly he sees, barely lit by his headlamps, a stooped fellow — a hitchhiker. He slows his car to a halt, being a Christian man and thinking he may be able to offer help. The hitchhiker opens the door. The driver cannot see his face, but his clothes appear old and tattered. Without a word, the hitchhiker gets in. An old, brimmed fedora hides his face.

"There is a smell to the hitchhiker not unlike this campfire here. The smell of brimstone. He raises the brim of his hat. Now the driver can see the hitchhiker is horribly disfigured: bloated like a hog's head, bruised, grey, dry with growths. The hitchhiker whispers that he has a terrible secret. He needs a confessor, someone who can make a difference. Someone to save him. Our man, the driver, agrees to learn the secret. So the hitcher hands him an old King George five-dollar note and says he must go to the local tavern in the next town. He is instructed to go in, buy refreshment with the note, and wait.

"The hitcher tells him to pull over, and he gets out of the car. 'Soon,' the hitcher says as he walks on, 'you will know all.'

"Our man drives along and finds the tavern, precisely as the hitchhiker said. He asks for a glass of ale, placing his old five-dollar note on the bar.

"The bartender looks up and says he cannot serve him.

"'Why not?' asks our man.

"The bartender says, 'The hitchhiker is never coming to tell you his secret.'

"The driver is shocked. How does this barkeep know about the hitchhiker? The bartender says the hitchhiker is dead, having died thirty years earlier in a fight with his brother. And the bartender knows this because he is that brother, and he killed him as Cain had killed Abel, and although his ghost continually tries to expose the heinous sin, the bartender must cover his tracks as he has done for years. And as he says this, he comes around with a rope, and strangles the young man, who has at last learned the secret, the last he will ever know."

I felt the lids of my eyes peel far into their sockets.

"And I know this because …" Father Sweet paused for effect. "I am that murderous brother!"

I shot to my feet, knees crouched ready to run. "Is that true?"

Father Sweet appeared gleeful at my panic. "Oh, my dear boy, of course not! It's just a silly story!"

Every sense I had was now on edge. Was I being watched? Beyond the ring of light provided by the fire, the woods were a huge black abyss. The fire warmed my face and hands, but my back felt vulnerable and cold. I looked over my shoulder.

I had an overwhelming urge to sit next to someone, and quietly toddled over to Father Sweet.

"Ah," he said. "There we are." Tilting, he shuffled his bum closer on the log and placed his arm on my back.

He stroked my hair. "Is this okay?" he said, softly. "Are you with me now, my Hyacinth? You are a good boy. A Greek ideal."

The fire was warm.

"You know, Jesus was a man. He knew us as a man," he said, gently caressing my head. "God made flesh. Loneliness. A passionate desire can become pleasure in pain itself, like a stiff ache that can only be soothed with the application of more pain. The bitter kiss of goodbye. All this God knows — as we know it deeply, my boy."

I entered a dreamy state, separated from my body.

My gaze was transfixed by the fire. I heard what he said. My head nodded, but I did not make it do so. Every breath was slow, deep. My body, numb. Father Sweet's eyes filled with emotion as he recited a soliloquy.

"Jesus came to be a man to understand the cravings and needs of a man, but also the embodiment of God's love. *Agape*. Unpolluted by animal lusts. The purest — purest and highest — truly the highest of God's gifts to men."

His voice sounded a note I hadn't heard before.

"The *atrament* is around us. It claws at us. Look at it. But here, in the warmth of His flame, we are safe. When Jesus rose, he entered us here," he said, tapping his heart.

"Our precious nepotism: the priest and his acolyte, avoiding any franchise with women. *Agape*, our secret, unpolluted, pristine love — handed down from priest to disciple for nearly two thousand years. Continent and manumitted from lust. God has made you special, but I will show you how to have an extraordinary life. Show you true love. No lust. True love, as God intended for our kind. For if one lies down alone, how can one have warmth? Ah, but if two should lie down. Two solitudes connecting in love. *Agape!* God Himself. *Agape!*"

I stood. "Let's put more logs on."

The fire crumbled down. He searched my eyes eagerly.

"I feel queasy," I said. Must have been the whisky.

23

I considered forcing myself to vomit. That way it might convince Father Sweet to take me home, but I pictured my parents and their wrath as he delivered me to them. Quivering, I resolved to ride out the remaining evening. The night became cool enough that I added a sweater. We crawled into the tent. Despite the temperature, Father Sweet chose to bed down in his old-fashioned underwear again. His body odour was strong as a snow boot.

I did not sleep, and I was unable to think. My mind slipped away hypnotically and off-kilter. Somehow, we were back in our old positions. I found myself at the edge of the canvas with my face to the ground. He spoke but I could not hear what he said. There was, again, that insistent sighing of his, and his menacing restlessness. Did last night ever end? I heard his arms moving. He whispered my name and I resorted to ignoring him. I was not there. I became a ghost.

Without a flashlight, it was blackness, and each sound rubbed close against the ears. I pinched my thumb.

He shuffled his body closer to me along the oilskin, and I heard him yelp when the sticks poked him in the ribs, the same sticks I remembered planting under the floor in the afternoon. It was as if someone else had done that, but it was a friend. I'd given myself a gift that I'd forgotten.

Growing relieved, I took a breath.

I could think. The fugue broke. I was alert.

He was mumbling. I breathed the air wafting in from the edge of the tent, which was fresh and cold and good.

In that cold air, breathing long and deep, I could relax a little.

At some point sleep came, but it was broken by a sudden, frantic movement above me.

I gasped.

His huge, smelly bulk was on top of my body. I was in the midst of a struggle.

He was babbling incoherently, like a lunatic. "*Continentiam! Agape, agape!*" I could not see his face, but I smelled his foul breath, his dirty, oily face and hair.

Then, with a crow-like shriek, he cried out, "No! No! Oh no! The lust, the lust! No. No."

And he rolled over, and he was still as the grave.

The moment passed.

He snored.

I was shaking. Back at the tent mouth, eyes wide open; this time, it was I who breathed hard, in shivery gasps. *What just happened?*

Quietly, I cried for a long time.

Why am I here?

Was he even awake?

Was I awake now?

24

When you are startled by a bear in the woods, there is a certain facial expression you make. You cannot help it. Bug-eyed, stretch-mouthed, red-cheeked. Your hair might even stand up. You won't scream. You're too frightened. You are paralyzed.

It's pure terror. You are staring down a monster. It may be your end.

That was how I found Father Sweet as I opened the tent that morning.

He was backed against a beech trunk as if — having been shot by arrows — he was breathing his last, gasping and moaning in agony.

I spun round, looking for the bear.

There was nothing.

I turned back, and it was then that I spotted the underwear around his ankles. Watching the first blob of muck fall, I heaved a sigh of relief knowing he was only using the tree as a toilet.

As for me, I had awakened that morning having wet myself. Something I had not done since I was four. It was shameful. Humiliating.

He wasn't in the tent, so I had quickly changed from my sopping underwear and camping trousers into a pair of shorts.

After a quick rinse in the river, I lay my wet clothes on a rock to sun-dry. But for a single, long airplane vapour trail, the morning sky was clear of any cloud. It was warm.

I had the shakes, though I was not cold. The first aid kit held Aspirin, so I took one with canteen water. The muscles twitched in my upper limbs as I raised the pill to my mouth.

Maybe I had a fever. Or I was losing my mind.

I got to work gathering kindling.

Everything with Father Sweet had gotten confusing and weird, exactly as I had warned my dad.

The rodent body was all but gone now, little more than a few tufts of fur. Mostly grass. No faces. Its carcass had become soil. There was only the return to Nature.

Nearby, Father Sweet was doing a series of awkward-looking squats and exercises in his underwear while humming cheerfully.

"And now, my 5BX!"

He ran in place for a few seconds then began doing sit-ups. Fully out of wind, he stopped.

"More like 2BX," I said.

"I beg your pardon," he said sternly, huffing. He seemed disappointed I was not impressed by his display. "Set up for Mass," he barked.

He disappeared into the tent.

Once I'd got the fire back in shape, I dutifully set up our log altar, enjoying the layout's symmetry. The curve of the forest, and the tall ash trees, created an apse. I built a church. Our Descended Lord of Nature.

He emerged and whipped his stole over his neck.

It was quick, in English, with no reading and he never looked me in the eye. Just Eucharist, rapid as can be. He grumbled that he would recite lauds on his own that morning, and I gladly traipsed off to clear and pack the altar.

I reassembled the case to the screeching of blue jays. Over my shoulder, I sensed him hovering.

He was done his prayers, but wandered around, aimless and impatient. "Why are you quivering?" he asked me, his breath sour as pickles with old pipe smoke. "Look at you. Shivering like an old lady. Why?"

"I don't know."

"Stop it."

I cleared my throat. "I can't."

"I said stop that. Stop it. You are being indulgent."

I didn't know how to appease him. I just wanted this last day to go by quickly. I was almost home.

"Yes, Father."

Father Sweet slumped down on a log near the fire.

He seemed disappointed. "The next time we spend the night together, we must become closer."

I didn't answer. He threw up his hands at me. "It's as if you understand nothing," he muttered. "Like nothing is true with you. You are deliberately desecrating your vocation."

For our breakfast we ate the last can of beans in silence. I washed out the pot and made tea for him. We still had the Kraft Dinner, which I planned as lunch before we could finally, finally go home.

He had a pipe and a cup of tea.

"Ours is a vocation of sacrifice, but we gain so much. We gain service of the Lord and we win each other. Listen to me," he said. "You will lose everything you value. But this is what God wants for you. And your parents."

My jaw trembled. What did I value?

"Within the Church there is complete freedom," he said. "We are ourselves. Don't you see how precious this is? God himself has anointed us, apart from the faithful."

A long smile came across his face and he perked up. Something occurred to him. He chuckled into the mug. Whatever blocked up his mood dislodged. All cheer now, he hummed and looked into his pack. He was eager to share an idea.

"There is a place nearby I would us to hike to. Something I want to show you."

I reached for my backpack.

"No, no," he said. "Leave that. I shall bring my rucksack. And all our needs. You need only bring yourself."

More weirdness, I thought. What could I do?

He pulled together his kit and seemed determined.

I filled my canteen and we were off, hiking upstream.

25

With no cloud cover, the sun made quick work of rising and getting hot.

We climbed up a moderate-sized escarpment that was difficult to hike. Below, the river got deep and then went rapid. The forest became thick, with plenty of old, felled trees, and the terrain forced us to the edge of the ravine. We walked a narrow ledge that was ragged and crumbly. There was no trail.

It kept getting rougher. The forest came right up to the edge of the ravine wall, which was dangerous and steep. I felt weak. My hands still quaked. He led on, making his way by grabbing at trees for balance like an orangutan. The terrain rose higher and I saw that the easier path would be across the river. There was no shore on this side. Because of the slope, I had to walk at a painful angle, and a single slip would have sent me down and my body would break on the rocks and all my blood would drain into the river.

How can he do this? Even managing to carry a pack at the same time? What gave him this sudden energy?

I saw the worst ahead, and clipped my canteen to my belt loop.

At its most treacherous part, the ledge disappeared, changing into a rocky and baked-mud slope — almost a vertical cliff — covered with ragged weeds. Dense forest overhung the top, putting the drop into shadow. At the crest of the slope, there was a crooked cedar blown by wind into an angled, lopsided cross. The ravine here had weedy vines and plants holding dirt. Far below, small rapids gushed along ready to drown you dutifully if you slipped.

"It might be easier to go into the bush and then swing back to the riverbank," I shouted to him, so far ahead of me.

"That would take hours!" he called back.

"Why don't we go back?"

"Almost there!"

I fell farther behind him, but at last I could see that the high ground was giving way ahead to a hill, and then a small open flood plain down to the river.

Finally, we descended. We came upon a flatter ravine bottom, where both river shores were obscured by bulrushes. The river here was shallow and gentle. There was another wide bend ahead.

Now we were more than a thirty-minute walk from the campsite. I was out of breath.

This new location was strange to me, with the high bulrushes and a bad smell. I did not feel the control a good Scout can have over his campsite. This was an open area not well-travelled by people, but maybe by animals.

"There." Father Sweet pointed at a minor, sulphurous spring that was drooling over some stones into the river with little more force than a drippy hose.

"See? *That*, my boy, is a font."

I stared blankly at the dribble. It smelled putrid.

He seemed proud and stood with his fists on his hips.

"Remember? We were discussing the font of life?"

It came back to me — the gore of the heart fountain.

"Oh! Right. So that's it?"

He nodded.

"A font," I said. "Okay. So that's a font."

"Do you understand now? Everything?"

I nodded cautiously, detecting he meant something momentous.

"Now," he said in a weighty voice, "let's get on with it."

He dropped his pack, withdrew two striped beach towels and set a long-lens Pentax camera on top.

"What's happening?" I asked.

"Let's go for a dip," he said, urgently pulling off his clothes.

"I haven't got a bathing suit."

"A skinny dip!"

"I don't like swimming."

"Now, now," he said, hopping and tugging off his pants and undergarments. "You must bathe, my lad. Hygiene."

He was naked now, wearing only a wooden cross on a thin leather cord, and beginning an awkward heron-walk into the chilly water. All the hairs of his back prickled alive down to the ditch of his arse.

"Come, my boy, the water is *glorious!*" he said, shivering, thigh-deep and splashing some handfuls onto his chest.

"Can't be. You've got goosebumps."

He smiled and bent over to dramatically inspect and pull at his balls. "Oh, you're looking that closely, eh?" he said.

When he stood up again, the shape of his dick had changed.

"Well, it's just the effect of temperature," he announced. "Now, you come in here."

"I haven't got a towel," I said, picking at my thumbnail.

"I brought you one."

"I don't want to get wet and cold."

"No, no! That's not it at all! Are you really so dense? Be open to experience! Aren't you an adventurer?"

"I've gone swimming in a river before."

"Don't be shy, my lad. You've got no reason. Why, you're Greek perfection!"

"It's fine for you, but I'm not going in. No way." I lowered myself to sit on a rock near the pack, eyeing his camera.

He stood for a while, hands on hips, breathing and thinking, his chest scrubby with charcoal hair and the grey flabby skin on his shapeless torso pale as an uncooked sausage.

"Oh, look! There's something interesting down here on the bottom," he said finally, making a big show of looking into the water. "Come see!"

I didn't answer. My thumb started to bleed with the picking.

"Come, come look! Ooh, I think it's a little crab or something."

I clutched a big chip of stone. "Crayfish, maybe."

"Yes, but I'm not sure. Come tell me."

I crossed my arms. "No, thanks."

He pondered me. Another expression crossed his face. Bitterness, maybe.

"Are you a shadow?" he asked. The question gave me chills, the way he spoke.

"What?"

Suddenly, his demeanour changed. "Now, you listen here," he said in a new voice, pointing at me. "Your parents will be very cross if they learn you were difficult…. And worse, that you did not bathe."

The pulse in my neck throbbed. My face grew hot.

"I've got responsibility. I *will* tell your parents you were a wilful, naughty … scamp!"

A big lump engorged my throat. My trembling fingers fiddled with the stone.

He held up his right arm, with its bandage from my accident with the hatchet. With his short, baby finger, he pointed at his wound. "We wouldn't want *anyone* to get in trouble."

Oh, god, I thought. *Dad will kill me.* I found that suddenly I was breathing hard as a runner.

Minutes passed. There he stood, naked, thigh-deep in the water with his beard quivering in the cold, staring fiercely into my eyes.

I felt weak. As if it would help me cling to gravity, I hugged my knees.

"After all this effort," he said, looking to the heavens. "It's true what they say. No good deed goes unpunished. Don't you understand I have beaten my heart empty for you?"

I kept stuck in position.

"You brought me to this place!"

I shook my head in confusion.

"I am Hylas! After all this, I should receive you. My deserts."

Squeezing my thumbnail was all I could do to keep my nerve.

"Perhaps you are not who I thought you were," he said with a long sigh and another gaze skyward. "Perhaps I have gone on holiday with the wrong brother."

I clutched the stone like an axe head.

"Leave him out of it," I cried.

He tilted his head and grinned.

"Yes. That must be it, eh? The wrong brother."

I pictured Jamie, shorter than me, weaker than me. One night in the tent such as the two I had just endured would have surely led to an epileptic fit. How would Father Sweet have responded to that? How would my baby brother make it out in one piece? As it was, it was not looking good for me, and I was bigger than him.

"Maybe I should plan a new trip," said Father Sweet, smirking. "With the little one. The correct brother."

I bit my lip and stared back.

"Or not?" He shrugged. "Prove it. Prove to me you are not the wilful brother." He leaned my way. "Come here."

It was Saturday morning. Right now, Jamie was probably sitting at the kitchen table, eating one of Mum's grilled-cheese sandwiches. Maybe she sat with him.

I thought of her, gossiping on the phone, chewing the paint off her nails and smoking. My heart broke, missing her. In the rare times I had hugged my mother — like last Christmas when we got the CCM bikes — she would stiffen at the touch and go all cold. But at that moment I longed for her to hold me close, so I could smell the Arpège and Du Maurier in her blouse while she protected me, and I could shut my eyes.

I swallowed hard and blinked away tears.

Sticky with my own sweat, the rock fell from my hand back to the other river-washed stones.

Up raised my head. This put a smile on Father Sweet's face and his arms opened wide. We stayed that way for a while, staring. Father Sweet licked at his lips.

Out of the blue, our moment was broken by a sound to my right. I heard a splash. Then another.

The noise startled us both.

It was coming from around the bend, hidden by the bulrushes. I craned to see what or who was splashing, and Father Sweet looked down and around, suddenly very aware of his nudity.

It got louder. Nearer.

Father Sweet and I recognized it together — paddling. It was nearing too quickly for Father Sweet to react. A boat was coming round the bend. Someone new was entering our claustrophobic two-man world.

26

Father Sweet stood naked as a mangy badger as two witnesses in a green canoe paddled into view, past the riverside weeds. They were two normal-looking people, to my eyes. It was a man and a woman — about my parents' age — paddling quietly along in their canoe. They were the first people we'd seen since leaving Blackburn Hamlet.

Hope drained from me almost immediately. They saw the bulbous and hairy body of a naked man standing in the shallow. On a rock, they saw a crying boy hugging his knees. Their mouths dropped to their chests in unison, like they were witnessing some occult back-country ritual. The woman squeaked and they both averted their eyes from us.

Father Sweet gave a chaotic performance trying to conceal his private parts. His left hand clutched at his groin. He crossed his legs, and with the other hand he waved goofily, smiling wide and bellowing a clownish "Hellooooo!" in a panicky attempt to appear normal and friendly.

The man looked at me, then to Father Sweet. He knotted his brows at us, as if to convey scornfully he didn't know what was going on, but that we were clearly up to no good.

Hoping to make a wordless appeal for rescue I locked eyes on the man, but he was not game and shot me a hard look. As if convinced that this — whatever *this* was — was equally my fault.

A flush of shame rose up my neck.

The man was right. How *did* I get involved in this mess?

Maybe the woman could help. But she squeezed her eyes shut tightly. Paddling blind, she made a faint whimpering noise like she was sitting on a tack. "Squeeeeeeeee!"

They paddled on; stroke, stroke, stroke. We remained frozen in place. They headed downstream, toward the mild rapids, but I still saw them, and for some time they remained within shouting distance.

They never even changed the pace of their paddling. They were like robots. I imagined they paddled us straight out of their minds, so they could resume normal life and forget about that creepy boy and that awful naked man.

Father Sweet glanced around frantically. The invasion had thrown him for a loop.

Finally, I opened my mouth to speak, but he beat me to it.

"Fine, then!" he said, throwing up his arms. "Your temerity has defeated me."

Once I saw him stomping out of the shallow, I felt great relief. Tears leaked from my eyes, which I quickly wiped away, and I snorted some mucous back up my nose.

He chuckled, wagging his finger as if we were playing chess and I just executed an unforeseen gambit. "You mercurial, teasing imp!" he said.

As he reached for his towel I giggled involuntarily, out of nervousness. Perhaps it was relief, or terror, I could not determine what I was feeling. All I knew was that feelings were happening to someone, and it may have been me, but at this time I was not acquainted with who that was.

"Oh," snapped Father Sweet, suddenly angry at my laughter. "Indeed, I see. Indulge in your cachinnation at my expense. All for your mirth, eh! All right, then."

"Why don't we head back to the camp? I'll start a fire," I said, exuding pity. He looked so soggy and pathetic. I'd made an enemy. My parents were going to be outraged. The worst was still waiting for me, and it would come from my mother and father. "You can get warmed up. I'll put the tea on for you, and you can smoke," I said, trying to sound meek.

His face softened.

"Ah, my lad. Why must we quarrel? Your solicitude is touching."

Lip quivering, I contemplated the couple paddling out of sight downstream. How could I paddle my own way out? Even back at camp, it would not be over, and there was his looming insinuation. His threat. I was desperate to return home, but Father Sweet turning to Jamie next was impossible to risk.

Looking at the camera, I decided to make a critical deal with him. Then something enormous happened, which I immediately packed away into the back of my mind, where its carcass could rot in eternity.

27

After drying his legs and chest he pulled on his shirt and socks and eventually his pants. We walked back toward camp, his arm resting heavily on my shoulders.

"Such a voyage we have had, eh?" he said. "Still quaking, I see. Hm. Perhaps you are merely cold!" His mood brightened. "Let's head back to the tent now, there is still time. I'd like to warm up, too. I have an idea!"

At that, my heart sank. What did he mean by a new idea? What new, baffling activity did he have in mind now?

Father Sweet was nearly skipping. He moved quicker and cantered ahead, higher up the embankment.

"Come on! Let's run!"

He ran, and I struggled to catch up. He got long ahead, past the highest and most treacherous part of the embankment, that awkward edge of the cliffside where a slip would do you in.

"Wait!" I said. Father Sweet had moved past the crook of the thin ledge and was gone, disappeared behind the forest and the angle.

I reached it myself, finally. The ledge was thin and crumbly, the trees awkward to hold and the drop to the river steep. There was about twenty feet of near-vertical dry-dirt slope, then sheer cliff another twenty feet. Maybe forty feet to the river below.

Father Sweet was nowhere to be seen.

The going was hard and slow because the sturdiest tree branches to hold were just out of reach for my arms. I could not grasp the lopsided cedar cross.

I pulled unsteadily forward, holding to a cedar branch that strained at my weight.

And that was when I smelled it.

Although I suffered from a humiliating phobia about bears, I had never, in fact, come face to face with one. Even if circumstances put me near a zoo, like that one in Kanehsatake, I simply avoided their pens.

But then, when the wind changed and blew at me, there was a shitty stink that came from nowhere. The stench was horrible and familiar at once.

Or was I simply confused? I did not trust myself anymore.

More than the scent, there was a presence. I could not fight it off further, and I felt my breathing start to go haywire again. Instinctually, I knew the presence was a threat and that if I continued along this path, nothing good would come.

I could go silent and hope it passed. If a bear was in the vicinity and found me, it would put my head in its mouth, and that would be it. It would devour me, stripping me like stringy chicken meat, right to the bone.

If I was to save myself, it would be at a painful cost.

I looked down. I could fall to the rocks and river below. Or luck may be onside and I could grab something on the way down. I could catch myself and not fall all the way. Either way, it was preferable to being eaten alive.

I stopped breathing, to hear more clearly, but it was only my heartbeat.

I could wait to see what emerged. Hang in here, waiting.

But the smell became stronger, and so I made my choice.

I had a tenuous grasp on a cedar branch — and my feet planted on the crumbly ledge of the escarpment. I let go and leaned back.

My heartbeat skipped, and I fell. Nothing was under my feet. I fell freely.

It felt endless.

Then I hit hard the mud and rock slope, with a smash. My body slid down the cliff and my bare legs ground into the pebbles, mud, and scree. Abruptly, with a wrenching jolt, I got caught in a tangle of nettles halfway down. My left leg was unnaturally crooked and jammed.

I was safe from tumbling all the way to the river. For now.

As quickly as I was relieved to stop sliding, the pain shot in one heartbeat later, like fire. I gasped for breath. Finally, I gulped enough air to holler a yawp into the ravine. I followed that with a hysterical series of French curses that echoed.

"*Maudit' câlice! Christ Jésus!*"

Blood was everywhere. What stopped me? It couldn't be just a clump of weeds. Something pressed hard against my leg.

It was a rusty metal wire that ripped into my thigh, deep into my crotch. An old part of a fence, a trapline, or maybe even a telegraph wire. I was sitting astride it, and it kept me from falling. I was like G.I. Joe, wounded and hanging on to a thin rope, desperate not to fall. The slope dropped into a full cliff just under my feet. My bare legs were wrapped in nettles that burned my raw skin. The pain started me panicking.

I screamed.

The nettles were too thick to rip, and I became mad to break free. My pulse accelerated as the burn worsened with each second.

My mind blanked and I went into a full-on panic. I screamed, my voice high and shrill.

I was a trapped rodent stupidly yanking at his legs and yipping like a squirrel.

If I got free, I would fall onto the rocks under the cliff. I did not care. All that mattered now was the burn of the nettles.

"I say, my boy, are you all right?" Father Sweet's face appeared on the ledge above. "My word! What are you doing down there?" His voice shocked me.

I gasped a few times to catch my breath.

"I fell," I yelled.

"Indeed you did. Is that blood? Are you all right?"

"No, I'm not all right." I looked at my legs, which were scummy with blood and mud. I was seeing stars and worried I might pass out.

"Here," he said, reaching down with a stick.

I couldn't believe it. The stick was completely useless. It was at least four feet too short, and it was a floppy green stick better used for marshmallows.

"Reach for it, my boy."

It was such a ridiculously poor effort on his part that I laughed. A flimsy, finger-width twig. Three feet long. Not even close to long enough. It did nothing for me. I felt crazy.

My laughing got squashed by the pain and turned into deranged weeping. Blood ran down my leg and pooled in my shoe.

"If Mike was here, he would know what to do."

"Who?" asked Father Sweet.

I realized I had spoken out loud without intending to. *I have lost my mind*, I thought. If I can get a grip, I can pull myself out of this mess. I just need to act carefully. Quickly.

"Well, if you won't even try to let me help you," said Father Sweet, sulking.

I would have to do this myself. The Holy Spirit of Practicality took hold. A Scout's instinct.

If I got free, a bad fall would be next. I would break my leg, or worse. First, I needed to cut the nettles off. The wire, painful as it was, would hold me in place.

I poured a bit of canteen water onto each of my legs as a wash. There was a wound on the left leg, and lots of scrapes and scratches. In fact, the cut hurt less than the scrapes. *It's just skin pain*, I told myself. The big wound was the only thing to worry about.

Wiping tears, I pulled out the Sucrets kit from my pocket. I pulled the tiny folding knife. I was shaking and dropped the tin, which bounced off the rocks as it fell to the river. The tiny knife was not serrated and the cutting was slow. Worse, it got slippery with blood.

"My dear boy, I cannot get to you," Father Sweet said, six feet above my head.

I kept trying to cut myself free, but then the little knife slipped out of my blood-wet hands and tumbled down the embankment into the river. I whimpered. I tried ripping myself free of the nettles, but they only bound me more tightly. I fought to stay calm and use whatever resources I could muster. I would need to delegate to Father Sweet.

"Run back to the tent," I told him. "In my pack on the outside pocket there is a Scout knife. Bring it to me."

"Straight away!"

"And also, bring my first aid kit. Bottom of my bag."

"Yes, sir!"

He ran off, leaving me alone. I stayed, entangled and trapped. The burn of the nettles became constant, and so hot with pain my skin felt cold. I violently shook.

It's shock, I thought. *I'm going into shock. I need to get this line off and apply pressure to the cut before I faint. Maybe if I can get the wire out of my leg, it may relieve some pressure.*

When I put my mind to it, the line was easy to take off. I moved my thigh to reduce the weight of my body on my wound. This lessened the pain in my left leg. With my bloody fingers, I pinched closed the wound, and shifted to sit on the wire.

I felt like I was outside my body, a spirit. The wind hit my ear so clear that I heard minuscule whistles within the breeze. The water below gurgled. Each edge of each plant leaf on the river-bank shone, lit by the dazzling sunlight. I knew every single one as if they each had a name.

Maybe I'm about to faint, I thought. *Maybe I already have.*

I leaned back, feeling surprisingly peaceful, though I was cold and dizzy.

Then, a new sound. Something rummaging through the forest.

I heard heavy footsteps edging closer.

I looked up, expecting to see Father Sweet.

Instead, it was a set of black shoulders that curved like a mountain into a head big as a truck wheel. Its brass snout and enormous mouth breathed lustily at me. Dark, glassy eyes sized me up. They were dead and mechanical, shark-like bear eyes.

A looming, silent black bear stared me down. My worst nightmare.

I knew what it wanted. Finally, it had come for me. We regarded one another.

Was I dreaming?

I returned the animal's straight gaze.

My pulse throbbed fast in my jaw and mouth. The bear bobbed and sniffed, trying to figure out how to reach me — a big, bloody morsel, hanging just out of reach. It was close enough I could smell its last meal of fishy garbage. But hopefully it was not close enough to reach me. Its bottom lip curled to show a row of its lower teeth.

If it did happen to slide off the edge, it would land on me, pull me off the slope with it, and we'd fall together into the river twenty feet below. A bear always goes for the head.

My bladder emptied. All the piss ran down my left leg, stinging the wound.

The bear shuffled on the crumbly ledge, and swatted the brim of the cliff with its claw, doing a front-paw dance. Dry mud fell on me. I spat a few crumbs from my lips.

I will faint, or I will vomit, I thought. *Somehow, though, it's up to me to fix this. Here I am, hanging by a thread. Can't go up. Long drop down.*

The bear was less than eight feet from my face.

From a long distance away, I heard a child bawling. Childlike, whimpering, ka-yipping in a high pitch. *Who brought a baby way out here?* I realized it was me. I was crying like a baby.

Hearing myself, I grew hot with rage. I broke. I growled the way one might try to scream awake from a nightmare. It was a low rumble, but when I found my voice, I was able to pull it like a rope. And I found a way out.

No one could get me out of this fix. No one, except me.

Aiming squarely at the bear, I hollered a deep and angry roar right out the pit of my guts.

The bear stopped moving and regarded me, a noisy little creature.

I shouted again, and the monster tilted its head.

With my right hand, I grabbed a handful of scrabbly rocks and dirt, throwing it in its face. The bear snorted as the dust hit. I yelled and threw some more. Now the bear backed up a bit, confused.

I felt a stone lodged in the scarp and pulled it free, a jagged, half-baseball of sandstone.

I roared one more time and heard my voice howl in a good, strong wolf call.

I hurled the rock hard as I could. It hit squarely on the bear's nose, which must have smarted plenty, judging by the paw it put up to its snout.

I shouted again, and the bear backed away, out of my sight. The giant head disappeared into the dark underbrush.

Seconds later, Father Sweet unexpectedly appeared.

"Why were you yelling?" he asked.

"Bear."

He spun around to look, then laughed at me. "No, my boy. You're imagining things!"

"There was a bear!" I said.

"Oh, come, come," he said. "Your imagination."

"It's not!" I yelled.

"Here is your knife, now," he said. "I'll drop it to you, but you must catch it."

"It can't be far away, that bear."

"Hm? Let's not be silly."

He genuflected and carefully lined up the knife to send it my way.

"Must have expert aim now," he said. "If I am to save you."

He steadied himself against the lopsided cedar tree for fear of falling into the ravine himself. At his back, the black trees hunched over him, as if they might push him over the edge.

"Be careful," I said, hoarsely.

"My boy, I am always careful."

He began to hum and sing a little, making more ruckus than I thought was necessary. He lined up the Scout knife the way he might if he were playing five-pin or darts.

I saw the branches rustle and shake over his right shoulder.

The knife dropped down as I watched behind his back. The bushes moved.

It's coming.

The knife hit my arm. I fumbled it. I was too transfixed by the movement in the bush. I was not even looking at what I was doing, only watching Father Sweet's back. Pulling my arm in close and pressing the side of it against my leg, I blindly grasped at the knife as it flipped around.

With a lucky grip, I caught it.

"There, you see?" Father said. "Easy as pie."

The branches moved roughly and suddenly.

"Watch out!"

He turned.

The bushes swayed, but did not open.

He stood, waiting. Nothing happened.

He tilted his head and looked into the darkness. Father Sweet turned back to me.

"Bit of a breeze, eh?" he said.

I stared for a long while. "Where did the bear go?"

"Right here," said Father Sweet, tapping his head. "I told you."

I shook my head and waited. But nothing came.

"Get on with it," said Father.

I opened my Scout knife and cut myself out of the stinging nettles, still sitting on the wire line. In addition to the dirt scrapes, my legs were covered in red hives. Worst of all was my left leg. Now that I could get a look at it, I could see it was not just cut. The muscles and skin of my thigh had been torn. It was an awful wound, snaking like a river so deep into my leg that fat could be seen squelching out of the deepest part of the cut, where the wire had gone in. Fortunately, though, there was no sign of an artery bleed.

"I need tetanus shots," I said.

"Come up now," he said. "I will give you a Band-Aid, and we can get on with it."

Carefully seizing weeds with my left hand and trying my best to avoid the nettles, I hoisted myself toward the ledge. With my right hand, I stabbed the knife into the slope for a grip. Father Sweet moved off toward a flat. Each movement of my left leg was agony; the knee felt broken and stiff and unable to bear weight. It was cocked at an unmoveable angle. I had to sidestroke my way up the ravine, heaving most of the weight with my arms.

Finally, I was at the flat. I lay out on my side, panting into the dust.

Father Sweet came over with the St. John's kit and a smile.

"Now let's see what all this silly fuss is about," he said, squatting down.

I rolled over and he saw the leg.

"Dear God," he said, recoiling. "But, your beautiful white skin … and the *blood*." Back on his elbows, he stared at me, blank.

He was unable to bear the blood and searched my face, his mouth opening and closing like a fish.

My knee joint was locked but I was able to pop it to the side and free it — with great relief — so I could get the knee straight.

The pain was sharp, and I couldn't help but cry a little. Again, I swore out loud, right in front of Father Sweet.

"*Christ Jésus*," I said.

I picked out the bigger bits of dirt from my wounds. There was iodine in the St. John's kit, and as I dabbed it on, I sobbed openly at the sting. If I had a needle and thread, which I'd lost when the Sucrets tin fell, I would have tried to stitch the wound shut; or at least the part going into my upper thigh, which was bleeding the worst. Instead, I wrapped the cut shut with bandages as best I could. My right leg got the sour end of the deal. I ran out of gauze and just had to leave it. Everything throbbed. It was probably the nettles that made the worst of it.

I kept my mind focused by doing my best Scoutcraft first aid, which I never thought of as something you did to yourself.

"Hand me that stick over there. The big one," I said. "I can't put weight on this leg."

Father Sweet silently brought me the deadwood, not quite as good as a Scout staff, but good enough for a crutch.

Then he bent and kissed my right leg tenderly, high, near my upper thigh where there weren't blisters or welts.

I was sure he was going to cry. "You've been disfigured."

I scowled at him. He seemed keen to make a speech.

"This has marked you. A sign of righteousness. An agreement between you and God. The outward sign of what's written on your heart, spiritually." His lips trembled, and tears spilled over his eyelids. When he said "agreement" he touched my breastbone. His hands made me very aware of my privates, and his focus on my upper crotch.

I cried. "Oh, why did we come here?"

He rubbed his neck. "Well, for you."

"Why are we here?"

All through the gash on my leg throbbed fat pain. "*Câlice!*" I cried.

I asked his help to hoist me up, and another *câlice* slipped from me as I winced from pain.

"Why do you let us do it?" I asked.

"Do what?"

"Swear. In French," I said. "You and the teachers."

He smiled at me in a genuine way that made me nearly forget the past three days. "Isn't it obvious, my boy?" he said, helping me rise. "It's because you're asking God for help. Now why would we stop that?"

28

We headed back to camp the long way, the safe way. He only tried to make conversation once. I got the impression he was going to suggest we do something together when we arrived back at the tent, but his voice trailed off.

At camp, I took the last of the fresh water and washed my leg of the nettles. Relief was temporary. The sting came roaring back.

I packed, as difficult as it was with my leg. Father Sweet sat on a rock and said his prayers.

When the tarp came up, and Father Sweet saw the pointed stakes I had laid under the tent floor, he gasped.

Well, there it is, I thought. *Wait until he tells Dad about this.*

Father Sweet merely sat, nodding to himself, frowning.

"I'm going to bring you home now," he said. "Home to your mum and dad."

I muttered.

"What's that, boy?"

"I cursed. I mean, I said I'm cursed. I'm cursed." I touched his arm and got blood on his shirt. "Cursed."

It was a wordless, radio-less ride back to Blackburn Hamlet.

29

Finally, the car passed the penitentiary outside Blackburn Hamlet and we turned onto Tauvette Road, coming nearby the forest Jamie and I loved so much, which caused my breathing to constrict, and I coughed.

"I don't know with you," Father said. "Life's choice is to listen or ignore God."

"Yes, Father."

Father Sweet pulled into our driveway. Mum was wiping her hands with a dishcloth as she walked out the front door. I saw her face drop from a very high precipice when she noticed Father Sweet's demeanour.

"Remember what I said about our deal," I whispered to Father Sweet, staring at my mother.

He crossed his heart.

Immediately, her eyes locked on mine and I got the impression for the first time in my life that my own mother might despise me.

I hopped on one foot, covered in caked blood.

Father Sweet helped me by holding my elbow. I sat down on the stoop as he unloaded my pack from under the hood of the car.

"What happened?" my mother asked him.

Father Sweet sighed. "Well … it did not go as I had hoped, I'm afraid."

"Oh no," she said.

My mother stared me down.

"I need to see a doctor," I said. "For stitches and a tetanus shot."

"Oh, Father, you've got blood on your shirt," she said.

"He's quite a handful," Father Sweet replied, shaking his head.

"Father, I'm so sorry," said my mother.

"Look after that leg, son." Then, to my mother he said, "He got … a nasty scratch."

"Yes, of course," said Mother. "Thank you."

Father Sweet put a hand on my shoulder and lifted my chin. "Don't give your mother any problems."

I looked him in the eye and crossed my heart discreetly, as a challenge. He nodded.

As my mother glanced at her watch, he climbed back into the Beetle. I entered the house with Mum not far behind.

"I'm glad to be home," I said to her. "Where's Jamie?"

"Don't you give me any of that, Mister Troublemaker. Now I've got to take you to the clinic and get back before dinner. You stay right here. Don't you get your bloody mud on my nice carpets."

She trotted into the kitchen to retrieve her keys.

In the letter basket on the sideboard, where Dad had last left the hatchet, I saw an envelope addressed to me. It was an official notice from the Scouts Canada HQ on Baseline Road. Without a word, I placed the hatchet back where Dad had left it, though it was now filthy.

"Mum … when did this letter come?"

"Friday. Let's go."

I folded myself into the front passenger seat, keeping my bad leg straight.

The letter lay across my bloody lap.

During the drive, Mum asked me no questions about the trip with Father Sweet or how my injury happened.

We got to the clinic and I decided to open the letter while we waited for the doctor. Better that than sit silently with my mother, who had steam rising from her ears. I felt terrible for putting her out.

Besides, it was an official letter demanding my attention.

It was from Mike Racine and was on Scouts Canada letterhead. Mike declared he had moved to Blackburn with his family. He described his long-time involvement in the Scouting movement and how he had started the first Scout troop on the reserve near Maniwaki. Now that he was here, he said, he was interested in sharing community and knowledge with young people. His own son would join our troop.

Mike had taken a job at Indian Affairs, where my father worked. That was why he had visited us, he was scouting out our troop for himself and his own son. He would be the Troop Leader, and his son would join one of our patrols.

The land was important to him, Mike wrote. We would spend our time together learning from the land, which is wiser than any one person.

According to the letter, Donny Blanter, our current Scout leader, was moving on and now Mike would be 1st Blackburn Troop's new scoutmaster. It was my old wish come true.

The doctor inspected my leg, complimented me on my bandaging. He got to work getting a tray ready to clean and stitch it shut. I leaned back while the doctor stitched, reading Mike's letter.

"Many things have inspired me during my life," he continued, "and I look forward to hearing what has inspired you."

Deep excitement bubbled up within me. Here was something different and true that rang out like a horn. Mike was not a confusing person who ambushed us with requests and motives.

He was straightforward. The news that he was coming to lead the troop was a wish come true for me. Yet it seemed to be intended for someone who was gone. If it was a bugle, I heard it as if from a vast distance.

Something had shifted, and had been lost. I told myself it was too late and resolved to resign from Scouts that week.

"So," the doctor asked my mother, "how did this happen?"

Mum replied, with a sigh, merely, "Boys."

30

A week later, Jamie encouraged me to get moving on my leg, but I only wanted to watch old episodes of *Gilligan's Island* in the basement on the black-and-white TV. I hobbled around the house while my parents growled at me to stop making it look worse than it was and stop feeling sorry for myself.

We sat in the back during Mass that Saturday evening. We even left after communion.

I saw the Lemieux family.

Our Scout troop met for the first session of the year with Mike Racine as Scout leader. I stayed home instead, and earned a hot reprimand about money, pride, and persistence from my father. I told Jamie to tell them I was quitting Scouts for good.

Moreover, I told my parents I didn't want to be an altar boy anymore and said I didn't care if they hated me for it.

I discovered that quitting was a simple thing to do. No amount of punishment could make me put on a cassock or do anything again. In a way, it was my true birth.

It would be the beginning of a cold war in our family.

"I don't know what in hell has gotten into you," my father said. "But I'm this close to giving up."

Before October got into full swing, my leg had healed enough for me to venture a bike ride before Dad got home and Mum noticed we were gone. Jamie was eager to finish the roof of the tree fort before winter set in. My brother snuck a bag of our father's tools from the basement.

Slowly, we biked to the edge of the greenbelt woods at Tauvette Road.

There was a tree nursery there next to the bush. I found that I could only stand as far as its first row, on the gravel. The last steps before you left the town and entered the country.

Jamie motioned to me from a few paces inside the forest, but I could not move.

"Is it your leg? Can't you walk?" he asked. And then, as a joke, he said, "You smell a bear?"

"I don't know," I said. I couldn't move.

Something awful was pulsing through me now.

Months earlier, I served a funeral Mass for Father Sweet. He delivered a homily that was oddly personal for him and it came to mind.

"There's a time to reap and a time to sow," he had said. "Death comes and we talk about a reaper, reaping our friends and family like wheat. Instead, Christ Jesus talked about shepherds, about fishermen. Our faith is confusing. Why does the shepherd tend his flock? Why do fishers fish? Is it for the good of the sheep? The good of the fish? And then, there is that one solitary lamb, for whom the Good Shepherd will choose to put all at risk, to go to the wilderness to fetch, simply to hold close.

"Why does the shepherd lay down his life for the very lamb he tends for sustenance?" Father Sweet asked that day. "Isn't it obvious the answer is for Love?"

My eyes filled and I shook my head at my brother.

Jamie walked his bike next to mine and set down the sack of tools with great care, as if any sudden movement could spark a catastrophe in me or an attack.

"I can't finish the tree fort," he said. "Not alone."

"I'm sorry."

Slowly and standing so that he could support me, Jamie hugged me, and I felt my body sag into his arms.

I breathed deeply, relaxing in the comfort he offered. Brotherly love, truer than any of Father Sweet's rhetoric.

Behind Jamie's back, the life of the forest carried on in the shadows. I felt that we were outside of that, though, both of us floating free, completely outside the world. A few short weeks earlier, the bush had appeared endless to me, but now it only looked dark and closed off.

part two

1

September 2003

Sometimes, when the light is just right, I see Jamie the way he looked when we were children. He can still seem like my baby brother, whom I adored and protected almost like a parent, and not the man who became the anchor of our family.

"Here's a good one," he said, handing me an old class photo. "My god. What sick social engineering experiment designed those school clothes?"

Picture day, 1977. All our clothes made of itchy, suffocating polyester: rompers, long lapels, velveteen dresses, bell-bottoms, Tarlek tweeds, mustard turtlenecks. Every head of hair brushed so full of static you'd spark every doorknob. Our smoked-out, coffee-breathed teacher, wall-eyed Mrs. Cattleford, looks on the verge of her own psychological China Syndrome.

"There you are, Mr. Serious," he said, pointing out my pout, bowl-cut, eyebrows pushing down my squint, and, of course, the sienna velour zip-up. "What a fashion show! Meena Thomas, Brian and Briar Birk, Rocky Robicheau, Kevin Nadeau, Lee, Ricky, Tonya, Marc, Terry. Can't believe I remember these names. They weren't even in my class."

"Chuck it," I replied. We were filling garbage bags in Dad's basement.

"Who's that one there?"

"No idea."

"Like you don't remember. You remember every useless triviality."

"C'mon, throw it out."

"No way!" said Jamie. "I want your niece and nephew to see what a dork you were!"

"Pretty sure they know that already."

"*I'm* keeping it, then."

I returned to stuffing garbage bags. My brother had created a "keep" pile, and he placed my school photo there. I had no "keep" pile. Well, not entirely. I had stored away a few keepsakes at my apartment already, such as the hand drum my dad got at his retirement, and which I believed was precious. Regardless, I was creating far more stuffed bags than Jamie was.

"If it can't be sold, and it can't be given away, it's garbage," I said.

"That which can't be sold or given away is priceless," he replied. I was going about this — cleaning out Dad's house — ruthlessly; it was something to get through, a chore like shovelling dirt. For him, it was all fond reminiscences. "And I don't buy that you don't remember. You remember."

I remember.

I picked up a copy of the *Catholic Book of Worship*. The one with Father Sweet's English hymns.

Most things I remember from the old days only became clearer in meaning to me when I grew to be an adult. I might overhear a piece of choral music, or read the classics, or smell certain tobacco smoke. I'd be troubled. Then, a small epiphany.

Later, I studied Latin during my brief university career, and along came full reminders. Phrases sounded familiar. I heard

Father Sweet's voice and I would have a sharp recollection. I shone a light on whatever remained in my mind. I'd have a flash of recognition.

I became a decoder of my own memories.

The first things I decoded were benign. Father Sweet quoted Eusebius in casual conversation with schoolboys. "Never discuss the wicked or their deeds, but follow only in the footsteps of good men," he said in his best stage voice. I remember the hungry look about him when he was coaching boys' soccer, prowling the sidelines in long, ugly Bermuda socks. And his overenthusiastic play-by-play in Latin for chess club, with plenty — perhaps too many — pats and neck rubs while we hunched over the boards.

He loved us. A love, he assured me, that was pure and lust-less. The key, you understand, to why sin didn't infect any of this. Understanding sin is any child's main task.

All of it would go back in the drawer, far back in my head. Slammed shut.

"Hey," said Jamie. "I remember this shirt." He held up a yellow dress shirt. "I can still picture Dad wearing that to work with that powder-blue suit. At the time, I didn't realize Dad was trying to be stylish. Funny what you remember."

It was Dad's shirt from the day I went on my camping trip with Father Sweet in 1978. Funny what you remember.

2

Blackburn Hamlet's English Catholic parish, the Good Shepherd, finally got its separate church building sometime in the 1980s. The building was a concrete bunker styled like three cinder blocks arranged as a bracket. Was it supposed to look like giant stone hands reaching to engulf you? Who knows. There were no picture windows. Light came in from long glass ribbons at the eighteen-foot ceiling, but the main feature was a breathtaking single blood-red stained-glass window illuminating the nave from behind the altar.

It was what stood out when I stepped inside the building.

My sister-in-law Clare, Jamie, and I stood in the sacristy with the local parish priest, a man I was meeting for the first time.

"Please call me 'Padre,'" said the priest. "Or Pete. I don't go for 'Father this and that.'"

"Me neither," I said.

"Padre," said Jamie. "Thanks for helping us." My brother shook his hand with sincerity.

Padre was a clean-cut man in his late fifties, I'd guess. He had a confident and brisk look about him, like a lawyer late to court. He smelled brightly of aftershave.

"I wish I'd gotten to know your father better," said Padre. "He seemed like a decent man."

"Thank you," Clare said, slipping her hand in Jamie's. "It's a kind thing to say."

I stared at the wall, my eyelids half lowered to keep my eyes from rolling. Jamie and Clare were far, far better at small talk than I was. Leagues ahead of me. My strict interest was getting this over with, and getting back to sorting the house so we could sell it. This, I vowed, was my first and last visit to this church, ever.

"Your father wanted a full funeral Mass. You can say a few words after the Gospel if you like. Not a eulogy, but maybe some comments before my homily."

My brother took a breath and reached up to pat me on the back. "My big brother's going to say a few words."

Padre looked me up and down. "Great! You've prepared remarks? Fond memories are always good. Funny stories."

"Just gonna wing it," I said.

Jamie grimaced. "My guy's not big on prep."

"What's the point?" I said.

Clare's face tightened. "What can go wrong?"

"Well, you're sending off your dad the right way," said Padre. He put his arms around us. "I'm sure he's here in spirit. He'd want you to carry on. Every day above ground is a good day. Right?"

"Thank you," said Jamie.

"Typical churchy horseshit," I whispered to Jamie once Padre had de-coupled from us. He moved to the wardrobe and pulled out a cassock.

"I'll tell you when the time's right for you to come up and say your piece," Padre said to me.

It was Jamie's idea I say a few words. He'd been pushing me to do it for days. I didn't even want a funeral Mass, but Jamie insisted this is what Dad would have wanted, which I agreed was true. Well, it was true that he would have wanted one of us to say something. I was a massive disappointment to our father, there was no denying it, so I had no idea why Jamie wanted me to give the speech. *Dad probably would have wanted something at the cathedral*, I thought, *and a send-off from the bishop. And colour guard; the casket being piped in. And a choir with horns.*

That wasn't true, I thought. Dad was not a showboater. Where was this coming from? Why was I angry at him? He was just a Catholic soldier, and, if anything, he probably would not want the pomp.

The petty thought made me blush with guilt. *I'm not being fair*, I admonished myself. The man was dead. All his faults were going to be in the ground soon. Mine I still had to lug around.

It's okay. It's okay. This will all be done and finished and over soon enough.

"Thanks for organizing all this, Clare," I said to her. "You're amazing."

Half-hearted, she gave a two-fingered salute — almost a Scout salute — glancing at me nervously. "Thanks for trimming your beard," she said.

I hadn't trimmed my beard. It wasn't even a beard, per se. I just hadn't shaved in three weeks. But I did take a shower before putting on a suit and tie. I tried hard to smile and she fake-smiled back at me. Her husband's dirtbag brother.

3

I hadn't set foot in a church in decades.

To begin the ceremony, the three of us — Jamie, his wife, and me — stood at the open casket with Padre and received guests, shaking hands at the back of the church. It was almost a wake before the Mass. A short visitation. But, unlike a good Irish reception, no booze.

Jamie was not comfortable with dead things, never had been. Even meat gave him the creeps until it was cooked. He could not eat roast bird of any kind because it resembled the carcass of the animal too much. So, he did not look at our father when the casket was opened, and he stood to the side in a way he would not accidentally catch a glimpse. Jamie was a master of tact and diplomacy. No one would notice that he wasn't standing near our dad or that he had not looked. Clare might not even have noticed. But I knew. I did the looking for us both.

They did a good job with Dad. He looked more placid than he ever appeared while alive.

I found the visitation uplifting and surprising. It had the air of a neighbourhood Christmas party, and it nearly made me cheerful. Many people I recognized from the old neighbourhood, school, or church. Brian Birk brought his mother, and she took my hand sweetly.

"Where is your mother, dear?" she asked. "I haven't seen her in ages."

"She's not well enough to come, Mrs. Birk," I said. "I doubt any of this would register with her, and if it did, probably only upset her."

"Good to see you, old boot," said Brian. "Bad circumstances and all that."

"Brian," I said, "you've gotten incredibly fat. And you're hideous." He laughed before moving along to Jamie and Clare.

The next pair were two Indigenous men. One walked with a cane, looking ancient as an apple doll. The other was a broad man about my age. The old gent was transfixed by Dad's chalky and stretched face, ignoring me as he approached.

I introduced myself. "Thank you for coming."

They hesitantly shook my hand.

"Did you work with my father at Indian Affairs?" I asked.

"Nope," the old man said. He bobbed his head as if trying to see my father's whole body through his trifocals. He stood wide-eyed and huffing like a horse for a good while. "Yep. That's him."

The younger man nodded and frowned, he squeezed the older man's shoulder in a gesture of support. They exchanged a few quiet words.

"Sorry for your loss, eh," the younger man said to me.

"How did you know our dad?" Jamie asked.

The old man inhaled shakily, and then he regarded me. "I came to see it," he cried. "To see that he's dead!" The old man burst out crying.

Clare gasped.

After a pause, I said carefully, "He's definitely that. Watched it happen myself."

The two men nodded in unison. "Good," said the old man. He seemed satisfied to see Dad lying out.

The younger man winced at me as if to kind of say sorry, I guess, and helped the older man off. They shuffled to the pews without more explanation. There were more hands for us to shake and people to hug, but I watched where they sat.

"What was that about?" Clare did not lower her voice. "That was rude," she said.

But before any further could come of it, there were faces from the tennis club, the bridge group, the Blackburn Arms (which the old bully, Squirm, now managed), our street, and people from work.

One of the two funeral ushers closed the casket and Jamie sighed with relief. He and I helped push Dad toward the sanctuary.

We settled into our front-row pew, and Mass started with Dad's casket at the crossing, a huge bouquet of white blossoms on top.

"You okay? You look like you're not feeling well," Jamie said.

"I wish you'd quit asking me that," I said.

Behind us, at the entrance of the church, I heard the door open and turned to see someone enter, then stand idly at the exit with his hand on the door bar.

Mass began with an adult altar server helping Padre.

The time came up. Padre nodded and pointed at me. *You're up.* Here was the opportunity to say a few words before the homily. As I rose to the chancel podium, I saw who it was standing at the back of the church. It was Mike Racine, the old Scout leader, in jeans and a flannel shirt. Mike was grey now, with a paunch, but he still had the same granite mien I remembered. The sight of him was both shocking and reassuring. Disorienting.

I traced my fingers along the edge of the podium and stared at all those faces watching me. Someone coughed.

"Uhm," I said, looking down at the red liturgical tome as if it could tell me what to do. I had no notes for my speech.

"Eulogies aren't a thing at Catholic funeral Masses," I said, eventually. "But Padre said I could say a few words about our dad. So here I go."

From the front pew, my smiling brother flashed a "be strong" fist pump. I felt nauseous.

"My brother and I knew our dad our whole lives.... Well, obviously.... But, really, I don't think we ever knew the guy. I don't think any of us know anyone. He didn't talk about his upbringing with us, and he spoke so little.... All I can really remember are the times that he was angry. Heh. Right now, I'm thinking he's going to come out of that box and glare at me or correct my grammar. Ha-ha." I cleared my throat. "I want to talk about happy times we shared as a family, and even times when I saw him happy, but I can't think of any. He wanted Jamie and I to grow up into men, and I guess we did that.... He was mad at us most of the time, and constantly giving us advice, and punishing us. I don't think he thought we ever did right. He sometimes spanked us, but I can't say we had a beating from him, not really, so that's good. My mother got yelled at, too, but he never hit her or anything."

My brother's eyes were cartoon-wide now and his mouth low. Speaking extemporaneously was, probably, not a good idea. My brother slowly shook his head, gobsmacked.

"But," I said, trying to win back the crowd. "I know he loved us. He must have loved my mother. And he loved his job. Because those were the things he seemed to focus all his energy on. When my mother had her first stroke, he kept her in the house and never complained about the extra workload.

And I can tell you that my niece, Kitty, and nephew, Harry, are his little sweeties, and for them he was their sweetie Grandpa." Where was I going with this? I felt the heat of the crowd on me. "There was … a lot unsaid, you know?"

My throat constricted.

"But what can you do?" I croaked, and stepped down from the chancel, and trudged the long march back to the front pew, carrying every heavy eye on me.

I sat down next to Jamie, who leaned over and whispered in my ear, "That was … fucking terrible."

I sighed.

Padre took the podium and thanked me.

"When someone passes away," he said, "there's always a lot unsaid. A lot undone. Unfinished business. In a way, that's what we heard in the gospel today. Lives don't seem long enough, do they? Because they are always evolving. There is always a tomorrow, isn't there…. Well, one day there will not be a tomorrow. Funeral Masses are here to remind us that when we say goodbye, we should recommit ourselves to a meaningful life, in Christ. Let us use our time here, and enrich ourselves to the fullest extent in the everlasting life guaranteed us by the death and resurrection of the Lord. God invites us to live a meaningful life, and to help each other do so. We're saddened by the departure of our brother. But we thank him for the gift he gives us today. Praise to you, Lord, through our sister Bodily Death, from whom no living man may escape. A reminder to treasure our lives, treasure each other, and to continue the work of building the Kingdom here on Earth."

At the end of Mass, as we moved Dad's casket out to the hearse, I saw Mike Racine speaking with the two men I saw earlier. I wanted to go over. The older man wept as he limped along. Mike showed no emotion and bowed his head to listen to the younger man.

By the time my role was complete, and the hearse had gotten on its way, I was swamped by well-wishers as they headed from the church.

I craned my neck to find them, but Mike and the two men were gone.

4

It was five o'clock on an autumn afternoon and the sun was nearly down. The roads and pavements were carpeted with yellow and red maple leaves blowing and collecting in piles. My brother met me at the Blackburn Arms for a pint. We slid into a booth across from one another.

"Dad's favourite place," Jamie said.

"Did you come with him, too?"

"Plenty of times. All his buddies knew the kids. You never came here with him, though, did you?"

I shook my head. I had never once entered the pub with him. I had never once bought my dad a beer. I was not even aware he frequented this place.

"To Dad," Jamie said, raising his glass.

I sighed and elevated my pint an inch off the table, nodding before taking a huge gulp.

"To things unsaid," I said.

"Like what?"

"After we're done selling the house, I don't ever want to come back here."

He nodded. "Don't see why you'd ever have to."

"Good riddance."

"It's not all bad. You and I had a lot of fun here.... I was thinking about what you said at the funeral. It's true we don't know anything about Dad. He had a forty-year career I know nothing about. Strange, no?"

"Don't care."

"Clare knows everything about her parents. I don't know how Mum and Dad met, I don't know what Dad did at Indian Affairs, I don't know anything about their childhoods. For that matter, I don't know a lot of whys. Missing all the whys."

"Too late to ask Mother anything."

"She might remember early stuff, like her childhood."

"Jamie, she doesn't even know who we are."

"I regret it," he said. He wasn't emotional, but his eyes were blank and I saw his sincerity. "I do. I wish I had gotten to know him better. Before he died. I don't know my dad. Not really. Now he's dead."

I caught the waitress's eye and gestured for two more pints.

"You?"

"Me?" I drained the last of my ale then rubbed my fingers, waiting for the next one to arrive. "If I had one more day, I don't know. I only regret not asking him ... why he was such an asshole."

Unexpectedly, I found my throat tight and tears in my eyes. "Shit. What is wrong with me?"

My brother squeezed my arm. I pulled it away.

The beer arrived, and I sucked it up.

5

The next day, I was alone in the basement.

Two dozen banker's boxes were piled like a half-ruined ziggurat, collapsed from age in the corner of the crawl space. I had brought my old pickup, a small Datsun Sport truck, specifically to unload everything at the dump.

The house was clearing out. Ghostly dark rectangles showed where pictures hung on the walls. The Swedish kitchen wallpaper was ravaged by nicks. In the living room, that revolting orange shag carpet had patches that looked brand new, where furniture had loitered for decades. Odd slips of paper and receipts lay everywhere. A few coins. Mother's smoking saturated every material so thoroughly it smelled like she might peek around the corner to criticize the way you lifted her china cabinet. Now, almost emptied, the house didn't resemble a home where you felt welcome to live your life. It's arguable it ever did.

I crouched and pulled the string in the crawl space. On flashed the light bulb. Propping up my spine by leaning on my knees, I waddled to the boxes and grabbed a waist-high one. It was heavy with paper and I could feel my lower back trigger and pop at the strain.

I hobbled into the laundry room, which was unfinished concrete illuminated by a high basement window and decorated with dust and spiderwebs.

Labelled *1964*, the box was stuffed to overflowing with files. It weighed a ton.

I eased it onto a folding lawn chair next to the dryer and lifted the lid.

Inside was a stack of folders, and I grabbed the top one.

The first page was a letter between my father and an Oblate priest running a school in Saskatchewan. Two things caught my eye.

The first was that my father's role at that time was as an "Indian Agent." The second was that the priest's name was Father Aloysius Gast, a name that tasted gross and familiar to my mind in an unspecified way, at first.

Then I remembered. I needed to sit down.

> ... Suffice it to say the two brothers were frozen to death by the time we found them. This fad to run away is yet more evidence of the incorrigibility we discussed. Also, I regret telling you our bet regarding the number of tubercular deaths this winter was won by you, and so I owe you a hot dog and a glass of milk when next we meet in Saskatoon. Fifteen of the little devils died before the final melt, just as you predicted. We lost track of which body was which, so we buried them last week all together after having them in cold storage. Sister Bartholomew will send you a list presently so you may alert any next of kin when you do your next "tour" through their encampments, if you see fit.

I slid the box to the floor and twisted my lower back on the nearly broken, yellow lawn chair. I opened another letter from Gast to Dad, dated 1972.

> ... I considered what you said about the word "school" to describe our humble little abbey. It's true we make no pretence to a proper British education such as you and I may know it, but consider these pupils. Their souls may yet be saved. We do our best to have them learn a trade, if possible, and of course never to speak that gibberish again. Is it not enough? Would they ever know any differently?

The crawl space next to the laundry was an especially creepy spot for me, since it was where our dad would punish us. If we failed him in some task, or were too loud, down we went. He would obligate us to kneel, and say decades of the rosary. We could hear life going on in the house above through the creaking floorboards. I always kept my eyes tightly shut and I quaked, imagining evil spirits around me. I don't know how Jamie felt because we never spoke of it once either of us could return upstairs.

So, the next letter I came upon from Gast seemed particularly chilling.

> ... when I arrived, they were using a wooden box to force contrition in the hearts of the especially naughty. Runaways, stealing out of the kitchen. The usual. I found the contrition excessive. And so, I have simply made our bad boys kneel in the dark cellar. Their expulsion to this lesser Hades near the coal room

is enough. Juvenile Indians seem especially
frightened of the dark and being alone ...

I wondered if Gast gave our dad his ideas. Or if they had
come the other way around.

There were no letters from my dad, so I could only read
Gast's side of the dialogue. This glimpse into a one-sided discussion was jarring. I could not imagine him — as I knew him
— having so in-depth a discussion with anyone to warrant such
detailed responses. I had only ever heard Dad say enough sentences in my lifetime to fill a newspaper column. Yet here was
evidence of a long, long correspondence outlining projects and
politics only the wordiest of schemers could manage. It wasn't
the man I knew, because the man I knew never said enough that
I might know him.

My shaking fingers set down the letter.

Instead of loading the pickup truck with boxes for the dump, I
spent the day reading in the basement, pausing only to text Jamie
at one o'clock that afternoon and asking him to meet me at the
Blackburn Arms for dinner that night.

What R U talking about? He texted.

Wait. C U @ 6, I replied.

I texted that if he wanted to know who his dad was, I would
tell him that evening.

After hours of reading, the ziggurat of boxes came to resemble a stack of coffins to me, and our silent house took on a feel of
a crypt. By the time I left the basement, it was twilight and I ran
up the stairs, frightened as if ghouls were chasing me and would
grab at my legs.

6

I beat Jamie to the Blackburn Arms and was already two glasses of Boddingtons in by the time he arrived. It had begun raining outside. He shook the drops from his overcoat when he entered.

"There you are, my dear!" he said to the pint of beer the waitress placed in front of him. Squirm winked and waved at Jamie from the bar and mouthed "on the house" with his hand over his heart. Squirm had been a minor celebrity very briefly, as he was on the kid's TV show *You Can't Do That on Television* in 1980. For a few years, he was the centre of attention. He found it uncomfortable, though, and it changed him for the better. The experience made him humble. His old compatriot Rob fared worse. He didn't live far away from Blackburn since he was doing ten years for multiple break-and-enter convictions at the Innes Road prison.

Jamie and I drank.

"I'm all atwitter," he said. "What did you want to tell me?"

Jamie looked fantastic in his suit. He was a corner-office partner at a law firm downtown, practising corporate law, so it was no surprise. He belonged to the Rideau Club, after all, and Clare was some sort of head nurse at the Children's Hospital of Eastern Ontario. They had twins, and a gorgeous river-view house in Rockcliffe, a stone's throw from Rideau Hall.

"That's a nice suit," I said. "Serious."

"Thanks."

"You look great. Navy is your colour."

"Clare got me this tie last year."

"It's perfect. Matches your eyes."

"Kind of, yah. You're right. I think it's Hermès."

"Spectacular."

"Thanks."

I wiped my eye, shook my head, and squashed down the lump in my throat with beer.

"Everything okay?"

"I love you."

"Okay …" Jamie looked around the pub. "I love you, too?"

"Good. Because I'm what you've got left. I wish I had more to give you."

My brother frowned. "Come on."

"You are the best thing to come out of our family, and I am so glad. So glad. I want to say I'm proud of you, but you did it all yourself, so how can I take pride in that?"

The waitress appeared. I ordered a chicken pie, with another beer. My brother ordered a salad. "Watching my waistline," he whispered dramatically to her, patting his belly.

He asked how many beers I'd had.

"I learned something important about our dad today," I said.

"Right, that's why we're here. Let's hear it."

"What do you remember about Dad's job growing up?"

"I remember when he retired, and they gave him that cool drum he hung in the living room."

"I took it. The drum. It's in my apartment now. What else?"

"I remember Mike Racine saying he would be working at Indian Affairs, and us wondering why Dad never mentioned him."

I nodded. "Mike came to the funeral."

"He did?"

"He stood at the back, just like he did when we first saw him at Scouts, way back when."

"I didn't see him."

"There were two other Indigenous guys who came to the funeral, too."

"Right! The old guy who almost cried and said he wanted to make sure Dad was dead or something like that. Very strange."

"Exactly."

The waitress arrived with my newest jar of ale.

"Seriously, how many have you had today?" Jamie asked.

"Who's counting?" I sipped and wiped beer head off my lips with my sleeve.

He stared at me. "You should be counting."

We watched the game on TV for a short while. A couple of plays.

"Those guys didn't say they worked with Dad, but I believe I know who they were."

Jamie looked at me and waited.

"The old guy said 'That's him' and pointed at Dad in the casket. He was emotional."

"You think the younger one was his son?"

"Sure. He was the one, I bet."

"What do you mean?"

I sighed and closed my eyes. "The one our father took."

Jamie blanched. "Sorry?"

"The one Dad took."

"Took where?"

"Today I went through a pile of boxes in Dad's basement. I expected bits and shits I could toss out. But they were files from his work. It was awful. I have no idea why he was keeping them at the house. I felt like I was discovering evidence of the Holocaust."

Jamie leaned back, looking confused and alarmed.

The waitress brought our dinners. I sat glumly watching the steam coil up from the hole in my chicken pie. My brother, staring at me, barely noticed the salad plate under his chin.

"What do you want to tell me?"

I grew clumsy-mouthed. "You remember, you know, our old parish priest? There's only one you know I could mean."

Jamie searched my eyes. "Father Sweet?" He stabbed some lettuce and a tomato. "'Course."

"I came across a name in Dad's files. The name of a guy you-know-who used to talk about a lot. At first I didn't know why the name seemed so familiar to me, then I remembered it was a priest he looked up to."

"What does this have to do with Dad's work?"

"Dad knew this priest and, and —" I stuttered, trying to find the right word "— sort of worked with him."

"I don't know what that means."

"It means we live in a very small world."

My brother sat up, suddenly more erect. His lips parted, and he looked at me with deep concern. He looked terrified.

"Oh no," he whispered.

"What's wrong?"

"Flash," he said quietly, and clenched his fists.

I bolted up and came around, easing him out of the booth and pulling his small body to the floor just in time for him to cry out an unholy shriek and go rigid. I held his head while his body seized, and his eyes rolled back.

The old man at the bar laughed. "What the hell!"

Squirm strode from behind the bar and briskly told the man to leave, pointing at the waitress to escort the gent out. He made a scene while Squirm knelt to hand me a few bar towels for Jamie's head.

"That guy just earned himself a permanent ban," said Squirm. "Too bad. He's a cook. I could use a new cook."

After a minute, Jamie let out a groan and began huffing like he'd run a marathon. Spittle ran from his mouth.

"You didn't bite your lip, at least," I said. Jamie was too out of it to respond.

The waitress finally got the loudmouth to leave, promising him his tab was on the house, but he wasn't welcome back. Another man helped her ease the fellow out the door.

"Thanks, Squirm," I said. "Appreciate it."

He waved me off. "You lads are always welcome here. This is home."

Blackburn had long stopped feeling like home to me, but Squirm still looked like the same thug I knew as a kid. He was fatter and slower, and softened by disappointment, which comforted me. I nodded.

Jamie had wet himself. I placed a towel over his lap as I rolled him onto his side.

The other man came over. It was Padre, the pastor from the Good Shepherd Church where we'd just had Dad's funeral.

"You fellas need a hand?" he asked.

"No, thanks. All under control here."

"Shit," Jamie said.

"Yah, buddy, I'm sure you feel shitty," I said.

"No," he said. "Shit."

"Oh," I said. "Understood."

7

Jamie had his workout kit in his bag. While he went to the toilet to change and clean up, Padre sat with me as I finished my chicken pie and beer.

"I knew your dad a little," said Padre. "He and I went golfing once or twice."

"Didn't know Dad golfed," I said, between forkfuls.

"He was proud of you," he said.

I stopped chewing and looked at the man — the priest — across from me. "Come on," I said. "Don't give me the pastor routine. I don't buy it."

"What do you mean?"

"Lookit, I don't know what your agenda is here, but whatever it is, I appreciate your help with my brother tonight and sending off our father, but I'm not a church guy, so whatever you're selling, I'm not buying. Yah?"

"No? Your dad told me you studied theology in university."

I threw my head back and laughed. "Figures he'd say that. I took one year of anthropology of religion. Big difference. You don't need to believe in God to get a degree in that. Which I did not get. Because I quit …"

"As for my agenda…. My agenda is you."

"Oh, I bet it is, black-shirt," I said, downing my beer.

Padre looked around the pub, squeezing his knuckles.

"Look, I'm sorry you had a bad experience with … but, if you ever need to talk," he said.

"With all due respect, you're the last person I would talk to."

He sighed and sipped his beer. "I've heard that a lot over the past three months."

"Oh yah?" I said, chewing. "What'd you do?"

"I'm new to the parish. You didn't know? The previous priest is on leave. So, I'm here to serve the parish and help out."

"'On leave,' eh?" I nodded sardonically. "You guys. When I was a kid, our priest was moved out under a cloud and an old Irish guy was brought in to fix us. Fix the parish."

"I know all about Father Sweet."

I stopped eating and examined Padre. "How's that?"

"He sponsored the previous parish priest into the seminary. I know all about Sweet."

My brother came back to our booth, uneasy on his feet. He stood balancing himself at the edge of the table.

"I'll take you home, Jamie," I said.

"I'd still like to talk with you," Padre said. "There's more to say. About your dad, and maybe about Father Sweet. And Father Lemieux."

"What are you talking about?" asked Jamie.

"Daniel Lemieux, the priest I'm relieving," said Padre.

My mouth dropped open. Danny Lemieux; our old neighbour and Father Sweet's favourite altar boy.

"Didn't we know a Danny Lemieux, back in the day?" Jamie asked me. "From hockey or something?"

I nodded slowly.

"I'm here to help," Padre said evenly, locking his eyes with mine.

"We need to go," I said. "Jamie's legless and I need to get him home."

"Don't worry about this," Padre said. "I'll take care of the bill."

Squirm came over to tell us the same thing.

"Squirm, you're having a bad night with all this gratuity," I said. "You can't keep comping everyone's bill."

"It's karma," he said dismissively. "What goes around comes around." Squirm grinned.

"I'm not going to argue with that," I said.

Outside, the only vehicle I recognized in the parking lot was my own. Jamie's S-Class Mercedes, which I was looking forward to driving, was nowhere to be seen.

"Where's your car?"

"I took a cab," Jamie said, shrugging. He wore his suit jacket for warmth, but otherwise was dressed as if to play soccer. "Don't drive me home," he said. "Let's sleep at the old house. I'll text Clare and let her know not to wait up."

8

The only pieces of furniture left in the den were a pink tweed sofa, and a yellow faux-leather stool worn by time into a grotesque, arsed-out brown. Jamie stretched his back on the chesterfield, a can of Coke balanced on his chest. I crouched on the stool, drinking Crown Royal from a "Greetings from Sunny Florida!" juice glass.

On the floor, I set up my father's old portable turntable and we listen to a scratchy copy of *2112*.

"Great album," I said. "Wish it was in better shape."

"That new priest seems like a nice guy," said Jamie.

I changed the subject. "How are you feeling?"

He looked at me. "How are *you* feeling? You've been drinking all night."

My thumb stroked the juice glass. "Remember when you-know-who left the parish?" I asked.

"Father Sweet?"

"Poof," I said. "Gone one Sunday and there was that new guy in there."

"Barely." Jamie shrugged and rubbed his face.

"Well, I remember," I said. It was about a year after our camping trip in 1978. "Suddenly, with no explanation, he was transferred to another church somewhere up north. That's what I overheard from the adults, anyway. His replacement was that dull Irish priest. Remember him? He didn't seem to really care about anything, just read his Agatha Christie stories, drank Bordeaux and soda ... and spent a lot of time with his live-in housekeeper. What was her name? Oh yah, Moira."

"What I remember," he said, "is you yelling at Mum and Dad when they wanted me to be an altar boy."

"I did?"

"Big time."

"When was that?"

"Before Sweet left. They wanted me to do it because you dropped out and wouldn't go."

We were sitting in the den, where we used watch TV as a family. We would all sit here silently watching some ridiculous sitcom like *King of Kensington* in the dark and saying nothing. Mother in the corner smoking and flipping through a magazine, Dad grinding his teeth, staring at the screen like it was an alien transmission. Emotionless as the laugh-track played.

"I don't remember that," I said.

"Boy, they were mad."

"What else do you remember?"

"I don't know." He sipped his Coke. "You quit Scouts, I remember that. You quit everything."

"You were their pride and joy," I said. "Mother and Dad."

"No. *You* were their pride and joy. I filled in when you gave up."

I looked down at my lap. "Whatever."

"Sorry, I didn't mean it quite the way it came out. But remember all the stuff we used to do? Before you became a hermit, locked in your room? We used to play hockey. Scouts, camp. Remember the tree fort? And the CCM Mustangs?"

I thought of the treehouse we built, perched and level in the trees with our glorious construction site hidden in the scrub.

That view. I sensed my heart rate pick up and my blood pressure fall. I did not like where this line of discussion was going. The memory of that summer smothered me, crushing and hot, full of nausea, regret, and grief.

"Dunno," I said.

We had already thrown out the shears, and so I watched the rain pelting the back patio in the garden, where a metal bistro table and chairs Mother bought decades earlier now lay in a rusty orange pile, lit by a weak outdoor lamp. When she bought them, she said we'd have dinner out there in the summertime, but I only recall it being used as a place for her to sit and smoke, and stew.

"I never quite got it … I still don't," Jamie said, slowly, finally, so the insinuation could hang in front of me.

I stood and ripped a macramé owl from the wall, throwing it back toward the garage door, where I had garbage piled.

"I wonder why they made us go," I said. "Church."

"Church? Pff. They never doubted that."

"Maybe they thought we'd be better people or something."

"You're an idiot. People don't think about what they do. They just do it, then they try and figure out all the trouble they get into later. That's why there's lawyers. And that's how lawyers get rich."

I dipped my head proudly as I sat back down. Jamie was a successful lawyer and I loved it when he sounded scrappy.

"I haven't seen you have a flash in a long while," I said.

"Another suit ruined."

"They'll be able to get that out. Your dry cleaner must have you on Air Miles."

My brother took a deep breath and looked at me.

"What? Bad joke?"

"There's something I need to tell you."

I stood to turn on the ceiling light.

The album was nearing the end of the side, when Geddy sings about where his life might be and the strain of carrying on.

"I'll just come out and say I don't want you to worry," Jamie said. "But I've been having more seizures and it's not the usual reasons."

His tone was serious — almost frightened. "What's the new reason?" I asked.

"There's a, like a thing in my head. It's … you know … like a growth."

I shifted uneasily in my chair and cleared my throat. I looked at the juice glass and wished I had not drank so much.

"A bad growth?"

He propped himself up and smiled teasingly. "There's a good kind?"

"I mean, is there anything they can do?"

"Yes. Surgery."

I muttered some gibberish I didn't even understand. Crazy talk, literally. Nervous, crazy talk.

"That's why I didn't drive tonight," he said. "That's why you've been seeing Clare drive us around. I can't drive. Not anymore."

His voice black as oil, he apologized for not telling me sooner.

"You tell Mother?"

Jamie laughed. "Last time I was there, Mum thought I was some kind of entertainer."

We both laughed. It devolved for me, into a deep, hollow place, until I sobbed and couldn't stop.

Jamie rose and retrieved a roll of paper towels Clare left when she was cleaning the windows last week. I blew my nose. He took the needle off the record and sat on the edge of the sofa. We were face to face.

"Look. I don't know if I'll be able to talk afterward." He swallowed, and his eyes dilated. "I hope so. But maybe not, they said. It's near the speech area of the frontal lobe. But not the comprehension area, which is weird. That's a different spot. I may be able to understand what people are saying, but not be able to respond in any way.... Oh god.... Fuck me."

I stared, incredulous. "How's Clare? The kids?"

"The kids," he said and touched his scalp. "You know I'm an optimistic person. But my worst nightmare is something happening to those kids.

I sipped my whisky. I had been thinking about how to tell him about Dad, about the boxes and what they held, but now doubts came.

He looked over and we both flexed our mouths, but said nothing. He worked up courage.

"Listen, I'm going to tell you this because I don't know if I'm ever going to get a chance to say it again," he said. "You're my brother and I love you. Haven't we always been honest?"

I didn't reply.

"I'm going to need your help with this," said Jamie. "I need you to do something."

"Anything."

"No, no. Listen." He bowed his head. "I don't know how to say this except to just come right out, but here it is. Clare is all right. The kids are all right. We are all right. Okay?"

I thought maybe he was saying this to convince himself. And that I was his witness. His confessor.

"Don't hate me for this, but *you're* not all right ... I feel like there's something that's been wrong for a long, long time. Something you haven't told me. I don't know what it is. And I worry I've run out of time to help. I want you to get help."

If anyone else had said this to me, I would have punched him in the face. But as it was, I could only listen, and sniffle. How things had turned.

"I don't know what to say," I mumbled. I wondered how to give him what he needed when I wasn't sure myself of the language.

"I can't say I'll be there to give you help," he said. "I wish I could. You've always been there for me. You are my best friend. You've protected me, you've cheated for me, you've scrounged for me. I can't say thank you enough. But I feel like this is the last chance I might have to say the only thing I want from you is for you to remove what it is that's — that's … blocking you. That has made you so unhappy." He attempted to catch my eyes. "I'm not talking about you not holding down a job. I don't care about that. What's kept you from living a life that makes you happy?"

He stood and went to his suit jacket, draped over a box near the front door.

"Here," he said. "They're shrinks. I know. Don't even say it. Therapists. Call someone. Please get help." He exhaled like he had just set down a barrel.

"You want someone to hear my confession?"

"I did *not* say that." Jamie raised a finger.

He was right, of course, and I was being childish.

"Do you have something to confess?" he said.

How could I say I did not even know where to begin to pull on the knot of yarn inside? I lied. I said I would call someone.

"Good," said Jamie. "I think it's overdue."

"I'll do it for you."

"Do it for yourself."

"Too late for that."

His head tilted, and I immediately regretted saying something so self-pitying. But he let it go. The rain let up a little outside. It was quiet.

"You were going to tell me something about Dad," Jamie said.

I shuffled to the kitchen to rinse my juice glass in the sink, stalling for time. I shook the Crown Royal bottle to see I'd drunk two-thirds of what was left. How could I pile on more worry when Jamie was fighting for his life?

"Right now, I've got a headache," I said, at last. "Too much Geddy Lee. And I just want to go to sleep."

We called it a night. Jamie pulled his mattress into my room to sleep on the floor beside my bed, as if we were back in school and weren't middle-aged men sleeping in an abandoned house, haunted by our own past.

There was a box of our old comics in the corner, and I dragged it over between us. If their covers weren't worn out like leather and the pages crumpled from overuse, they would be priceless. Jamie found *X-Men* 98, holding it as reverently as scripture, and I read *New Gods*. We silently flipped through these precious artifacts, each of us propped up on an elbow like the old days. I sighed with satisfaction.

Finally, Jamie rolled over and I clicked off the light.

9

Next morning, Jamie was up and gone before dawn.
Later that afternoon, I tackled the garage.

"For Christ's sake," I said to the junk pile. Dad had a brand new set of golf clubs, or so they looked to me. Shiny and cleaned. A treasured possession. A half-dozen tags showed off the courses he'd played all over the region, from Gatineau semi-privates to the Hunt Club and Royal Ottawa. Dad was not an idle golfer.

I moved some boards. There they stood. The CCM Mustang bikes Jamie and I cherished as kids, beaten, scraped, and dented into clobbered-up steel bones, all four tires flat. The bicycles were smaller than I remembered, though they were perfectly fit for two strong boys. I wiped dust from mine and admired the yellow chrome paint clinging to the frame. Both saddles worn smooth by our bums and the stuffing coming out the back edges.

The past is not dead, it's right here. It's always here. It won't die like it ought to. Not until it gets what it wants. Gets its bill paid.

I hefted the golf bag onto my shoulder and placed it in the bed of my pickup.

Less than ten minutes later I rang the doorbell of Padre's rectory.

On his front lawn, a collection of sparrows was frantic to eat the remains of something I bent closer to see.

Padre opened the door and a big smile lifted his face. "What a nice surprise to see you!"

I pointed at the birds. "What you think these birds have convinced themselves of? That to get the seeds they're after is worth eating the shit they're buried in, or that eating a pile of raccoon turd is no shame if you're hungry?"

Padre blinked at me, narrowing his eyes. He frowned and examined the birds before looking up at me. He shrugged. "I guess, lunch is lunch to get by?"

"That's faith," I said.

His smile vanished. "Look. How can I help you? I'm busy."

"I brought you a gift," I said, blushing. I didn't know why I started off so hostile. "You mentioned golf. I don't play golf myself and Jamie can't use these clubs."

"Okay, okay. Come in." His face softened, and he nodded. "I'm glad you came. I've wanted to talk with you."

"Sorry," I said.

"There's someone here."

"And the clubs?"

"Just set them there."

He patted my shoulder as I crossed the stoop. I put the golf bag down.

"Hey, brother," said a voice. Behind Padre, a middle-aged man stood in the hallway with a playoff beard and the same unstyled, unwashed hair as mine. He wore dirty jeans and a sweatshirt with a big clown announcing the Blackburn Funfair. Around the eyes, which were shaded under brown-tinted lenses, I recognized a deeply familiar visage.

"Hello, Danny," I said. "Awful long time."

"Danny's … I'm letting him stay here a few days till he gets sorted," said Padre. "But that's a secret. From the parish."

"I'm a danger to society," said Danny in a plain, flat drone.

"Don't joke," Padre said into his armpit.

Danny and Padre looked down, but I held up my hand to my forehead and watched them.

"Come in, I've got something for you," said Padre.

Padre's rectory was sparse. I remembered the florid, maximalist clutter of Father Sweet's home, stuffed like an enchanted curio shop with urns, books, musical instruments, and statuary. This rectory, in a different, modernist building from the one I knew as a kid, felt as welcoming as a men's hostel. Or a halfway house. Long after I stopped going to church, the parish finally built their heavy concrete bunker to worship in, and to house its priest in connected apartments.

"Too early for beer?" Padre called, leading us to the Scandinavian-furnished lounge.

"Never too early for beer," I replied.

We sat and Padre joined us, carrying three bottles of Export and an opener. We each took our turn.

"Better tomorrows," said Padre, raising his bottle. We drank.

"So, Danny," I said, "you a priest or something?"

Padre stared long and hard at Danny, who turned on the television and flipped through channels from his chair until landing on the sports channel showing highlights from yesterday.

"Danny is taking a leave of absence," Padre said.

I drank and asked why.

"Working through some things," Padre said.

It sounded suspicious and my eyes automatically shifted into a squint. "Like what?"

"Almost forgot!" Abruptly, Padre stood and left the room.

I observed Danny, transfixed and silent, watching a soccer clip. He chewed his bottom lip, making the whiskers of his beard prickle and bend.

Padre returned with a magazine.

"Look at this," he said, handing it to me and pointing out a feature article to which he'd bent the magazine open. It was a story on Griff Kelsey, the Hollywood actor. I peered over at Danny, who seemed in a fugue.

"My mother reads this sort of magazine," I said to Padre.

"You'll want to read that," droned Danny, not taking his eyes from the television.

I looked down. It was an article about the creation of *King of Blood*, a Jesus-flick that hit cinemas last year. Griff Kelsey was the director.

"Look," said Padre, and lowered his fingertip to the article.

Padre's finger traced down the sentences until it rested on a name that made a sibilant hiss in my mind, coiled around twenty-five-year-old memories.

> The production's resident pastor is Traditionalist Catholic Reverend Benjamin Sweet, who performs Mass for the production every morning before shooting begins.

The article came at me as hieroglyphics, at first. That name wouldn't go into my mind, so I read past it, though the sentences unsettled me without understanding. It dawned on me, though, how much Padre may know about me. "Why are you showing me this?"

Danny, eyes still glued to the television, said, "Father Sweet's not satisfied playing the small-town circuit anymore. He's gone Hollywood."

"What do I care?" I said.

"Aren't you interested?" Padre asked, searching my eyes.

"No. I don't care to know," I said, pushing the magazine back at him. He refused to take it.

"Keep it."

"You're mentioned," Danny said.

"Danny!" Padre snapped.

"What does that mean?"

"Not you *per se*, but you'll recognize someone," Danny said. "I know I did."

I stood and rolled the magazine into a club. Danny, infuriating and sloth-like, rolled his eyeballs up and rose from his seat while I towered over Padre and felt the heat in my face, ready to fight.

"Danny, I will spin your jaw. I don't know what you two —"

Padre cut me off. He raised his hands as if to embrace me and whispered, "Peace. Peace. I know how upsetting this is."

"It's not," I shouted. "Not at all. I don't care."

"Don't think about it. Just take the mag. You'll want to talk."

Somehow, gently, he guided me to the front door, where the afternoon sun greeted me like a light at the end of a tunnel. We walked past the clubs.

"Let's talk golf another time," he said.

I gave him an affirmative look.

He waved me goodbye as I started up the Datsun Sport truck and drove back to the house, with the copy of *Tinsel Circus* curled on the seat beside me. I regretted leaving that beer on Padre's coffee table.

10

I brought chocolates for my mother, which she didn't touch and peered suspiciously at like they might be poisoned. I immediately regretted not getting donuts for the nursing staff, who were upbeat and hard-working and deserved donuts. Bad planning.

On the best days, Mother could walk perfectly fine, but she stayed in her room unless the nurses coaxed her out, or there was a meal in the common room. She sat on her bed and stared out the window. Clare had decorated her room with pictures of the children and their drawings. One picture, drawn by Harry, showed us all as stick figures. My dad, mother, and me all wore sad faces, and Clare, the kids, and Jamie had happy faces.

She said nothing as I gently reminded her who I was. I moved the chocolates to the bedside table. Her eyes remained on the treetops outside.

I sat down beside her and placed my hand gently on her knuckles. She recoiled a little. I waited for her to acclimatize, the way an iguana might assume the temperature of its environment.

"Mother, I wanted to tell you about what happened this week," I said, deciding at last to be simple and come out with it. "Jamie and I had Dad's memorial service, and we buried him at Notre Dame on Montreal Road. I thought, maybe I could take you there one day, if you like?" That last part I regretted the instant I said it. Why would I say such a thing? I did not want to take her anywhere. Maybe I wanted to lessen the blow a little?

"Who?"

"Your husband."

"What about him?"

"I know you don't remember but we talked about this last week.... It doesn't matter. When the time is right, you'll be next to him. Jamie ordered a space on the headstone."

"What the heck are you talking about?"

"Sorry Jamie couldn't be here," I said.

"Who's that?"

"Your son," I said. "I'm your son. We are your sons."

"Pff. I don't have any children."

I sighed. "You don't, eh?"

"No, no. My husband is coming to get me later today. We're going to Mustique."

It was an interesting and very specific choice of location, I thought. I looked down at the stack of old *Hello!* magazines on her bedside table. None were from the past three years. Why bother?

Mother had been a fan of Princess Margaret and used to follow her jet-set lifestyle in the magazines, never passing up a copy of *Hello!* or *People*, especially if it held a photo spread of Margaret and her holidays.

"Must be nice," I said, and I meant it.

"Oh, yes. We have a sailboat. A big one. There are lots of parties on the boat. We have many, many friends. I love champagne and I drink as much as I like."

The delusion cheered her. The mind, as it fails, seizes on to the most powerful bits of a person. In her case, the power of celebrity. I imagined other adult children in this place might have parents fighting dementia and brain damage from stroke with all their might, angry and raging at their world's demise. Mother had feathered for herself a happy and glamorous fantasy. I found it comforting. Better that than enduring her yelling at me, fighting me, which is what one would have predicted, based on her cheerless personality.

"That sounds lovely," I said.

"You wish," Mother said, suddenly filled with spite. "You're not invited. Our friends are all rich. You're not rich."

"No, I'm not," I said. "I live in a mouldy apartment in Old South. And I'm on the dole."

To me, she looked the same as ever: bone-thin, with a long neck and coarse hair like warped steel, grey as it had always been. When she jerked her head, I got the impression of an angry turkey.

"My husband is a movie star."

"He must be busy."

"Oh, he is. He's working on a new movie right now. He's very famous. I bet you'd like to meet him, wouldn't you? But you can't."

"Okay."

"You got a cigarette?"

"No, Mother, you don't smoke anymore."

"The hell I don't. What good are you?"

I sighed.

"Mother, do you have any recollection of Dad's job? Your husband's job before — uh — before he became a movie star? Maybe he worked for the Canadian government? Does that ring any bells?"

She laughed scornfully. "You gormless little twat. Who do you think you're talking to?"

I grit my teeth.

I had come to tell her about Jamie's pending surgery, but that seemed absurd now. It occurred to me if I never came back to see my mother, her shambolic mind couldn't care less. I suddenly worried the same might happen to Jamie afterward. After he went in for his procedure.

A chill went up my spine.

Mother being this way I could handle. Not Jamie.

But a thought relaxed me. The kids would carry on. Kitty and Harry. It didn't matter about us. The kids were safe.

Clare would save them. Clare, whom Mother hated from day one, regardless of everything Clare had done for our family to keep it functioning. Without her, our family would be nothing. Jamie and Clare had already saved their children by giving them a good foundation, good insurance for life. More than that. They gave them the trajectory for a brilliant life. They were sensational parents who provided a good home. That's what mattered, right? The thought strengthened me. I smiled, relieved that my parents' twisted piety hadn't poisoned Jamie's kids.

"Remember, Mother, every day above ground is a good day," I said.

"Ha! That's a laugh."

On my way out, I stopped at the nursing station and thanked them for looking after my mother.

"That's the job description," said the head nurse, a powerful-looking woman in Hello Kitty scrubs and a hoodie.

"Does she ever ask to go to church?"

The question made her blink. "She's not mentioned it. Would you like us to add that to her routine? There's a chapel on the ground floor."

"No, I'm just surprised," I said quietly. "The lady I knew would have put priority on that."

"People change all the time."

So here she was at the end of her life and all the churching had come to this. "Suppose so."

The nurse gave me a double take. My face must have looked portentous because she stopped reading her file and seemed to suspect something was up. Something suspicious, with me. I stood there too long, chewing my lip like an idiot. Likely, as a palliative nurse, she'd seen it all. "You know, she's in good hands," the woman said, a searching note in her voice.

"My niece would love that shirt," I said, and headed for the elevators with no intent to ever return.

11

It was two years after the wedding, and Clare was having difficulty getting pregnant. It turned out she and Jamie both had fertility problems, and so they relied on in-vitro wizards at a Sussex Drive clinic to help fulfill their family wishes. Personally, I suspected the difficulty getting pregnant was a sign from God that our family was not meant to nurture children. That our poisoned line was not meant to survive.

The twins were born five years ago.

Back when Clare was expecting, I asked Jamie how he thought he could possibly qualify as a father. How would it be possible after the childhood we had.

"Why would you ask? I'm going to be a great dad." He smiled confidently as if there was a comedic reason he was trying to cover up.

"Let me guess. You'll do the opposite of how Dad raised us?"

"No," said Jamie. "Remember when we were young? You used to tell me to trust my instincts, look at the environment, listen. You were a real Boy Scout. You trusted me."

I smiled at him. His notion felt distant to me, but true. Distant from where I was now, but I remembered the boy who was able to lead calmly a shaking and terrified Jamie away from bullies like

Rob and Squirm, who were planning to rub a racoon carcass on him, and bring him to where rain falling on leaves was miraculous and reassuring. My eyes lowered at remembering that boy.

Jamie was, in fact, a warm, strong father who could lead his own children in the same way. And it made me feel good that I inspired him, even a little. But jammed in hard against that feeling was shame. What did I know about anything? I knew that you're supposed to do the right thing, but I instead allowed myself to rot into a derelict. I'd been cowardly all my life since then.

I wish it was a kidney or his heart that was the problem with Jamie because that way I could help. I could donate. It would be a big thing that I could feel good about, something I could use as a step for my courage and become the man that I should have been.

I could have done something significant with my life.

Jamie always hated being close to dead things. Now he was facing death himself. It should be me. Would his own corpse disgust him as much as Dad's did? Or would he understand it was a part of himself? If he could stand next to his own body, what would it be to him but a horror?

What did I have going on? And I had no fears of dead things such as he had. I had a fantasy that I could hold him while he was cremated — me burning alive — so that he would not have to be alone in the furnace. Me, a martyr. That would make up for all the time of my life I had wasted.

As if on cue, my phone pinged with a text from him.

Where R U?

House, I texted back. I had been sleeping at the house for three days now and had started wearing Dad's clean underwear, T-shirts, and socks. My own apartment sat empty a twenty-minute drive away.

Cleaning or reading?

I didn't respond.

On the kitchen counter was the copy of *Tinsel Circus* and its bonkers article about Griff Kelsey and Father Sweet. I'd read it twice last night. In fact, I had to read it twice because seeing Father Sweet's name in print made me ill, and my eyes kept skipping over the parts about him. I had to force myself to read about his can't-make-this-stuff-up journey from Canada to Vatican II to Hollywood, where he led a remarkably old-fashioned parish, funded by Griff Kelsey, and lived with his new young acolyte, Antony.

The article was mostly about Griff Kelsey and the scandals surrounding him prior to the release of *King of Blood*, a movie I have only vague recollections of being in theatres, but according to my quick internet search, was a big hit.

Every time Father Sweet's name appeared in the article, and once I could drag my eyes over the lines, I felt personally slapped and galled that he was in such a grand spotlight as a glossy American magazine. My mother, if she could have understood, would have been over the moon.

He was quoted speaking about two things: Vatican II and its dreadful effect on the Church, and Antony.

> "Judgment entered the Church. But not the judgment of God, the judgment by the individual congregant. It is why liberalism is the enemy of the Almighty, and anyone faithful to Him."
>
> Sweet is earnest and serious. Antony tugs at his sleeve and whispers to him.
>
> "Ah, my acolyte. Antony's family are Catholics in the best sense." He smiles at Antony and strokes his back. "His father and mother gave him to me to complete his education."

It was that last part that stuck with me more than anything. Although there was another portion that specifically related to something I knew plenty about, something that existed deep in the cellars of my mind.

> "It was the weekend Pope Paul VI died," says Sweet. "I had just returned from an extremely disappointing camping trip. I had been thinking about my dear friend and mentor the Monsignor Aloysius Gast. Then it was revealed to me that everything I loved about my vocation, I had fought to destroy."

I felt I understood well "what he loved."

I brewed a pot of stale Nabob and opened a can of beans for breakfast. Between cold spoonfuls, I slurped black coffee and stared into the back garden. A drip of brown sauce fell from the spoon to my sweatshirt. I wiped it with my thumb and licked it clean.

The article showed a big picture of Griff Kelsey's sun-roughened, Botoxed, once-handsome mug. He was as big a celebrity as one could imagine. And a nutbar Catholic rebel who fought Rome with a regressive, crazy form of the religion that believed the pope was the Antichrist and translating Mass from Latin was the reason for all the corruption in the world. This was where Father Sweet, who used to lecture me on modernism and the importance of Vatican II, had wound up. This was the guy who said the traditions he shared with his old mentor Aloysius Gast somehow involved me sharing a sleeping bag with him under the delighted eyes of God.

After a few tries, attempting to put the words right, I pressed send, asking Jamie if he knew whether our father had any last requests or plans. Did he say anything about what he wanted done after he died?

Woulda told U, he texted, after a while.

It was almost eleven, and the sun was shining. Jamming the rolled *Tinsel Circus* into my back pocket, I took my coffee and bean can out back, setting them down to prop up one of the rusted patio chairs.

I had a suffocating desire to do nothing and breathe and stare at the fence Dad had neglected to paint for twenty years. At the base, the wood had gone so soft and rotted that squirrels barely paused on their way into the neighbours' garden on Woodburn Road.

I sipped at my coffee, rapidly cooling outside.

The kids are all right.

Still need to tell you about Dad, I texted him. *Tonite?*

There was a long break during which nothing came back, and I stared at my phone.

Hi, came the text. *It's Clare. I've got Jamie's phone.*

I sat up.

What's happening? Where is he?

We're at the neuro.

Can I call?

He fainted. He's fine. I'll call you. Wait.

Suddenly, the garden's derelict calm changed complexion and the sun glared hard into my eyes. I stood and reread the texts. Then I dialed Jamie's number.

Exasperated, Clare's voice answered by telling me not to worry.

"Can I help?" I asked. "Who's looking after the kids?"

"Stop. Don't worry. They're at the neighbours'."

"Why didn't you ask me to help?"

"You've got a lot going on; I didn't think it made sense."

I surveyed the wreckage of my unemployed midday: eating beans from a tin can in my parents' backyard and drinking stale coffee from a Smurf mug that asked me if it was break time yet.

"I've got nothing going on," I said.

I could picture Clare at the doctor's office, shaking her head trying not to tell me the truth, and then giving up.

"Listen, we didn't want to bother you."

There it was. "I get it," I said.

She groaned. "I didn't mean it like that."

"No, no. I get it."

"But the kids are all right," she said.

"That's good. It's what matters."

"Are *you* okay?"

I took a deep breath. "I am so sick of hearing that question. I feel guilty people keep asking me that when it's clear there are so many important things happening."

"Jamie's worried about you."

"Can I talk with him?"

"He's lying down in another room.... Let's just chat, me and you."

"I'm sorry, Clare. I wish I had the tumour instead of him. It would be so much easier."

Clare said nothing. It would, truly, be easier for everyone. I could picture her nodding her head, admitting it was true.

"Jamie's a great dad," I said. "You both. How do you do it?"

Clare hemmed a little. I hoped she was pleased with the compliment. She thought before responding. "I suppose ... it's not my job to build their life. I believe — and Jamie — we must help the kids find what works for them. Yah? And then get out of the way. It's their lives, not ours."

"Have you told the kids? About, you know?"

"Of course. In a manner that makes sense for them. I told them in the car when driving to school one day like it was no big deal."

"What on earth did you say?"

"That Daddy's got something wrong with his head and the doctors are going to try to make him better, but he may be different afterward and might not be able to talk. But I said we'll still love him and look after him. And that was it. They asked a few questions, said they loved Daddy, then moved on. They were fine."

"Wow."

"With five-year-olds if you don't make something into a big deal, they take the cue from you. It doesn't help if you freak out."

"Our parents wouldn't have told us anything. They would have thought it was for adults to deal with. In silence."

"Right," she said. "Well. It's the twenty-first century. And Jamie and I figure the kids can deal with it."

"What did the kids think of the funeral? Were they scared?"

"Afterward Kitty asked me — it was cute — she said, 'Mum, you know church? What's that all about?'"

My indomitable niece, Kitty. Amazing confidence and presence of mind. "I wouldn't know how to answer that one."

"I said it was like a club where people get together to sing songs and talk about life."

I laughed so loud I scared birds out of the trees. "If only."

"She's a child. It works."

"I don't mean to sound pissy," I said.

"Your parents had different ideas," she said. "Jamie always felt like you got worn down by it."

Unlike Jamie and Clare's approach with the kids — to help them design their own emerging lives — my folks used church as the dictating focus to structure and habilitate my life.

"He says you used to stand up to them more and protected him when you were growing up. Then, right before you went to high school, you sort of gave up on everything. Stopped caring. He figured your parents' negative vibes finally got to you."

"It's not fair to blame them," I said. "The only one to blame is me. It's me."

"Things adults say to kids work like a spell on a person for their whole lives."

"I've had plenty of opportunity to get my act together."

"I won't lie, I would feel better if I saw you happy. Maybe not even happy. Just doing something engaging. You know? Engaged with something you thought was … meaningful."

I took a breath. "Jamie said the same thing. I want that. I'm trying."

"You know, I gave Jamie some — oh, wait. Here's someone who wants to talk with you."

She handed the phone over.

"Hey, man," said Jamie. "How are you?"

"I heard you fainted."

"Just running some tests and planning the big day. Coming up soon, like a couple weeks."

"I can look after the kids," I offered.

"Nah. We've got a neighbour next door with kids of her own. No biggie. They just make it a play date. They'll have a sleepover. Besides, I was hoping you'd be there when I woke up."

I told him I wouldn't miss it.

"Are you nervous?"

"About brain surgery? Why would that make me nervous?"

"I've been thinking about what we talked about. I've got an idea."

"Good."

"Don't get too excited. I think it's a start on — well — you know."

"You going to see a therapist?"

"Not exactly. More of my own way of, I don't know … working through things."

He exhaled. "Okay. Good start. This sounds good."

"Don't get too excited."

"Well, let's hear it."

"I've been thinking. Like maybe I want to do something."

"That almost sounds like planning and preparation. Who is this guy and where is my brother?"

"Well, there's something I want," I said. "But it's complicated."

12

That evening, Danny and Padre planned to watch the Habs-Boston game and Padre called to ask if I would like to join them.

"But first I need a favour if you could stomach it," he said.

"Depends."

"I need an altar server for tonight's Mass," he said. "And I was wondering if you'd mind."

"I'd mind."

"It would help me out."

"Get another kid from the bench."

"Kid? We don't use kids anymore. You haven't been to Mass in a while, have you?"

"Just the funeral."

"Well, you saw Andy. He's in his forties."

"Andy not available?"

"His son's got a ringette game at the arena tonight."

"Boys play ringette now?"

"Why not?"

"What about Andy's wife?"

"Well, the bishop doesn't like female altar servers."

"Danny?"

"Nobody knows Danny's staying here."

"Can't help you."

I decided to run some errands that afternoon, but showed up in time for puck drop. Padre met me at the door and was startled by my new look.

"Wow," said Padre. "Shave and a haircut. I didn't recognize you."

"I'll take that as a compliment."

"Can I get you a drink?"

"Whisky."

"A man after my own heart."

Danny remained in the same chair I'd left him in a day and a half earlier, his eyes still glued to the screen, his lips still chewing the edges of his whiskers. At first, I thought he wore the same Blackburn Funfair sweatshirt, but it was different. He sat low in the chair with his legs wide apart. I got the impression of a teenager trapped in the loose sinews of a hobo's body.

The reason I'd gotten a haircut and shaved my face was because of the unmistakable resemblance in our appearances. It depressed me. It worried me.

Padre delivered to me a generous glass of whisky in an icy tumbler.

"What'd you think of the article?" he asked.

I cleared my throat and raised my glass. "Look," I said. "I don't want to be here, but … here's to a difficult discussion." I downed a few gulps.

Danny looked at me. For the first time, his eyes seemed to focus. My toast brought a smile to Padre's face.

"The article was …" I said, taking a big breath. "It floored me. For a lot of reasons. First, I can't believe or understand why you-know-who was excommunicated and why he's become some sort of activist promoting such weird shit. Second, how on earth did he wind up in Hollywood with Griff Kelsey? And then third, I can't believe how blatantly obvious ..." I stopped.

Padre sat on the edge of the sofa and grumbled agreeing noises. *Go on*, he seemed to say.

"Like, the celebrity thing," I said, feeling lost. My train of thought was broken. "I mean, I remember how charming he was and, Danny probably remembers, he was like a celebrity himself in Blackburn Hamlet. Probably all over Ottawa." I didn't look at Danny.

"That's not what you were gonna say," Danny said and turned back to the TV.

I felt my face go hot. "This was a mistake," I whispered into my glass.

Padre took a breath.

"Sweet was excommunicated years ago," he said. "Amazing considering he was a delegate at Vatican II."

"Yah, I knew that. Everyone knew that. So what?"

"In fact, he's the last living Canadian delegate to Vatican II. That was his life's work. Until he was excommunicated."

"That guy's full of shit."

"He was on a committee that changed the Mass into Canadian English. Many felt they went too far in modernizing the Church. You know, trying to be more accommodating and open. There was hope that Vatican II would revitalize the Church. Make it fun and appealing. That's what Sweet and his friends thought. And Protestants would convert, and it would sweep the world."

"Ha!" Danny said. "That didn't happen."

"No. And when that didn't happen, Sweet and his ilk believed they failed the Church. Destroyed the mystery. So he started saying homilies against it, and saying the Tridentine Mass — the one they used before Vatican II. He came to regret his role in changing the liturgy and wanted to fight to change it all back.

"Imagine regretting your life's greatest achievement? He joined the Pius X society, which is a group of Traditionalist renegades who believe the Church started going wrong after the death of Pius X.

"The bishop told him to quit the society or he'd be kicked out of the Church. He wrote a letter essentially telling him to go to hell, and they excommunicated him."

"But that's not the whole story," Danny said.

"You know Maccabees?"

I was scrutinizing Danny, and it took a moment before I came to realize the question was for me. "Remind me," I said.

"Judas Maccabee led a revolt to restore Jewish worship at the temple after pagans had seized it. That's how these guys think of themselves versus Rome. They even call the pope the Antichrist."

"I don't care about any of this. All of this is useless. Useless information. How did he meet Griff Kelsey?"

"Sweet loves celebrities and people with power. He's a real star-worshipper. Griff Kelsey is rich. He funds the Pius X society. Naturally, when he heard that a Vatican II delegate was recanting everything, he wanted him for his own pastor. And off goes little Benjamin Sweet of Cape Breton to Hollywood."

"You don't care that some clergy think the pope is the Antichrist?" said Danny.

"Something you want to say, mister?" Padre snapped at him. "Sweet has always been in a group of eccentrics. There are a lot of sub-communities among the clergy. He and plenty of others are now rogues."

"Boo-hoo."

"Personally, I couldn't be a priest if Vatican II had never happened. The old Church was too secretive, too weird. Not enough of a focus on ministry and too much focus on mystery. Somehow, though, the Church has been dying in Canada all the same. When I started as a priest, the pews were full, there were liberals and conservatives. A broad swath of people. Nowadays the pews are nearly empty and only conservatives remain. But guys like Sweet and Gast, they always felt like outsiders."

"Aloysius Gast," I said.

"A well-placed, slippery man with political connections in Rome. He would have thrived in medieval Europe."

"I know all about Gast."

"How's that?"

"I'll tell you later. First, tell me about the kids. I want to know about the kids."

Padre and Danny shared glum looks. I repeated the question.

"There's no doubt," Padre said. "That unquestioning loyalty of the priestly class is one thing these guys miss about the pre–Vatican II days."

"You mean it was easier for them to get away with it on a massive scale?"

Padre shifted in his seat. I wondered if he would answer my question or dodge.

"They think the openness of Vatican II is what's killing the Church. They might be right. Catholicism is a secret institution. Think of how big the change was. Once parishioners understood Mass, looked the priest in the face during confession, and engaged with the world, light was shone into the shadows. It was ugly, what it showed. John XXIII wanted the focus of the Church to be justice. That is what happened."

"Justice, eh?" I said. Dodge.

Danny stood up and walked to the kitchen, leaving Padre and I alone in the lounge with the TV.

I pointed sharply where Danny had walked. "Justice?"

Padre held up his hands as if to say *slow down*.

"I know why you're here," I growled to him. "With Danny. I've seen this show before. When you-know-who was sent out of our parish, another priest like you came in to clean up the mess. That's what you're doing here. I'm going to kick his fucking head in."

"You can do that, but I'll stop you. I can tell you what happened, but you have to promise me you won't hurt him. There's more here than you realize, and you need to believe me that I'm here to help. There's help here for you, too. I know why *you're* here."

"Danny," I called in a hot, chippy voice. "Get in here. Think it's time you came clean with me, bud."

"You know more about all of this than you let on," said Padre to me gently. "I can imagine how angry you are right now. I want to talk with you."

Danny shuffled in from the kitchen, holding a beer bottle to his lips. Padre and I were in the lounge chairs and observed Danny lean against the wall, keeping his distance. He scratched the back of his calf with his foot, socked in a dirty white athletic tube.

"So, we're doing this now?" asked Danny. "Is this the kumbaya moment?"

I stared at him. The pot lights hit his tinted glasses exactly right so I could see the outline of myself as a reflection. The effect was so creepy I shivered. "What did you do?" I asked.

Padre held up his hand. "Before you judge Danny, I'd like you to think about how it was for you when you were young."

"The fuck are you talking about?" I said. "You don't know a goddamned thing about me."

"Sure he does, brother," said Danny. "Takes one to know one."

My hands clenched into fists and I sprang up out of the chair to charge at Danny but was stopped by Padre, who slammed me to the floor and pinned me around the neck.

I was immobilized, more from the shock of this sudden violence than its actual mechanics.

"Just because I've got this," Padre said, pointing at the Roman collar of his shirt, "shouldn't make you assume anything."

"Listen, brother," Danny said. "Padre knows — people like you and me. He knows it because he hatched from the same egg. Different Sweet. Same Father."

Padre released his grip.

I sat up and found myself shaking uncontrollably. Danny shuffled back to the lounge chair and watched the TV.

"Don't say you and I are the same," I said to Danny, not looking at him. "We are not. You hear?"

"You need some time," said Padre. "Want some water?"

I shook my head. I slid one fingernail deep under the lid of another and felt pain in the quick. Padre gestured for me to sit on the sofa, as far as I could get from Danny without leaving the room.

"I don't want to talk about it," I said. "About me."

"I understand," said Padre.

"I could get a haircut and wash, too, brother."

"What did you do, Danny?" I asked, quieter now. "You tell me now."

He drank.

"That's not gonna change what you did," I insisted.

"Who's afraid to talk about his sins?" Danny said, licking dry lips. "At the school, I was there for a grade three art class. I was helping one of the little girls out of her painting smock."

Danny stopped talking and stared at his beer, peeling the label in one single piece.

"I ran my hands under her shirt. I didn't mean to do it. But I did. It was like I was on automatic pilot. I was like a robot. It scared the living shit out of me. I ran out of the school."

I gagged. I could smell Father Sweet's rancid breath in the tent.

"Then he called the bishop," Padre said, calling me back. "And then the bishop called me."

I took a deep breath. "What about the parents?"

Padre and Danny were silent.

"So noble. Both of you," I hissed. "You fondle a kid and skulk away. And you help him hide."

"I don't think she knew that something happened," Danny said.

"Danny says he's never done this before, and I believe him."

"And that makes it okay?" I said.

"I don't think it's okay," said Danny quietly.

I called him a coward, then looked at Padre. "You say it's important to teach kids about right and wrong, that their souls are on some sort of cosmic merchant's scale. You scare the piss out of them with hell, and treat them like sinners, and meanwhile, here you are with your shitty, exploiting, pornographic habits."

After a while, Danny spoke in a low voice. "If I could, I'd just leave and go live far away," he said.

Padre held out his palms. "All things in due course," he said.

"Call the parents right now," I said. "You're hypocrites! You say you're looking out for God's children, but you're predators." My hands trembled. I felt a rabbit's urge to run.

"We've been talking," Danny said, looking at Padre. "A lot. About the past, about what's next, about the best thing to do."

"Oh yah? The best thing for *you*," I said. "Nicely played. For you."

Padre sat back and handed me my whisky glass. "Okay. Okay. Let me ask you, what is it that you want?"

Here was the reason I came, and I had yet to stake the position and ask for the help I needed.

"I read the article," I said. "And I need to do something about it."

"Okay.... What?"

"I want to talk to the parents. The parents of that kid, Antony. I need to know how to get to him. Get to them." I jammed the fingernail in deep. "I need to do this," I said. "Not for myself, you understand. But because my brother asked me to. I have to do this for my brother."

"Odd," said Padre. "Why wouldn't you do this for the parents? For Antony? What would you say?"

"Can you help me find them? Not Danny. I'll be calling the police shortly. Just you."

Danny and Padre said nothing. They blinked at one another, seemingly confused by my comments. To me it was clear as day.

"The two of you have convinced yourselves of something that isn't legitimate," I said. "The whole goddamned thing should come down. You need to go to the police."

"All in due course," said Padre.

I pulled myself to my feet. "All in due course, eh? I'll tell you something. My dad worked thirty years for the government. Here's what he did, good Christian man that he was. He rode through reserves with a posse of armed men and took kids away from their parents. He gave them to the Church, to raise and educate. Guess who was his favourite priest?"

"The thing is, it's not just Sweet," Danny said. "Sweet used to be at Gast's school in Saskatchewan, too."

My mouth snapped shut and I set my jaw.

"Gast thinks Danny is one of them," Padre said.

"Danny, you *are* one of them," I cried. "You just said it." I felt faint. "Wait a minute. That guy is still alive?"

"Monsignor Gast has got to be over a hundred," Danny said. "He lives in Mexico now."

"In a Traditionalist Catholic compound," continued Padre. "An Apostolic Society. Some of the priests have been excommunicated, some have not. But all of them are there because Latin American Catholics still keep their bad apples hidden."

"I was invited. To come to Gast," said Danny.

I shook my head. "Bad apples," I said. "It's not the apples, it's the orchard." I had never felt so filthy. Well ... maybe never.

"Will you help me find Antony's parents?" I asked Padre.

"Yes," Padre said. He looked at Danny, and the glance worried me. "But I — we — want something from you in return."

13

"I'll be going away for a while," I said to Clare. "My little project to … you know."

"Get on track?" she asked.

I sighed. "Brought some stuff for the kids," I said, nodding at the box in my arms.

Every time we spoke, Clare and I had eye-contact problems. We said things we wanted to take back. But underneath it, I loved her. I valued her more than she probably realized. I don't know if she shared the sentiment.

She smiled. "I like the haircut. You look good like that," she said, holding the door open for me.

I stepped onto the polished marble tiles of the house and set down the box.

"So, what's with all the mystery? Are you taking your dad's inheritance and joining a commune in California? Going on a retreat? Becoming a Scientologist?"

It was fair game, I felt, given that she had a right to know, both as my sister-in-law and as someone who had tried to help. "Sorry for the mystery," I said. "I could do better."

"As long as," she said without looking at me, "you're trying."

Kitty entered from the kitchen, with a sticky face and a bowl of apple slices. She gave me a hug, spilling fruit on the floor, and invited me inside, trying to pull me by the hand.

"No, honey," I said, squatting down. "I just came to drop something off. I'm going on a trip."

"What in the box?" she asked.

I lifted the lid. "For when you're older. These are books that Daddy and I had when we were young. See? There's Hardy Boys and Encyclopedia Brown and a huge pile of comics."

"Huh," she said.

"What do you say?" said Clare.

"Thank you," she said over her shoulder as she left.

"There's something about this," said Clare quietly, "that makes me think you aren't coming back. And I hope that's not so."

I did my best to smile reassuringly. "I'll see you for Jamie's operation."

14

I was sleeping in my old room in Blackburn Hamlet. I had stopped packing up and removing dad's belongings from the house for the time being. It felt like a half-empty time capsule and felt like I belonged nowhere. But I felt closer to the kid I was — the person I was — than I had felt in decades.

I went to the grocery store to restock the fridge, parking my car near the Legion hall where Jamie and I used to attend Scout meetings. Just beyond the hall, south of the town was a trail into the greenbelt that led to the Mer Bleue bog. It was on that trail I remember Mike Racine taking the troop on our walks into the bush.

In my hand was a brand new Blackberry. First thing in the morning I traded in my old, cracked Blackberry for a new phone and opened the calendar application for the first time. I had never bothered to put anything in the calendar before, but now I had one specific date and time to plunk in. Jamie's surgery date was set. I needed to be up and at the Civic Hospital for Wednesday morning, 6:00 a.m., in two weeks' time. The app created a dark-red monolith to mark the twelve hours of the day I'd be sitting with Clare in the waiting room.

I had plenty to get done beforehand.

In the late afternoon I drove to Gloucester city centre and picked up my new passport. I had never owned one in my life. I sat in my truck and looked at the portrait, official, clean-cut and serious. Sanctioned by Her Majesty and the Government of Canada and dressed with a hexadecimal number. Like I knew what I was doing and should be trusted by authorities to cross borders and conduct affairs.

The sun was setting as I drove back to Blackburn, crossed over the Green's Creek bridge, and felt my jaw tighten confidently into a smile. I tilted the rear-view mirror down to look at my face to be sure. There it was. A smile.

I drove to the rectory and spotted Padre on the front lawn, chipping walnut husks with a nine iron.

"If you're truly offering," he said as I walked to him, "I will take all these clubs. They are ten times better than the set I've been using."

"They're yours. Use them in good health," I said.

"Did you get your passport?" Padre asked, chipping a walnut into the hedge.

"And the tickets. For me and Danny. Though I don't know why he has to come."

"Well, that's the deal. Still. You're generous."

"What my dad left me is more than I need."

"You might think you're saving Antony, but in so doing these things you're saving much more. You know that Jewish saying that he who saves a life saves the world?"

"That's a bit much."

"Well, you're saving yourself, aren't you?"

"I thought you black-shirts would say only God can save any of us?"

"I would never say that. That's bullshit," said Padre. "God helps those who help themselves. Ben Franklin."

I poked at the golf bag with my foot and chuckled.

"Somebody," I said, "a long time ago … told me you cannot save yourself. Salvation only comes from above."

"Who says there's one kind of salvation? What a lousy world it would be, where everyone should be passive. Waiting to be saved like the cavalry is coming to save the settlers from the Natives."

I was stung by the Native comment. "My dad did the opposite." I pictured my father, passionless, with a set jaw, pulling a young boy away from his screaming mother, and handing him to Father Sweet. For his own good.

That image — a priest receiving a child from my father — made me shudder. It was such a horrible thing. Especially when it occurred to me that the parent of that child — unlike the way Jamie and I felt our parents cared for us — might actually love him, the way we loved Kitty and Harry.

"People should know better," said Padre.

"What people should do," I said, "is fuck off. Everyone's got an idea about what everyone else should do."

Padre stopped golfing and regarded me evenly. "A man who saves a life saves a world. Nobody's life is without injury. I'm talking about you now. The best medicine for your kind of injury is to do a good turn in exchange. That's how decency gets its footing. And I see what you're doing."

"No, you don't." I dug into my thumbnail. "You don't know me."

"I know principles. It's not about what harm you received, but what decency you can do for someone else."

He beckoned me inside. In the lounge, there sat Danny rotting before the television, still.

"You and Danny both want to live good lives, but it doesn't take anything momentous to make the change. Choose to have a life with purpose," Padre said. "That's it."

"Easy for you to say," Danny said. "That's your job."

"No, it's *your* job," Padre said, suddenly loud, stabbing a finger at him. The outburst startled me.

"You think that he doesn't need any momentous change to stop touching little girls?" I said to him.

Padre seemed exasperated. "No, no. You don't get it."

Danny crossed his legs and breathed heavily, but didn't take his eyes from the TV. To me, he seemed as inscrutable as a lizard.

"That's what religious people always say when you confront them with their choices."

"Of course, I think it's a momentous change. Grace comes when you choose to have a meaningful life."

"I've been trying my whole life to solve that one," I said, making peace with him. It occurred to me that Padre might have his own drama going on with Danny, and my arrival stoked the coals.

"Most people see meaning in what they do, not the other way around. That's sin," said Padre. "God wants us to do the right thing. Sin is justifying doing the wrong thing."

"I'm trying," I said, sitting down and unsure if he directed his comments at me, or at Danny. "I'm trying to."

"Danny, turn off the TV," said Padre.

Danny clicked the remote and the room got quiet.

"You said justifying doing the wrong thing ..." I paused. "I know that. I know it. My dad made me believe he valued good. And that he was good because he knew good from evil, and I didn't. And he had power. He was relentless for a hard, unkind good. A 'good-for-you' good. Like medicine that tastes like poison."

"All people have dark and light in them," Padre said.

"Really? He was suspicious of anything sweet. My dad trusted poison. And I think he believed I deserved —" I said, stopping short, suddenly unable to finish.

Padre waited for me, hands folded.

"You are justifying the wrong thing," I said to Danny without looking at him.

We were quiet.

Padre was the sort of man who was untroubled by sitting in a room across from someone unwilling to talk. I could see his appeal as a confessor and distrusted myself.

"You know," he said, "we have to feed goodness. You can't repress the bad. We need to understand our sins and reconcile ourselves with them."

It was seductive.

I flushed hot. "Please," I said, "I'm not your parishioner. Don't give me that shit. Your idea of … morality is none of my business."

"All right. I'll use your words then. People think they can find the good and avoid the evil, but they can't. Instead of fighting, sit with it. Acknowledge it. Then, you have to feed the good impulse and starve evil. I'd ask you to please give some thought about how you view your dad."

"I don't have to do anything," I said. "He's in the ground. And I'm sifting through what he's left behind. Taken several trips to the dump already with my truck, and dozens of bags to Goodwill."

"You may not realize it, but you are trying to reconcile with him. It's why you're here. One reason, I know. Why you want to talk to Antony's parents. We want to think everything is black and white, but often that's how situations — stay with me now — such as what happened here with you and Father Sweet occur."

I felt faint. I looked at Danny, whose eyes were on the carpet before him. The room had dropped away to be little more than a black space filled with Padre's voice close to my ear.

"You are good," Padre said, and he leaned toward me. "Children are good. We have no right telling them they are sinful and their souls are at stake over good and evil. Adults created this mess. I knew your dad. I heard his confession. I can tell you he wasn't without shame."

"My dad did awful, awful things," I said. Barely above a whisper. "He worked for the government doing bad things. His career was taking kids away from their families, and giving them to the Church. Native kids who lived in the sticks with their parents and hunted and fished for a living. They gave them to the priests and the nuns, who sterilized those kids, beat them and starved them until they died, or died running away." I looked at Padre. "Kids died."

Neither Danny nor Padre looked surprised by what I said.

"How do you know?" Padre said.

"I've seen letters between my dad and that priest."

"Gast?"

"And others. I am in possession of a lot of … damning evidence."

"How much evidence?"

"Boxes and boxes."

"And what do you plan to do? With this evidence?" Padre's voice went cold.

I looked up. "I'm not sure yet."

Padre sought my eyes. "I could help you, take care of those boxes for you."

I looked away. "I have stuff that I could write down. I also have my own experience. And because I know —" I stuttered "— I know exactly what I know — there was more done to these kids. Stuff justified with some flowery language about Greek beauty and the Bible. Children are sinful and need to be *corrected*. But in the end, Padre, it's just plain old molestation, isn't it?"

Danny put his head in his hands.

"I don't understand why," I said. "Teaching children that they are sinful and need to confess. Teaching children to be guilty. Even while lives are being ruined. Kids are dying. And I don't understand why you, you *priests* are … so goddamned confident you are right."

Padre leaned back. He was quiet. "Well," he said at last. "I'm not. And even though I might have ideas about why, I can't say either that I understand."

"Then what good is any of this," I asked. "And what good are you? Just more bullshit gabbing and blocking. Idiotic complexity."

Padre sighed. A few moments went by, then he spoke slowly. "You'll hear people say it's a modern phenomenon," he said. "Caused by the evil liberties of modern society. You know, pornography, casual Fridays, all that. Vatican II."

"Ridiculous," I pronounced.

"It's not true, no. But it *has* gotten harder to handle."

"See? Right there. *Handle*. Handle what? *What* are you talking about?"

"All I mean is the Church has fewer tools to solve these problems. I'll give you an example. There was one pope — Gregory IX — who got word from Alsace about a full-scale revolt. A priest had been burned at the stake by villagers. Now, the official record says this priest had been '*immodicus*' with some young people. Boys. It's clear enough to see what happened if you read between the lines. A group of families were up in arms. With good reason, I imagine. Gregory sends a substitute priest to the village, who is killed upon arrival. Protestors tear down the local church. Gregory's worried this could spread. So, he sends in the Inquisition. They quickly label the angry families as heretics, and all of them are burned — virtually the whole village — and then another priest goes in to rebuild the community. From scratch. Destroy the village to save it. The whole story was sealed up, locked away, and Bob's your uncle."

"My god. When was that?"

Padre's eyes zeroed in on mine. "One thousand years ago."

I stared at Padre until my eyes stung.

"That wasn't the last time this happened," I said.

"Heavens, no," said Padre. "But, you see, things are improving. We don't destroy villages anymore."

"That's not funny," I said. "You want to treat symptoms, not provide the cure."

"Oh, come now. The Church *is* the cure. The political history of the Church," Padre said, "is the history of Western civilization. And the outcome is we've *got* a civilization."

My lips curled at the word *civilization*.

"Order over chaos. But there are ... leftovers. Inside the Church some ancient traditions still lurk, like this ... Hellenistic problem, if you like. Come on. You know all this. Why did you study anthropology of religion?"

"I don't know," I said. "I honestly don't."

He stared back with suspicion. "The best of the Church — to any one of us — is this, what we have right now. Two guys sharing some time together, making the world less lonely, more meaningful. The Church is good for that. But if you believe the Church is God on Earth, and people do believe that, then you've got people who will do anything to protect it."

I sighed and shook my head at him. I hated this discussion and wanted it to stop. Padre was trying to convince me. "The whole apparatus needs to come down," I said. "The Church is the problem."

"Catholics believe in forgiveness, but also in the inheritance of sin. So if you're going to call yourself Catholic you take the good and the bad."

"I'm not Catholic," I said.

"Sure you are. You were baptized in the Catholic faith. You were raised Catholic. You're in until the Church says you're out.

You can concentrate on the bad if you want. People want a safe place where they can talk about goodness. I'm here to make things better. You are Catholic. It's nice to go some place once a week where people are nice to each other."

I bit my lip at the insinuation. Nice to each other. Sure. Like in the sacristy when Father Sweet would pinch the altar servers' bottoms — nice.

"Don't call me that."

"You were trying to understand Father Sweet," said Danny to me, as if he had been thinking about it the whole time. "That's why you studied religion. You were trying to understand what happened."

"You don't know anything," I snarled. "Shut up."

"Just trying to help."

"Well, stop. I don't know why I do anything."

"That makes two of us," Danny said.

"Good Lord," said Padre, sipping his beer. "What a pair, you two."

"But I'll tell you," I said, directing it over his shoulder, mostly at Danny. "I know what I'm doing now."

"Give some thought," Padre said. "About those boxes. I can take them for you."

None of what this man says is genuine, I thought. *He's someone with charm and big words, but behind the smile is someone all in to "handle" this situation. And perhaps light a fire, if I'm not careful.*

"One more thing," I said. "I'm not in until you say I'm out. I'm out because I say I'm out."

15

At the house, I did laundry in the basement. As I removed clothes from the dryer, I laid them out on the linoleum floor. Five pairs of underwear. Five pairs of socks. One pair of jeans. One pair of khaki trousers. One nice shirt. Five T-shirts or polos. Toothbrush, paste, deodorant, et cetera. Aspirin. Notebook and pen. Bottle of whisky.

I folded my gear into my old vinyl Adidas bag I'd found earlier then went upstairs. I dialed Jamie's number and told him I would see him in a week or so.

"Text me when you get there," he said.

"I'll be back in time for your surgery."

After closing up the house, I drove to the rectory. Danny answered the door, holding a mug of coffee.

"You look so professional. All clean-cut like you are," he said.

"You oughta try it," I replied.

In addition to his mess of hair and prospector's beard, Danny was not wearing deodorant, which was evident despite my being outdoors while he stood on the transom.

"Where's your comrade?"

"Padre? Doing hospital rounds. Should be back any minute. He wanted to catch you."

Padre's Camry came up the drive and parked next to mine. He wiped his eyes and approached us.

"You don't look happy," I said.

A weary grin briefly wafted across his face. "Rough morning."

"Yah? Not enough in the collection plate or something?"

Danny backed up. "Hey, man, that is not cool."

I felt ready now. I would hit Danny.

Padre's eyes levelled with mine, and they were cold. "No, it's okay. Our friend here simply doesn't understand what it's like to sit in an embrace with parents on a hospital bed while their child dies in their arms. And that's what I did this morning. And, yes, it's exactly as bad as it sounds."

"I'm sorry," I said quietly. "I guess.... Well, maybe it's a hard job. Sometimes."

"Keeps getting harder," Padre said brushing past me into the house.

He left Danny and I standing alone together saying nothing. When he returned, I was relieved to see him.

Padre handed me a piece of paper.

"This woman's name is Melody Cary," Padre said. "Here's her email, phone number, and everything. I spoke with her already. When you guys get to Los Angeles she'll help you with your bear hunt. You'll find Sweet."

"No, no, no. I want nothing to do with him," I said. "I told you I want to talk with Antony's parents."

"Yah, yah. She'll help with that. I gave her a heads-up. She'll meet you at the airport when you land."

"Do you understand that I only want the parents? It's important to me to talk to those parents."

"I understand."

"Do you?"

He took a step closer to me. "I try."

I looked at the paper with Melody Cary's contact info. "You're a cleaner," I said to Padre without looking at him. "Sent to clean a mess."

Padre shifted his weight and folded his arms.

"What if I am?"

"National Center for Missing and Exploited Children. Wow. And what's SNAP?" I said, pointing to one of Melody Cary's two email addresses.

"It's a group that you might be interested in. Melody can tell you more. They have interest in justice. They help people who have been ... mistreated by clergy. She's a local volunteer in California with experience. A former detective. She worked with state police and now works with that missing and exploited children outfit. You'll want to talk with her."

"What's in this for you?"

"Think about what you're trying to do."

"Yah, what are you doing, man?" Danny sounded like a stupid parrot.

"A good turn every day," I said, unsure why those words left my mouth. "For the first time in a long while. I'm trying to protect a little kid."

"Me, too," said Padre. "I became a priest after Vatican II. Building the Church openly, and doing good is my life."

"You mean doing good for the Church."

We eyed one another. Padre took my hand in his and mumbled a few words. He was praying. Maybe even blessing me.

"Whatsoever you do for the least of us, you do for the Lord. Be a channel of peace." He looked up and smiled. "You won't like it if I say trust in God, so instead I'll say don't be afraid."

"Okay," I said. Then I surprised myself and said, "Thank you."

"Have you given any thought about those boxes of your dad's?"

I shook my head. "You're asking about this again."

"Where are they?"

"My dad's house."

"If you leave me a key I can go through them for you."

This was the third time he had asked after them. He saw the answer in my face. Like my father, I projected disapproval with great conviction. It's all in the eyes and brows. Like Clint Eastwood.

"Can you at least believe, just a little bit, that I want to replace systems of oppression with systems of goodness and kindness?" he asked. "Creating an open, natural spirituality where we can encounter God as a friend. That should be the journey of our pilgrim Church."

"I don't give two shits for your pilgrim Church," I said. I turned to Danny and took a breath the way you do before walking into the dentist's office. "You ready to go?"

I threw his duffel violently into the Sport truck.

"Hey, look at that old Adidas bag," Danny said, full of cheer and climbing into the passenger seat. "That really brings me back! Reminds me of the old days."

"Fuck the old days," I said.

16

Southern California was not lush as I imagined it to be. In my mind, and my mother's celebrity glossies, Los Angeles appeared green, golden, and teeming with beautiful women, art deco villas, and shiny sports cars. As our plane began the descent on a cloudless afternoon, I watched the dusty yellow hills and sooty bushes roll under us, and I wondered why I expected it to appear more as a jungle. Two fires burned on hills to the north, sending long grey plumes out over the ramshackle clutter of the city, sunbaked as a desert junkyard.

The plane landed. Danny turned to me and said, "Our first priority has got to be replenishing the supply."

Airport security had taken my whisky bottle back in Ottawa, which is where I discovered Danny had made the same mistake and tried to sneak in a forty-pounder. We didn't buy booze at the duty-free because we were inexperienced travellers and unsure if we would go through security again at the other end.

We followed our cohort of passengers along the terminal's overcrowded and greasy hallways to the baggage carousel, and that's where we discovered Melody Cary searching for us. Like a shield, she held a homemade sign with Danny's and my name on it, bracketed by a heart on one side and a smiley face on the other.

She was a tall woman with short, frizzy hair who used barely any makeup. Her eyes were enormous and bright. She wore what looked like expensive white jeans and a bright pink crew neck that made her flawless, rich brown skin pop like gold. When I waved at her, she broke into a colossal, welcoming smile that made my face tingle.

"You look like my sister-in-law," I said.

"Then c'mere, give me a hug, since we're family," she said in a happy drawl. We embraced and I breathed in a fresh, wonderful scent. She wore bangles on one wrist and they jangled in my ear. Clare's hair was long and straightened, but Melody and Clare did, in fact, share a resemblance.

Danny got a hug, too.

"I'm always glad to meet some fellow travellers," she said, laughing.

Outside, the dry heat felt like treasure, and Danny whistled at the summertime vibe. Then the Los Angeles air hit us, smelling of diesel fuel and cigarette smoke. We dodged eight hot lanes of arrested and honking traffic to reach the parking garage.

Melody walked with great speed and purpose as we struggled to keep up. She led us to her pale Highlander SUV on a low floor. I got in the front passenger seat.

"I'm going to take you boys to your hotel. Then let's go for early suppertime so we can make plans," she said.

"We're at Motel 6 in Reseda."

"I know. I live in Simi Valley. It's on the way for me. Griff Kelsey's church is in Thousand Oaks."

"Is that where Father Sweet is?" asked Danny.

"I understand you both have a history," said Melody, cautiously. "With him."

"Sure do!" Danny said, upbeat and strange.

I turned to look at him. "I'm not so jubilant," I said.

We drove into an urban landscape carved more out of asphalt and concrete than soil.

"There's palm trees," Danny said. They lined the roads like straws a hundred feet tall, tasselled with single, Seuss-like pom-poms of fronds. Heat distortion wafted over the highway.

"Urban sprawl," I said.

"It's like that Joni Mitchell song," Melody said. "They paved paradise."

"She's Canadian," Danny said.

"Is that a fact?" Melody said. "I thought she was from California."

"No, it's true," I said. "Somehow, all Canadians know every famous or semi-famous Canadian in the world. I don't know how, but we do."

Melody chuckled. "First time you all have been in California?" It was.

"Your friend Padre is an interesting fellow. You know he's the first priest ever to reach out to SNAP to help? Usually they just try to block us, but he seems awfully keen to bring this Father Sweet of yours to justice."

"He's not mine," I said.

"Guess I'll take him, then," Danny said. I turned in my seat to look at Danny who returned my gaze, almost as a challenge.

"My husband passed away a number of years ago. It's for him I do this work," said Melody. "I'm not even Catholic."

"Neither am I," I said.

"I am," said Danny. "I'm a parish priest."

"Mm-hm. I heard that," Melody said. "This here's an interesting project, I'll say. Padre told me he hopes you boys will testify against Benjamin Sweet."

The comment startled me. "Dunno why he'd say that," I said. "I never suggested I would."

"You know other victims?"

I lowered my head. I must have appeared beaten down because I sensed she changed her tone and became so gentle it gave me chills.

"I'm sorry to be so forward, sugar. Nothing surprises me anymore, but I know for you this is all new."

I regained some composure. After a few blocks of driving, I asked, "How did you get into this?"

"I was an investigator with the County Police. Long ago. My husband was an altar boy. I volunteer to keep him close to me."

"So, SNAP. What is it?"

"A survivor's network. For people like my husband. We meet with survivors — doesn't matter how long ago it was, by the way — we run a helpline, do support groups, and sometimes we advocate with the law when we can. That's my specialty. It's been growing. Ever since Boston last year, people feel safer coming forward, but we're just scratching the surface."

"What happened to your husband?"

"His priest got onto him when he was about eight or nine."

I glanced at Danny in the backseat. He stared out the window as shops zipped by.

"I mean, how did your husband pass away?"

"Oh," she said. "He had a terrible psychological depression, you understand. We could not get enough help. Or prayers. I didn't know if there were enough in the world. See here, this is life-or-death we're dealing with. The Lord Jesus blesses our work, but sometimes I wonder if he isn't paying attention."

"Melody," said Danny, "can you stop at that liquor store up there?"

"Of course, sugar," she said calmly.

She pulled the car into a BevMo parking lot.

"Mind if I wait in the car?" she said. "Not much of a drinker, myself."

"Hey," Danny said, tapping my shoulder, "can I have some money?"

"Only because I'll drink it, too," I said. I gave him fifty dollars and he jumped out.

Melody turned on the radio.

"Sorry about your husband," I said.

"I do appreciate that. But it was nearly ten years ago. He watches over me. My angel's got my back."

"My father just passed away," I said, regretting the words as soon as they left me. I didn't want her to feel like I was angling for sympathy. I had merely been making conversation. "We weren't close," I added quickly.

"Isn't that a shame. I imagine you have some powerful feelings. Especially with your past."

"No, no. I'm fine. Really. I'm fine."

"Sure you are, sugar. Of course you are," she said, looking at me with her enormous, kind eyes. "But that doesn't mean you aren't hurt."

"No, no. I'm good."

"You don't like to be touched, do you? I could tell when I hugged you."

"Ha! Guilty."

"You want to talk, you know, I'm an awful good listener," she said quietly. Melody had a slow and benevolent voice unlike any I had heard before and I wanted to oblige her.

"Thank you," I replied. Barely.

Danny burst through the BevMo doors carrying a bag of bottles. He lifted a gallon-sized Jack Daniel's and made a show of its volume for me. He returned to the back seat.

"I love America!" he cried. "Everything's so cheap and easy!"

"You can say that again," said Melody.

17

I was footing the bill for everything so far, and though Dad had left me plenty of money, I did not feel comfortable paying for two rooms at a hundred dollars each. Therefore, my inner cheapskate won over my better instincts, and decided that Danny and I would share a room in the Motel 6. Danny was penniless and — I learned — so clueless about money as to seem like a child.

After settling our bags onto the twin beds, Melody drove us to dinner at a nearby Bob's Big Boy.

The diner was low-ceilinged and buzzing with families and servers. We all admitted to being starving. The vinyl-seated booth squeaked and farted as we scooted in on our butts. It wasn't a classy spot, but the view was nice, sort of. A pretty sunset reflected on a colourful hood over the sparkle of cars that began clogging up the road at rush hour. Danny and I ordered American cheeseburgers, which were massive. Melody chose a salad the size of a turkey platter.

"You boys familiar with Griff Kelsey's church?" she asked.

We shook our heads. I said I'd read the article in *Tinsel Circus*.

"It's a Traditionalist Catholic church. Paid for by Kelsey himself, but it's his father who's really the driving force. Do you all have conspiracy theorists in Canada?"

"Oh yah," I said.

"Then you probably know some of what they go on about. The world is an obvious place," said Melody. "God reveals himself in many ways, and it's up to us to take those cues. But people like Kelsey Senior look for a bigger, more convoluted meaning than what's really there. Why make things so complicated?"

Danny took his Coke down between his legs and poured Jack Daniel's furtively into the cup. He offered it to me, but I shook my head.

"You think you'll be here long enough to join me for a hike?" asked Melody.

"Sorry?" I said.

"Myself, I like to spend time in the hills around Simi Valley," said Melody. "That's my favourite kind of church. I go hiking. Nature's where you can feel God holding life and death together. Very simple."

Danny raised his glass to her in a toast.

She turned to me. "Canada's a beautiful place, I hear. Do you all like nature?"

"I don't think about it," I said, hoping she'd drop the subject

"Weren't you one of those bush rats in the greenbelt?" asked Danny. "You and your brother?"

I loudly sighed, and they took the hint.

"You don't feel like talking," said Melody. "Just business?"

"Sorry," I said quietly.

"Padre said you wanted to talk with the boy's parents. The boy from the *Tinsel Circus* article. Antony."

I shoved fries in my mouth and nodded. "Both parents. The mother and father."

"I've done my homework. I met Mrs. Paquime. That's Antony's mother. She is one of the ladies who cleans the church."

I stopped chewing. "What'd you tell her?" I asked.

"What a good job she was doing, and I needed a cleaning lady. That's true, by the way. I do need a cleaning lady. Not sure if she can come to Simi Valley."

"A simple ruse."

"It's the truth," she said. "And some small talk.... They attend Mass every Sunday."

"So, they'll be there tomorrow."

Melody prodded at her salad. "I'll pick up you boys early and we'll go to the first Mass at eight thirty. If the Paquimes aren't there for first Mass, we'll go to the ten o'clock, and the noon. We'll find them."

"Father Sweet there, too?" Danny asked, packing cheeseburger into his cheek.

Melody's eyes darted to mine.

To find Antony's parents, probably, I could not avoid Sweet. Is that why Danny had to come as part of the deal? So he could connect with Sweet? Dread washed over me. This cataclysmic appearance would be tomorrow. I looked at Danny, who was trying to read my face. *Tomorrow I will probably see Father Sweet*, I thought.

Suddenly, I felt the diner fade away to silence, and the air become depressurized. My balance skewed. Instinctively, I tried to shake it off like a dog. Things had become muffled and queer.

Melody put her hand on top of mine and squeezed. I raised my eyes to her and saw a halo of darkness around her face.

I fainted.

When I awoke, I was on my back on the floor of the Big Boy, with Danny and Melody crouching over me. A crowd of people hunched over them. A circle of faces.

"There he is," Melody said, smiling. "See? Just a little pass-out."

"I feel terrible," I said.

"You had too much of a big day with the travel and all."

Danny reached into my pants and took out my wallet.

"Don't worry," he said. "I'll take care of the cheque."

18

Back at the motel, Danny and I lay on our beds drinking whisky from plastic cups while the TV lit the room. The Nets were playing a home game against the Pacers and roundly defeating them.

The whisky tasted good. I was two cups in. Danny was half the bottle.

"That Melody is something, eh?" I said.

"Yah. Good lady."

"If he's there tomorrow, you know I don't want to go anywhere near him. I don't want to see him or talk to him."

"I know."

"That's your job," I said. "That's why you're here. To run interference."

Danny sighed. "Glad I'm good for something," he muttered.

I ignored his self-pity.

"You remember that old altar boy prayer," Danny said, "we did in the sacristy? The jokey one, back in the old days?"

"Which?"

Danny raised his cup and blurted out, "'Arse father, who farts in heaven. Shallow'ed be inhaled. Thy stinky bum, thy finger scum, under pricks as they are leavened.' No?"

"No."

He took a deep, raggedy breath. He looked darkly out the window and tilted the cup into his lips. "Well, we did."

I had a pit-of-the-stomach feeling. Nothing as benign as butterflies. More like a writhing, cannibalistic battle. I wanted to go home and climb into a hole. I thought of my apartment sitting dark and stale. My parents' house half-empty and cluttered by my indoor campsite. Everything halfway done, and poorly at that.

I drank to push it down, and I dug at my nails.

"You're a real strange guy, Danny," I said. "You turned out ... odd."

"Right back at you, brother."

"What are you going to do," I said, "with your life, now?"

He scoffed and shook his head. "I'm trapped. The bishop wants me to go to a retreat centre run by the Servants of the Paraclete."

"Parakeets? What's that mean?"

"It's where they put guys ... you know, *like me* for a while, before they put me back in rotation."

I grabbed the bottle of whisky from the table between us and poured some into my cup. "You should not be 'in rotation.'"

He grumbled.

"You need help."

"I just want to get away."

"Why did you do this? Go priest?"

His head swayed to show he was uneager to narrate this tale, but he spoke all the same. "After Ben ..."

I noticed Danny used Father Sweet's first name, but I didn't want to comment because I felt uncomfortable with the familiarity. I hoped he would not do it again.

"After he was gone, he wrote me letters, you know. Then as I got older he said I should go to the seminary. Nobody gave me any better ideas. I went."

"That's it? Because that old creep told you?"

"Later, I saw him. Before I was ordained. It was at a party, in the library at St Paul's. I couldn't believe it. Here he was. I was shaking like a leaf. So excited to see him. He took a long look at me and … got this disgusted look on his face," Danny said, staring to the right of the television, as if Father Sweet stood there, glaring. "He said I had grown up ugly."

I peered through the TV light at Danny, his face carved-out and fatless, with wispy facial hair clinging to his acne-scarred cheeks. His tinted glasses made it impossible to get a good look at his eyes. He sniffled.

"I went back to my room that night and I thought seriously about running away. Or jumping off the Alexandra Bridge. I was so ashamed." Danny picked at a stain on his shirt. "I don't know why I stayed."

Danny wore a Blackburn Stingers T-shirt. In everything he wore, I saw echoes of our childhood in Blackburn Hamlet. Though we weren't exactly friends, we had lived parallel lives there. Both of us now forty-ish, stretched thin trying to claw our way out of the pit, as the past pulled us mightily backward, and down.

"I haven't seen a Stingers shirt in years," I said. "You were wearing the Funfair sweatshirt the other day. I'm half expecting to see you wearing a Hornet's Nest hoodie tomorrow."

"Just crap I got from the St. Vincent de Paul bin," he said. "I haven't got many non-clerical shirts."

"What did your parents think about … you know?"

"My parents? Nothing. They never talked about it."

"Did they know? Were they angry? Did they hate you for it? Themselves for letting it happen?"

He contemplated the questions. After a while he shrugged. "Nothing," he said.

"Nothing? Nothing what?"

"You know why Ben was sent away from our parish? No?" His neck tilted back, and he talked at the spackled ceiling. "It was because of me. In the sacristy one afternoon, I kissed him on the mouth in front of Mrs. Gain. I'm sure she told on us. My parents never spoke to me about it, ever. It's all my fault."

"Is that bad?" I said, confused.

Danny's long and weathered face and Dahmer-esque glasses made him sinister to me. And yet, I could not help feeling a twinge of something new. Almost like, but not quite, empathy.

"Nobody else ever ..." His voice trailed off.

I heard the rest of his sentence in my head. *Loved me.*

"When you went into the seminary," I said, hating that word. "Surely, your parents had something to say."

"My mother went to her grave never saying a meaningful word to me. About anything, really. And my dad moved back to Îles de la Madeleine after she died. My sister invites him to Christmas, but I never join them."

The Pacers made a three-pointer and the game turned. I took a sip and wondered what his parents could have said, at the time, that would have made any difference. I started to think of Blackburn Hamlet in the late seventies. The Formica counter-tops and wood-panelled dens. I pictured Mother, feeding Jamie and me warm Weetabix with honey and milk, then leaning back, lighting up a smoke and staring through us with a zookeeper's faraway gaze. What was she thinking? I grew cold at the thought of all the secrets under the cheery surface of those dark homes.

"Would you tell me what happened? With him? You and him." I heard my voice as if it came from someone else. I could not believe I had asked. Maybe I was able to hear this, after all. Perhaps Melody had inspired me.

Danny spoke in a monotone, but his voice seemed to perk a bit.

"We would hold hands and walk in Centre Park, keeping to the trees and out of sight. One time he took me to see *Bad News Bears* and we snuck sips of beer in the dark. He liked that movie," said Danny.

"No, no, I mean ..."

"You mean the good times?" He took a breath. "No, you mean the so-called abuse."

I nodded.

"The thing you don't understand is Ben was the first person to make me feel ... I dunno ... special. He told me he loved me. I can't even remember my mother saying my name unless I was in trouble. It was different for me. You had parents who loved you."

I kept silent. There was no point telling Danny that no, he wasn't right about my parents. I couldn't tell him how I felt. I didn't know whether their sense of proprietorship over me was close enough to love to call it that. I didn't tell him because I had Jamie, which was all I needed, truly. I felt lucky to have such a great brother. I had someone, so I had no right to complain. Danny, it seemed, only had Father Sweet.

"You don't really want to know," he said. "And I don't really want to talk about it."

"Try me," I said.

He sighed and took a big gulp. He leaned over to grab the bottle and refill his cup. "Well, for one thing, he liked blowjobs and wanted me to hum anything by Handel while I sucked him off."

It was a shocking douse of cold water. The room spun on me. I felt like I might vomit. "Actually, you're right. Stop talking," I said. "Just shut up. Please."

Danny quaked. He panted through his nose for a few moments of anger.

"What about you?" he said, turning to me, growling through his choked-up throat. "You got something to say?"

"No," I said, meekly. "I don't."

"Try me," he said, in a way that poured molten hot shame on my face. "Pussy."

I sank the dregs of my whisky and poured myself another drink. "Sorry," I muttered.

Just as I was about to leave the room and get away from Danny, my phone pinged. It was Jamie on text.

hey — howzit goin there?

WEIRD, I replied.

U in hotel?

Y

how's danny?

>:-(

and u?

:-(

sounds fun … what r u doing?

working

on what

my problem

how can I help?

will let u know

man of mystery

how are you doing?

fine

how can I help?

touche

i met someone

??? Wtf?

a girl

!!!! Call now!!!

no too much going on

I don't know why I texted about Melody. I wanted to say something positive for a change. But I lost my nerve to go further. I wasn't even sure what I meant by it. It probably fell somewhere between wishful thinking and a lie. I was willing to say anything to make Jamie not worry.

Danny was snoring, sitting up in bed. I took the cup from his hand and shut off the TV.

Jamie kept pinging me on text, but I turned off the phone and plugged in the charger. I rolled over and slept in my clothes.

19

I awoke before dawn with a headache and squinted at the lamp. Danny was sitting at the table, saying Mass for himself in his underwear with a Big Boy saltine and some BevMo Discount Sherry.

I shivered with the hangover, but the sight of Danny pulled the nausea to the top of my head and I bolted out of bed and caught the toilet in time to puke.

"You okay, man?" he called from the room.

I closed the bathroom door with my foot and flushed. Danny knocked on the door. "You okay?"

"Go away!"

I turned on the taps for a shower.

Danny was a priest. A fact I knew, but had not really acknowledged. In fact, he was exactly the kind of priest I was determined to warn parents about, starting with Antony's. Catholic priests — these monk-like, celibate eccentrics whose job is to interpret cosmic morality for a community of amateurs — naturally develop mystique that protects them from scrutiny. Their lifestyles are simply too different from the family-life parishioners they serve, whom they sometimes openly compare to a flock of sheep. Sheep like the parents of the little girl Danny fondled at school.

And all that talk about forgiveness and reconciliation? It's in a format that the priest utterly controls, in a compartment — literally a compartment — of secrecy and dread.

I turned the shower to lukewarm. Why was it so important to Danny that he come? This was my project, not his. He was bound to get in the way. Did Padre send him here to spy on me while I spoke with Antony's parents? I was here with this guy, and we'd barely exchanged enough talk to establish an acquaintance.

There, that's a font, I thought, looking at the showerhead.

I felt better after my shower. I walked into the room wearing only a towel around my waist.

"Here," Danny said. He was dressed now. "I got you some Aspirin."

"Thanks," I said, taking it from him. He smiled.

"They're yours. I got them out of your bag."

"I figured."

"Here's some water."

I took the pills.

"Do you want to start the day receiving the Eucharist? I saved one for you."

"That's a cracker."

"It's a consecrated host," he insisted.

"No, I'm good, thanks."

Danny took my hand in his and said a short prayer. "Almighty God, protect us as we discharge our duties, keep us safe from evil and harm and let us return to those who love us. We ask this through Christ our Lord. Amen."

I pulled my hand back. "I want to get dressed," I said.

"I'm going to find coffee for us while you get ready," said Danny.

"Do you need money?"

"No, I still have some."

"You mean leftover from yesterday. My money."

"Right," he said, pulling the door shut behind him.

I put on a collared shirt, not wanting to seem out of place at church.

In the mirror, I saw my face as a disfigured and distorted child. I squinted, ashamed of my ugly self.

I pulled open the drapes.

Danny returned with two Styrofoam cups of coffee. "They're giving away coffee in the lobby! Free! And donuts! I got you one."

I bit into the donut and slurped the coffee. We stood in the open doorway with the California sunrise lighting our breakfast.

20

At seven forty-five, Melody's car entered the courtyard parking lot. She waved at me. I was happy to have strapped on a collared shirt, since she was outfitted charmingly in a royal blue dress. Kind of old-fashioned, I thought, like something out of the fifties. Her Sunday best.

Danny came onto the breezeway in the Stingers hockey jersey he slept in.

"My word," Melody said as she approached us. "Danny, are you wearing that awful thing? You're going to church. Go on in there and change."

She looked at me. "You look nice."

"I shaved," I said.

"I do believe you boys need a nanny."

"Not me," I said. "Not at all."

"Mmm-hm? You can look after yourself, huh?"

No. I could not. Melody could look after herself. I had proven that I was unable to look after anything. I pointed to the Sunday-morning road, waking up with local traffic.

"Driving looks easy this morning."

"How are you coming along with your talk?"

"What do you mean?"

"I mean exactly what I said. You want to talk to the Paquimes. Do you have some notes?"

I sipped the last of my coffee. Melody reached into her purse and handed me a small book called *Talking to Parents About Abuse.*

"You got time to flip through that," she said. "Might help you some."

I gasped at the title. "I don't know about this," I heard myself say.

Danny came out wearing a T-shirt announcing Miller Time. "This is the cleanest thing I've got."

I rummaged in my Adidas bag. "I will let you borrow — I said *borrow* — a golf shirt. Here."

"Thanks, man."

I jammed the booklet into my back pocket. Melody frowned a little.

We headed off to church in silence. The sun was up and heating the dead grass and roadside garbage. Seen-better-days strip malls and pawn shops whizzed by us, covered in grime. I clicked on the radio to change the dial on the mood.

"It's dirty here, but I like it," I said. "It looks lived in. And wow, this sunshine. You know back home it's getting cold now? It gets dark and no one goes on the streets if they can help it."

"My, my," she said.

"Reminds me of Pluto in the afternoon when the sun's setting. Or a war zone, the Battle of Stalingrad. Ice. Slush. Salt. No one can breathe. It can be pretty depressing."

"I imagine so," Melody said. "We're going to a more cheerful area now."

21

Griff Kelsey's Thousand Oaks church had a mouthful of a name: Basilica of Our Lady Immaculate of the Visitation, Traditionalist Roman Catholic Parish. It was designed to appear as a Spanish mission, but super-sized, American style. The structure was beige stucco, trying to simulate adobe and stone, and the tiled roof was some sort of synthetic cast material made to look like terracotta. Even the bell, I could see, was an aluminum facsimile that could neither turn on a yoke nor ring. A loudspeaker played a pre-recorded chime.

Melody wrapped a silk scarf over her head as we entered.

We were underdressed.

The entire congregation wore Sunday best. A pair of greeters at the door welcomed us. Melody was all smiles and charisma. Danny and I hung back with our heads down.

We shuffled into a pew and sat on the far aisle.

"Look," said Danny. "There's Griff Kelsey. The movie star."

Kelsey sat in the front row. I could make out a dark suit and a perfectly symmetrical bald spot. His eyes were wild and wide. It was my first encounter with a real-life celebrity. My mother would love it.

"Bingo," Melody said, and rose to her feet. She approached a family of squat people and embraced the mother, who seemed glad to see her. The lady introduced a man and a boy. Were they the Paquimes? Was that Antony? Melody pointed at me. The family nodded. Melody returned to the pew.

"After Mass, we are going to take them out for coffee," she said. "And then, you can say what you need to, sugar." She patted my leg.

"Is that Antony?" I asked. "The boy?"

"That's Matias, Antonio's brother."

I felt thirsty, and dizzy. "I'm not sure I can do this." Melody took my hand.

The procession started. We rose. I stood with my head down, squeezing Melody's hand like a baby while Danny watched. I began to quake and felt my knees buckling.

The procession moved past, and Danny whispered to me, "No Sweet."

I looked up. Father Sweet was not either of the two priests at the altar.

"Where is he?" I said.

Melody shushed us. And we went through the entire Tridentine Mass. Danny was excited as a dog, yipping out the Latin responses. As the ceremony wore on, I grew frustrated, and the nervousness of meeting with the Paquimes began to fester into nausea. The smell of the incense made me gag. When it came time for communion, which was done at the barrier *in lingua*, I snuck outside.

I sat on a concrete bench and sunk my head between my knees.

When Mass ended, a flurry of congregants bustled outside, and Melody approached me.

"You collecting your thoughts?"

"Sure," I said.

"You're up in thirty minutes. Will you be okay?"

I didn't reply.

"Do you know what you're going to say?"

I blinked. "Gonna wing it."

She put her hands on her hips and tilted her head.

"Remember what I said to you before? This is life-and-death. I'm not confident this is something you should 'wing.'" She sat down next to me. "Will you listen to suggestions?"

"No," I said.

She tsked. "For what it's worth," she said, "here's something my husband used to tell people in your situation. Will you listen to that?" When I nodded, she continued, "I think it's important to say you are a survivor yourself. You're speaking from experience. It's not their fault. People tend to feel guilty. I don't think anybody takes kindly to advice, just as you don't. But you are living proof that people can make it out, to the other side."

I lifted my head to look at her. "I am no evidence of anything. Except how to blow opportunities and live your life wrong."

"Bogus," she said, and smacked me lightly on the arm. "You don't have to do this if you don't feel up to it. I can do most of the talking. I've done this before."

I shook my head.

"I bet they won't know what you are talking about with Father Sweet. Do you want to pretend I'm the parents and you talk with me? Like a rehearsal?"

"Seems silly."

I sensed her disapproval descending over me. Deep down, I knew she was right.

"Well, well. Here you are, then," she said. "Unprepared for a conversation that might hurt some nice people real bad. No range practice, huh? For the gun? Range practice? You know what I mean?"

"I came all this way. I need to do this. And it's the right thing for Antony."

"I am with you on that. All I'm saying is you need to face this twice. Maybe more. At least face this in your head once before you face it for real. Don't walk into the lion's den without thinking about the lion."

"It's a bear," I mumbled.

"Remember, everyone is trying to do their best," she said. "Nobody means to do badly by anyone. It's mistakes and poor thinking that causes all the hurt."

It was solid advice and I told her so.

"I hope you know I support you. Let's be optimists. See what happens and let the Lord guide us." She put her arm around my shoulders. "Sugar, today is a good day, and here you are pushing for goodness instead of badness. To me that's clear evidence of angels at work."

My eyes began to throb. "I'm going to try," I said.

"Now come on," she said. "There's a bakery at Thousand Oaks and Los Elbes we need to get to before they arrive. I want to get a table."

22

Melody had arranged to meet the Paquime family at a bakery café called Knead to Rise, in a strip mall between a 7-Eleven and a dry cleaners.

Inside, ten loud people ate scones and muffins and drank tea. Melody waltzed in and commanded a corner table, directing Danny and me to pull six wrought-iron café chairs across the tiles. I bought some foam-plate pastries and put them in the middle of the blue gingham tablecloth.

The bakery counter attracted a constant lineup for take-away breads and rolls.

While we waited for the Paquimes, Danny ate a cranberry muffin.

As the minutes passed, my stomach sank at regular diving intervals. Click. Clack. Clock.

At last, the Paquimes entered, pausing at the doorway, scanning the shop nervously. Mrs. Paquime wore a yellow flower-print dress that embellished her round figure into a giant, doily-wearing coffee mug. Mr. Paquime had discarded the suit jacket he wore earlier and rolled his sweaty sleeves up to his elbows. The boy had followed his dad's lead, but gone further and taken off his necktie, too.

Melody rose and came to them, taking big friendly strides with her long legs across the tiles. Mrs. Paquime broke into a relaxed smile at the sight of her.

We shook hands as Melody introduced us.

"This our son, Matias," said Mr. Paquime with heavy Latino consonants.

"Antony's brother?" Danny asked.

"Yes. Antonio younger brother."

The boy looked about ten. "Hi, nice to meet you," he said in a breezy, confident American accent. He looked us in the eyes with the maturity of a young person accustomed to acting on behalf of his parents, I assumed, as a translator.

Danny offered to get them tea or a scone, but they waved him away and asked for water. He fetched three glasses.

My hands felt slippery. I looked down at my shaking fingers and saw I took it too far and lacerated the quick of my left thumbnail. Without fuss, I calmly pulled a napkin from the dispenser and wrapped my thumb into a wad.

"So glad you could join us, Mr. and Mrs. Paquime," said Melody. "There's a matter we really felt obliged to speak with you about. But also Mrs. Paquime, I meant what I said about needing some housework done during the week and I don't want to forget about that! My house is in Simi Valley, are you able to get there?"

"Yes! I can take bus or Mateo can drive when he not working."

"That's just perfect! How much do you charge?"

She appeared frightened by the question. "How much you pay?"

"Is twenty dollars an hour too little?"

Mrs. Paquime smiled. The price was good.

"Mr. Paquime, where do you work?"

"I am cook. Restaurant is in Thousand Oak."

The small talk sounded a million miles away to me. My throat was dry, I swallowed dust, and concentrated on breathing. Steady in. Steady out. I squeezed my thumb to staunch the blood. My leg bounced up and down alongside Danny's.

"You okay, man?" asked Danny. "Easy."

Mr. Paquime's mouth was agape and I saw the dawning recognition on his face. I must have tipped him off. Something was up. He tugged at Mrs. Paquime's elbow and she read his expression. They spoke rapidly at each other in Spanish.

"Wait," Melody said. "Wait. It's true, yes, there's something else we want to talk with you about."

"Immigration?" Mr. Paquime said.

"Huh?" said Danny.

"Immigration?"

"No," said Melody. "We aren't immigration. Relax, it's okay. They think we're from immigration enforcement. We're not."

"We're from Canada," said Danny. "Me and him. Canada."

"Canada?" asked Mr. Paquime.

"Si," said Danny. "Canada."

I coughed and it made me speak in a loud, unexpected voice. "Why'd you do it?" I heard myself ask. My face felt hot.

Melody and Danny swung their heads my way.

"How could you? Give your son to that man? Why?"

"Eh? No *entiendo*," Mr. Paquime said.

"Why did you do it?" I barked. Tears fell out of my eyes and surprised me. "How could you? I mean, what was it?"

Melody interrupted. "My friend here is worried about Antonio, and we'd like to talk with you about Father Sweet." She looked panicked.

At once, as she spoke his name, I felt myself go calm in the way extreme danger can make you perceive the world running in slow motion. I leaned back to the wall. The traffic outside seemed like a funeral procession. Hard glaring surfaces everywhere. Everything in sight made of asphalt. Not a plant anywhere. I felt my arms go heavy, as though I was buried up to my neck in concrete. I had blown it. But, possibly, I could try again.

"Mr. and Mrs. Paquime," said Danny, "we are worried Father Sweet may treat Antony in a way he doesn't like."

"Father Sweet is good man. He *love* Antonio."

"It's so difficult to hear," said Melody, "but these two men were abused by Father Sweet when they were boys."

"No," said Mrs. Paquime. "Father Sweet is man of God."

I took a long, serene breath. "*You* are good people," I said. "I know you are good. We all can see it. And you are dedicated to the Church because you believe it is good, and you trust your priest because you trust in God. You want the best for your children. I know that because my parents were like you. They wanted the best for me and for my brother. But the man who your son is with, I know does not have the best interests of your son at heart. I know this because I was once like your son."

Mrs. Paquime leaned toward me. "You know Father Sweet?"

"Mrs. Paquime, it is not your fault," I said. "But please listen. Your son needs help. He needs to be away from that man and back with his family. Back with the people who love him for who he is. Back with you."

"What you mean?"

"Father Sweet does not love Antonio the way you do," said Melody. "He loves him in a sexual way. A bad way."

"No!" said Mrs. Paquime, hitting the table. Her eyes darted like a cornered fox between the three of us.

Mr. Paquime handed Matias five dollars and said something in Spanish.

"Just for a short spell, sugar," said Melody. "Let us talk with your mum and dad."

The young boy glanced at us suspiciously before going to the counter to buy a jelly donut, which he took to a table across the room, out of earshot.

Melody and Danny nodded their encouragement. Mr. Paquime did not share his wife's panic; he leaned back and folded his brawny forearms over his chest.

"If I could go back in time and talk with my parents," I said. "I would tell them what I am telling you now. Talk with Antonio. I promise you he does not understand what is happening. Tell him it's not his fault. Tell him that you will get him help, and that he can get through this. Tell him you believe him. Tell him you trust him and that he is more important than church, or priests, or all of this."

A flame lit in Mrs. Paquime's eyes. "You think you more important than God?"

"He didn't say that," said Melody.

"You not more important than God."

"It has nothing to do with God," I said, secretly shocked I was still in control of myself and sharp of mind. "That's just an excuse he is using so he can — keep your son."

"Antonio is good boy," Mr. Paquime said. "He would not do what you say."

"It's not Antony," said Danny. "It's Father Sweet who is doing this."

"No, no. Antonio wanted go with Father Sweet," Mrs. Paquime said. "Father Sweet is a good man."

I felt sunk. "Having trust and being faithful people is good," I said. "I believe you are good, decent people. This man took advantage of your decency."

Mr. Paquime said. "I don't understand. What you mean?"

Danny interjected. "Wait a minute, did you say 'go with Father Sweet'?"

"Father Sweet is a good man," said Mrs. Paquime. "Mr. Kelsey, he love him."

Melody spoke in a low, sing-song voice that was very soothing. Mrs. Paquime clutched at her words, desperate to understand.

"Mr. Kelsey may not know what we know," said Melody. "It is not your fault. It is not Antonio's fault. But the important thing now is that Antonio is brought home to you, and that Father Sweet gets help."

"Antonio will not be able to talk with you about what happened, and that's okay," I said. "You will need to let him get over this. It will take time, but now he needs to get out of there."

"Hang on," said Danny. "Where are they? Where did they go?"

Mrs. Paquime wagged her finger in anger at me. "You not know anything what happen. This is your head. You read article and you make imagination."

"No, Mrs. Paquime. You must hear it. I know," I said. "Because Danny and I know. We know. We lived it. And, we have come out the other side. But it is very difficult. We want to help so that Antonio does not have to find it as hard as … we did."

"Father Sweet touch you?" asked Mr. Paquime quietly.

"Mrs. Paquime," said Danny. "You have to trust us."

"You, too?"

"Yes, me, too." Danny smiled and nodded cheerily. His face made me shiver.

Mrs. Paquime surveyed our eyes and reflected. "There is what you say, and what I say," she said slowly and pointed to the ceiling. "And what God sees."

Everyone slumped back in their chairs. The life of the bakery carried on around us, people laughing, chatting, and clattering plates and cups. The cash register dinged.

"You go to police?" asked Mr. Paquime, after a pause.

"Right now, the important thing is we get Antonio safe."

"We cannot talk to police," said Mrs. Paquime.

"I understand," I said. "This is moving very fast. I can imagine how confusing this is. We don't need to talk about that now."

"No, no. We no talk to police," Mr. Paquime said, unfolding his arms and appealing to Melody. His eyes pleaded. "We cannot talk to police."

We were silent while Melody examined their faces. She tilted her head slightly. "You're undocumented," she said quietly. "Aren't you? And that's why."

"What does that mean?" I said.

"Are you undocumented?" Melody asked.

"Matias born here," said Mrs. Paquime.

"How long have you been in California?"

"Ten years. Almost."

"We not go back," said Mr. Paquime. "We come here for good education. Opportunity. Matias and Antonio, they don't know Mexico. Mexico is dangerous."

"I don't understand what's going on," I said.

Melody patted Mrs. Paquime's hand. "They could be sent back to Mexico. That's why they don't want to talk with police."

Danny shovelled scone into his mouth with wide eyes, looking like he was watching an exciting movie.

"Even to get their son back?" I asked.

"Where has Father Sweet taken Antony?" said Danny, his mouth full. Everyone stopped talking and looked at him. "Well, I've been asking and no one has answered!"

Mrs. Paquime sobbed into her hands.

Melody leaned toward her. "Is it true? Did he take Antonio? Where are they?"

"He is safe," she said, weeping. "God looks after him."

"See, I told you," Danny said. "He's flown the coop."

"We don't know," croaked Mr. Paquime, at last. "We don't know where they go. They leave last week. He say Antonio education his responsibility."

"Oh my god," I said. I pictured myself as a boy sitting next to Father Sweet in his Beetle, passing a bottle of Coke between us. I came to his shoulder then, and I had to look up at the dark-bearded man driving the jalopy. Father Sweet was intoxicated with glee as he drove us far away into Quebec and away from Blackburn Hamlet. Who knows where he was taking Antony.

"Has Antonio got a phone with him?" I asked.

Mr. Paquime shook his head. His face twitched, as the burden settled over him. He sighed and sank lower in his chair.

"I might know," said Danny, raising a finger. "Where they're going."

Suddenly, Mrs. Paquime shot to her feet, sending her chair squeaking across the tiles. "I not listen to this," she said. "You are not good people. You are liars."

She spoke loudly and heads turned her way. Matias looked shocked by his mother's outburst. She stepped across the room and fetched Matias, seizing his hand and tugging him to his feet and out the door.

Mr. Paquime exhaled, but he did not rise.

"What do you think, Mr. Paquime?" asked Melody.

"I need to think," he said, looking at me. "I think about this."

Melody pulled a business card out of her purse and gave it to him, indicating that her mobile number was available to him at any hour.

He stood, and I saw for the first time the considerable size of the crucifix he wore around his neck.

23

Melody drove us back to the motel, I took my seat in the front and Danny perched his head near my shoulder like a parrot.

"Let's call Padre," I said.

"What for?" asked Danny, screwing up his face into an ugly knot of disapproval.

"I dunno. Report? Get advice?"

"Pff. I've got a better idea."

"I want to hear it, sugar," said Melody.

"I know where they are," said Danny. "Or where they're going at least. It's Tijuana. They're heading to Gast's place."

"How do you know that?"

"Because, I told you before, I got the invite, too. You want Sweet, that's where you'll find him."

"I have no interest in him. I just want to make sure Antonio gets away from him."

"Well, whatever. That's where you'll find him."

"What's in Tijuana?" asked Melody. She shook her head. "That is one sorry town if you ask me."

"Monsignor Gast has a compound there. Most of his followers are rebels and exiles. Priests who think the Church has lost its way."

"Lost its way? Where should it be?" I asked.

"It's become too liberal. Too progressive."

"I don't know what the point is if Antonio's parents aren't involved," I said. "What are we going to do? Kidnap the kid, give him back to his parents and then go to jail while they give him right back to Sweet?"

"Would you boys testify?"

"Me? Fuck that. No way," I said.

"Danny?"

He said nothing.

"Do you know other survivors?" Melody asked.

I looked at my thumb, still wrapped in napkin. "I blew it. We'll head back home tomorrow."

"It's early to give up yet," said Melody.

"What's the point?" I said. "Besides, my brother's having surgery. I need to get back. I screwed this up."

"I don't think you did," said Melody.

We arrived at the motel. Melody slid the car into an open spot under our second-floor room, near the stairs to the breezeway.

"Thanks for everything, Melody," I said, avoiding her eyes. "You're a good person. Sorry you put in all that effort for nothing."

"It wasn't for nothing. I'm not done."

"I am," I said. "They win."

"Are you sure feeling sorry for yourself is going to help you accomplish something?"

I shot her a look. "I'm not."

"Suit yourself," she said.

I opened the car door and walked up the stairs to our room.

The bed had been made and looked inviting. I poured myself a cup of whisky, lay down, and clicked through the channels looking for hockey.

Eventually, Danny entered.

"She's gone," he said.

"We'll leave tomorrow," I said. "I'll get our flights sorted in a bit. I need to rest."

Danny poured himself the last of the whisky. "That's it for the booze," he said. "I don't want to touch the wine."

"Let's leave tonight then."

"For Tijuana?"

"No, you idiot. For home," I shouted. "Fuck Tijuana. I'm not going to fucking Mexico. This is over. I blew it, I didn't convince them of anything, fuck. They don't get it. Nobody gets it."

Danny lay back on the bed and we watched high-school lacrosse on a public access station, sipping our warm whisky.

"How do you know?" he asked. "I mean, what to do?"

I groaned. "What are you talking about?"

"You seem sure it's time to give up. How do you know?"

I propped myself up on an elbow to confront him. "I don't get it. What do you want? Why are you in this?"

"Trying to be a good Catholic."

The words took a while to surface, and when they came I spoke in a hard voice. "Bullshit. All of it. Just a machine for exploiting and manipulating people, exalting habits into pointless rituals and protecting lying shitbags. And now, you're one of the lying shitbags who needs protection."

"There are a lot of reasons why someone might find a spiritual life worth living. What are you trying to do with Antony? You're making amends with your life, and it will benefit someone else. That's spiritual. It's good. It's God."

"Ugh. Enough." I turned back to the television.

"Whatever you call it. It's reconciliation, it's love."

"Shut up. Just be quiet. Fuck. You got a lot of problems, Danny. You're fucked up. And I bet it doesn't start and end with what you did to that little girl."

He froze. "I believe in justice," said Danny slowly. "That includes me … I will get what's coming to me. Catholics also believe in forgiveness. You asked what's in it for me, I'm part of the problem. I know that. I know about Father Sweet. I inherited it. But I'm not blaming him. If you're going to call yourself a Catholic, you take the good and the bad."

"I don't call myself anything," I replied. "You and your Padre taking the good and the bad. Why? Hasn't it proved to you now to be rotten to the core?"

"I'm not hiding. I'm not shirking anything. Like I said, there are a lot of reasons why people come to church."

"You are cowering in the rectory. Hiding."

He shrugged.

"I hear your bishop doesn't like female altar servers," I said.

"He's against the feminization of the Church. Moral relevancy and all that. He thinks we're all going to be homosexuals in skirts soon."

"Look in the mirror."

Danny drank the last of his cup and hopped off the bed.

"I'm going to get some more booze. Can I have some money?"

I handed him fifty dollars.

"Thanks, brother."

"Don't call me that."

"Whatever you say, brother."

24

We drank another bottle of whisky and fell asleep with the television on. Knocked out from all the booze, we both slept through the morning and rose at eleven thirty. My head throbbed, and the uneven ground torqued under me.

I fetched Aspirin from my bag. Danny moaned and cried out for water. As soon as I could get vertical, I had a shower and got dressed. Danny said Mass with his head held low.

I took a walk around the block with a stale lobby coffee. I kept my eyes down against the sunlight. The noise from traffic did nothing for my headache. Car after car buzzed past. Hangovers were a familiar state for me and — typically— I became anti-social to the point of hatred. Where are these cars going? What on earth could be so important for all these people to be out rushing around? What's the point?

When I returned, Danny was back in bed, lying with his back to the door.

My phone rang. It was Jamie. I took the call on the breeze-way, leaning on the railing overlooking the parking lot.

"Hey," I said, impersonating enthusiasm. "How are you feeling?"

"Good! Psyched. Ready. Just finished up a bunch of things at the office, wrote some letters in case … you know. One week to go. How is your project going?"

"Badly. It's over. I blew it."

Jamie spent a few moments before venturing the big question. "Can you tell me now what you were doing?"

"Maybe over a beer sometime."

"That might be as good as saying never, you know."

"Then, not on the phone," I said. "Not now. But I'll be home soon."

"Can you tell me about the woman you met?"

Another call was coming in. It was Melody.

"Perfect timing, it's her on the other line," I said. "But it's not what you think. I screwed that up, too. I'll be home like today or tomorrow and will tell you. Gotta go."

I switched the lines and took Melody's call. She whooped happily when I picked up.

"Are you still in town?" she asked. "Because I had a very interesting discussion with someone this morning."

The housekeeping cart was outside the room next to mine and the maid, who looked strikingly like Mrs. Paquime herself, waved at me.

"Who?" I asked Melody.

"Mateo Paquime. That's the dad. He told me what you said meant a lot. He said it was like talking to Antonio as an adult, asking for help. He understands what's happening and he said he'll testify even if it means all of them are deported back to Mexico and lose everything."

"Wow," I said. I walked closer to the housekeeping cart and saw the maid had placed there a photograph of two little girls in Catholic-school garb, holding hands before a hedgerow. Daughters? Granddaughters?

"Do you understand? You got to him," Melody said. "You did it."

A weary grin came upon my face and I stretched my back and one arm. "Can we go to the police and be done with it?"

"We could. But if we push a bit more we can get Antonio out. Any way to find out where Sweet is, exactly?" Melody asked. "Without tipping him off?"

This was pushing me further than I wanted.

"I'll ask Danny," I said, after a long pause. "But I think he'll just say Tijuana."

"Ask me what?" Danny said over my shoulder. He had snuck up behind me and stood on the breezeway in his underwear.

"If there's a way to find out exactly where Antonio is," I said to Danny. "And you-know-who. Are they still in America? Can you call Tijuana and find out?"

Danny's shoulders slumped and he shuffled back to the room.

"There's a good chance the Paquimes will be deported to Mexico," said Melody.

"You aren't friends with the police? Why would they rat them out?"

"They're cracking down on illegals, sugar. But Antonio will be safe and with his family wherever they wind up."

"I'll find out where they are," I said, walking back to the room. "Then you take it from there."

I got off the call and approached Danny, watching TV from bed.

"Here," I said, offering my phone. "Call and find out where they are, so I can go back home."

Danny sighed. "Not that simple, bud," he said, scratching his nose and adjusting his tinted glasses. "I can't just call up and say, 'Hey, is Sweet there with his boy toy?'"

"Why not?"

"Think about it," he said. When I didn't respond, he carried on. "He'd run. And besides, if he's there in Mexico, my guess is Gast will have more friends in the police than Melody will."

"This is just a bunch of bumbling priests who don't know we're looking for Sweet. Just tell them you want to find him for … yourself."

"Wish I could, bud."

I gritted my teeth. "So, if he's down there already we can't do anything?"

"I'm sure he's not there … yet."

"How on earth do you know?"

"I've got an idea, but you've got to trust me. If we're friends, you owe me that much." Danny looked for the television remote.

"I would not call us friends. I don't trust you. I don't know what to call you, frankly," I said. "I think you're a creep."

Danny shrunk at the comment.

"If you say so," he said, wheezing. "But I'm not." He avoided my eyes and found the TV remote.

"There's more to this than you're telling me." Even before I finished my sentence Danny had sat up and turned his back on me. "You hear me?" I pressed. "I know that."

Danny switched off the television. "What do you think you know?" he cried.

"I know what you're about."

He took a while to respond.

"No, you don't. You don't know what pastoral work is," he said finally, quietly facing the wall. "Helping someone find an experience through prayer — like an otherworldly, Godly experience — that gives them hope. I live for that. You know there's a bereavement group at the church, we laugh, we hug." He twisted himself sideways. "Sometimes, I get a chance to do a homily that helps someone work their way out of a moral crisis. I can see it.

You don't know how good it feels to see someone nod or smile at something I said, to help them to be inspired. Being a pastor is the love of my life. I help people live life. I love it."

"That's not what I mean. When you called the bishop after you molested that girl," I said, and he cringed at my words, "it wasn't because it was the first time. There were others. I know it. You're as bad as he is. And you know it. I know it."

Danny's face was blank.

"There was never another time," he said slowly. "That I would serve my own pleasure … the way Ben did with me — with us. That's why I called the bishop. That is why Pete came to remove me. Father Sweet made me into this. He told me he became a priest because he had too much love to give. I didn't know what he was saying. My vocation came from my injury. I am here to help. I want to be a vessel of peace and healing. I know you don't believe me. Or maybe you don't understand. But I swear that's the truth."

"Who cares if you only acted on it once?" I said. "It's in there."

"When it happened with little Emily — that was her name, by the way — I was terrified. I left the school. I cried at the rectory. I was sick." Danny removed his spectacles and I saw his sunken and dark eyes swelling. He struggled to continue. "I have been celibate, and true since my ordination. I think of myself as bedevilled."

"Bedevilled. Like it's not you, it's your devil."

"No. It was me."

"Then why did you do it?"

He opened his mouth and eyes as if to scream and shook his head in desperation. "I don't know," he whispered. "But it scared me."

Having let his words hang in the room, I waited while he cried.

"Danny, I'm not letting you off the hook. I can't. But if what you say is true, then help me now. Make the call."

He looked at my outstretched hand for a second, then shook his head.

"Fine. No trust," Danny said, wiping his eyes with a thumb. "But if you believe I'm here to help, allow it my way. You'll get what you want, I promise."

"What will it cost me?"

"Only a drive to Tijuana."

25

I rented a Ford Focus from Avis and we left the next morning at dawn.

I set a twenty-dollar bill on the nightstand and headed to the car. The maid approached on the breezeway.

"*Gracias por todos*," I said to her, pointing at the room. "I left you a little something in there."

She smiled. "Ah! Thank you."

For a moment I felt the warm peace of a small kindness.

Finally, Danny appeared. We drove onto the freeway in silence. Ten minutes later he said something. "I saw you spoke to the cleaning lady. You told her about the toilet?"

"What do you mean? What about the toilet?"

"Clogged. I left a huge turd in there. Couldn't get it down."

I sighed. Danny handed me twenty dollars.

"Here," he said. "I appreciate that you've been paying for everything."

"Where did you get this?"

"You forgot it on the nightstand."

I grit my teeth while my shame argued with our travel momentum. We did not turn around.

It took four hours to reach the border at San Ysidro. Long enough for the radio stations to change. The heat enchanted the highway into a blurry mirage as we made our way south. Los Angeles's extended concrete suburbs gave way to dirt and scrubby roadside bushes festooned with Cheetos and potato chip wrappers like ribbons.

The border itself came upon us as a multi-lane parking lot worthy of a Boxing Day sale. The American side wasn't too bad, but the Mexican side was an ocean of cars. It wasn't true, of course — it must have been a mirage of the heat creating a hallucination — but I was certain cars were piled on top of each other, scrambling to get across the border like beetles crawling over fresh dung.

Danny and I parked to visit the border facility washrooms. Inside, I saw desperate men strip down and bathe themselves using paper towels. Beside the car lanes there was an officious and inefficient pedestrian crossing, where exhausted children seemed to outnumber exasperated parents in a sweaty parade entering the United States on foot. It was noisy, and the heat and honking from cars was annoying, but I noted that I heard no child cry. It was as if this was normal, and no one found it chaotic and heartbreaking.

The lineup of men, women, and children marching into the U.S. on foot was a few hundred metres long. Some had small encampments within the lineup, with umbrellas and picnics set up. As if to encourage symbolic interpretation, a ziggurat-like ramp system forced the migrants to exert their leg muscles to enter the U.S. It looked like a little tower of Babel.

"These are the legal immigrants, I guess," Danny said. "Better life. For their kids."

"Looks like the apocalypse," I said, climbing back into the driver's seat. "Where are all these people going?"

"Wish they had a shop or something," Danny said. "I would sell my soul for a cold Coke right now."

"There's a Coke machine right there," I said. He looked at me, and I handed him a five-dollar bill.

A customs guard wandering through the parking lot nodded at me from behind his mirror sunglasses. His jawline showed he thought we looked suspicious. Probably figured we were druggies of some kind. That's what I would have thought.

"Where you boys from?"

"Canada," I said.

"Canada?" he cried, suddenly jovial and amused. "Canada! What on earth are you doing here?"

"Well, we —" I only just started to respond, when he interrupted me, laughing.

"Now, you two be careful. Tijuana ain't Mon-tree-all! These people will rob you blind and make *tortas ahogadas* of you!"

"Okay."

Danny got his Coke and we entered Mexico. There was no real inspection at the border. They saw our Canadian passports and simply waved us through.

We drove past the multi-lane car queue which, by my calculation, stretched for the length of Ottawa, from the beginning of Nepean to the edge of Gloucester.

Tijuana looked like a suburb of Los Angeles. Low-rise and concrete, but overgrown with plants that could survive the heat. There were as many auto-body shops as houses. The people looked identical to most of the Angelenos we'd left behind. The border struck me as incredibly arbitrary.

"Why would anyone fight with their life to leave here, only to wind up in the American version of this same place?"

"California used to be part of Mexico," said Danny. "And the Natives and Mayans, or whoever was here before that. Everyone's moving around like they always did. Only there's a fence now."

Our destination was through Tijuana, and with traffic it took us nearly forty-five minutes. It was three o'clock, and it dawned on me that returning would involve a longer wait at the border. I was exhausted, but dreaded the thought of staying here to sleep.

Danny pulled out a worn-out piece of photocopied paper he consulted while I drove.

"Jesus," I said, pointing at a swollen pink motel with fluorescent green trim, festooned with hearts and wedding bands. "Look at that forsaken place."

"Turn here," said Danny, pointing at the street by the motel. We drove three blocks of dry, fenced-in bungalows and car repair shops before Danny asked me to pull over.

It felt unsafe, this neighbourhood. Every window was barred, and whatever yards there may have been were hidden behind breeze-block walls or enmeshed with military-grade wire. At the corner was a razor-wire fence enclosing three lots. It was the most significant structure of the neighbourhood: two houses and a giant, windowless cube. Everything was painted beige. A cross made of two iron beams towered over the highest roof and a half-dozen flags flapped from the buildings.

Half the flags were the Vatican yellow and white, and the other half were pink, emblazoned with the words *ÉL TE AMA*. *He loves you*.

"That's it," said Danny, opening the car door. "You coming?"

He darted out like a puppy racing to the off-leash. There were no pedestrians on the street, and I left the Focus tight against the curb. The air had a sultry, leaded quality to it. I locked the car and followed Danny to the steel gate.

Danny buzzed the intercom. "Tell the monsignor that Reverend Daniel Lemieux is here to see him," he said. He needed to repeat his name two more times before the gate clicked open for us.

We were greeted at the door by a tall, cassocked man with short black hair. He blessed Danny, who introduced me in turn, and we were whisked into a small vestibule with a half-pew.

"This feels familiar, somehow," I said.

It was underlit and the walls were covered in a red velvet wallpaper. It was the same taste in decor from Father Sweet's rectory. The dim lighting, the collection of framed Victorian etchings, classical replicas and pottery, the suffocating miasma of incense.

"Leave the talking to me," he whispered. "Don't mention Sweet straightaway."

"I'm going to be sick."

A boy entered, no more than ten. He wore a white-and-green cassock, like a choirboy. His hair was clipped Marine-short. "Gentlemen, please follow me," he said.

The boy led us down a dark hallway into the outdoors, across a small patio. A burbling Home Depot fountain stood in the patio's centre. Against one wall, an old bathtub was turned up on its end, creating a makeshift grotto to cover a figure of the Virgin Mary. The geraniums planted there clung desperately to life, withering in the sun.

We entered the second, dark house, which was not air-conditioned and had a fishy smell under the frankincense. The boy led us to a long, dark room, the end of which featured a rococo wooden desk. The boy stopped us before we entered.

"The Reverend Monsignor Aloysius Gast," the boy said.

In the darkness, I could make out a figure behind the desk.

"Come," said Gast, waving his arm at us. "Come to me."

26

Another boy, outfitted in the white-and-green cassock, entered the room with a silver tray and three glasses of lemonade.

"Thank you, *pusio*," said Gast, taking a lemonade

In the shadows. I was unable to make him out except to see he was scrawny. Danny and I lounged in creaky leather chairs opposite his desk. This was his office. One wall was lined with books, the other with bright, vivid art.

The old man's voice was reedy as a stick of rawhide. "Canada," he said. "Bah. Backwater. A lost cause. At one time I thought Canada had a future. Government support of Catholic schools, the bishops in command of Quebec, and so on. I imagined America's inevitable conversion. Latin America below and Canada above, the pressure would be too great. Imagine: a Catholic Hemisphere. Oh! Then, poof! Roncalli's ridiculous revolution, we lost Quebec, and it was over."

"Some of us have faith, Monsignor," said Danny.

"That's quite an art collection," I said, gesturing at the large canvases filling every space, ceiling to floor. It was a display of mostly naked saints and swooning Christs, bleeding and suffering.

"Here, in Latin America, there is an appreciation for the mortification of the body. This is lost in the North. The Latino understands flesh. They understand poverty and pain. It is in this appreciation for the passion of Christ Jesus, the suffering, that the commons are connected to God." Gast rose, stooped and crooked, and clutched a cane. He crept over to a large oil, a pubescent, erotic-looking Saint Sebastian. He paused before moving on to a forsaken Christ crucified, the eyes rolled orgasmically upward, sweat and blood coursing over the lurid body. "In a hot clime, there is thirst, you see? There is poverty, fervor, lust, and pain. All those things that bring Jesus close to the skin. Yes? The body. The Latino knows suffering. Bodily suffering. *That* is the Mediterranean Christ. Look. We have lost this in our so-called 'First World.'" His fingers, brittle as dried bone, traced the form of Jesus's nude hip. "'The fruit of such spirit is Joy.' That is from Galatians."

"Beautiful," said Danny.

"What is this place?" I asked.

"An adulteress was to be stoned," said Gast. "And the Lord scratched in the dirt, a message. Perhaps the most mysterious moment in the gospel. What did he write in the dirt? Hm?"

He was asking me. I said, "I don't know."

"Everything that is not recorded," he said, raising his finger. Light passed through the long tip of his fingernail. "All the grants to our noble tradition. Everything that is secretly passed through apostolic revelation."

"Bishop Jean-Marc wants me to go to the Servants of the Paraclete," said Danny.

Gast's face curdled at the sound of an enemy. "The Paraclete. Bah. Such a fraternity would be unnecessary but for that abominable Second Vatican Council, which emboldened the flock against their priests. Every common parishioner believes he can judge the servants of God on his own. Unthinkable to previous generations…. What do they know about our ways?"

The boy re-entered the office, bringing a plate of cookies and cashews.

"Ah," said Gast. "Biscochitos. Michael, bring those outside. We'll go sit in the sun."

Michael bowed and gave Gast his arm for support. "The faithful thinks the Church is what they see on Earth," Gast said. "Hope. Faith. Charity. Manifestations of 'kindness' and so on. They do not know what our sacred charge is. And that is what Roncalli got wrong. The faithful thought *they* had been given the keys. They had not. They do not understand what mysticism we manage."

In the sunlight of the patio I got my first real look at the man.

Gast was just under five feet tall and wore a black cassock with red trim and purple sash. On his head he placed a wide-brimmed parson's hat against the sunshine. It gave him the appearance of a nineteenth-century missionary. His skin was a sun-cured leopard pelt of moles, liver spots, and de-pigmented blotches. His eyes glinted, rheumy and yellow behind his greasy spectacles. Sideburns and ear-hair combined loosely to create a small fringe under his hat. His glasses sat on his face crookedly, propped up by an enormous cluster of verrucae on his cheek, like a fleshy cauliflower floret. As someone who had willed himself to live more than one hundred years through spite and spellcraft, it was no wonder he looked the way he did.

"Thank you," he said to Michael. "Soon he will become *exoletum* and will cease to be my Ganymede. He will join the seminary. I shall miss him."

Michael led Gast to a small, rusty loveseat. Danny and I pulled up café chairs not unlike the ones my mother left in her backyard. Gast and Michael sat holding hands, and the boy placed his head on Gast's shoulder.

I felt complicit for witnessing such a display.

"Before Roncalli, there was a place for us in communities," he said, touching his breast. "We were accepted and welcomed into homes. They listened to us. Obeyed us. We smoothed the rough edges of society. Appeal to the law and the educators, and they would give us their sons. Now, we are outsiders."

Gast selected a cashew from the little bowl. "Do you enjoy cashews? They resemble homunculi. Nascent potential. An embryo," he said, fondling one with his fingertips and contemplating its "face." "May they remind us to protect the life of the unborn so that they may reach the salvation of the Lord." He puckered his lips to receive it on the tip of his tongue.

I was making a face, because Danny prodded me with his shoulder. "Have you heard news about Father Sweet?" Danny asked.

"Ah, the mercurial Benjamin Sweet and his boustrophedon life," Gast said, shaking his head. "Which side is he on now? We shall see. We shall see."

"What does that mean?" I said.

"Do you know him?"

I fought the urge to say anything revealing, thinking only of Antonio, and instead nodded at Gast. He seemed cheered by this.

"Then you know his story, I imagine?"

I wondered what, specifically, he meant and concluded it didn't matter. "I believe so," I said.

"Haven't you wondered how such a young man, barely out of the seminary, could become a delegate to Vatican II on such an important committee?"

"All part of the legend, I figured. His legend."

"Bah. My extensive connections secured a place for Sweet. I and my brethren had delegates throughout the conference. They were sent to fight perversions — to keep celibacy intact, to prevent female acolytes, to maintain the monastic cloisters. Our guard to fight against liberalization."

"Of course," I said. "The important things, right?"

Gast turned to me. He eyed me like one unaccustomed to insolence. "The habits of our doctrine have not survived thousands of years from the lips of Jesus because of reform. Roncalli and Montini were perverts who destroyed that which was built on the rock of ages."

"You're the good guys in this story. I understand." Roncalli and Montini were the pre-papal names of Popes John XXIII and Paul VI.

"Sweet was young. Foolish. Dazzled by the opulence of Rome. He came to believe Roncalli's nonsense about modernizing the Church. The growth in the faithful that was meant to come, if only it became a 'hippie' church. Bah. He betrayed us. Betrayed his mission. He lost the thread out of the labyrinth, but now he sees the error in his ways. He sees the Church is weaker, and controlled by perverts."

"But why are *they* perverts?" I asked.

"They turned their back on the sublime culture established by the Christ God himself to breed vocations. From boys to men. It has been thus since Paul Tarsus bent to circumcise Timothy." Gast stroked Michael's hair with his hand. The boy closed his eyes. "Instead, they focus on silliness. Marriage. Women. Bah. Feminization destroys everything God sent his only Son to implant."

"Right. *That's* perverted," I said, rubbing my temples. Danny gave me a warning look. "What is with this system of processing kids? Get 'em young? What's the point of making kids think of sin?"

My question took Gast aback.

"What are you?"

"I'm a visitor. What do you mean?"

Danny shifted in his seat and tried to speak, but Gast cut him off.

"I mean, where are you from?"

"Ottawa."

"Yes, yes. But, I mean, your people. Where are your people from?"

"My mother's family is from Cornwall. I think my dad was born in Ottawa."

Gast appeared irritated and waved his hand. "I can't quite see it. Some French arrogance? Perhaps Welsh? Around the jowls. No, German. That would explain your stern expression."

I looked at Danny, who appeared dumbfounded. "What does it matter?" I asked.

"Bah. You sound like my old nemesis, Charles de Koninck," he sighed and shook his head. After a pause, Gast resumed his diatribe. "The system worked for thousands of years, until it reached the filthy clutches of Roncalli and Montini. They never understood pure love. Only lust. Lust pollutes. Jesus's sublime love for his disciples purifies them."

The words — like wooing I heard thirty years ago — resurrected Father Sweet's voice to me, and I relived the arcane logic of my old parish priest's romantic ideas. I watched Michael's perfectly combed hair succumb to Gast's grooming claw.

"Transubstantiation is the same as having a pure heart," said Gast. "The mystery of the Eucharist, which is the heart of our faith. Pure intention makes pure any action. It is functional and it works, just as transubstantiation works. The death and suffering of the Christ were made good by His pure intention to free us of sin. Thus, bread becomes body. But only if the objective is pure and its intent pure."

Gast noticed my observation of his petting. "I believe the children are an invaluable commodity for our future," he said.

"How poetic," I said. "Didn't you write lyrics for Whitney Houston?"

Danny leaned over to me and whispered. "Careful. Remember, he who saves one life saves the world. Think of Antony."

For a moment, Gast appeared confused, but carried on. "The faithful here are quite good," he said. "The families are pious. Obedient to the authority of the Christ God. It's in the breeding. When the Spaniards converted them, it was not like those savages of the Fair Dominion I had to deal with. Oh no. Bare-skinned natives here already lived under imperial rule. Their priests, though heathen, nonetheless inculcated in their flock a fear of God. Today, our Church has solid footing everywhere south of this latitude, to the pole. Thanks to the Lord's gift of a preparatory hierarchy and the good work of the missionary Society of Jesus."

"You talk as if this happened yesterday."

"You know, I did extensive missionary work," Gast said, self-satisfied. "The Latino is a species not unlike the lost souls I encountered in your Canada, yet different in one major respect. The natives there were too infatuated with wilderness. They had no fear of God. They saw spirits and egalitarianism everywhere. Everything was a negotiation. Everything a dialogue. I struggled constantly to convince them of the very deep urgency to their souls' fate. The black-and-white decision they faced in their own dire salvation. They have a primitive, shades-of-grey view of reality. A repugnant moral relevancy."

At one time, I thought I found no better clarity in life than to stand in the bush and breathe in the natural air exhaled by plants. It was the suffocating order of the Church that seemed repugnant to me. Mike Racine's kind face came to mind as he explained to me and the other Scouts edible plants and berries. The thought of Mike caused my heart to sink.

"I know of your work there," I said.

Gast's saggy face constricted. "How so?"

"You corresponded with my father. You worked on some … projects together."

He squinted at me. "Your father?"

"He was an Indian Agent in the sixties and seventies."

I uttered our family name and told Gast he had recently died.

"I remember him. A good Catholic. Strong sense of duty. I admired his ingenuity." Gast chuckled at a memory. "Consider this sticky situation. I recall a small village in the Northwest Territories. Some vulgar little encampment. Say, a dozen cabins. We sent all the children to school in Saskatchewan. Months later, there was some unfortunate business that does not merit repeating here, but suffice it to say, it disturbed the parents. And they rebelled. Demanded the children back. The Mounties were quite annoyed!" He paused for lemonade. "We sent a priest to balm the Indians' spiritual needs. It came close to an armed conflict. The priest himself became embroiled.… An outbreak of typhus swept the school that year and many of this village's offspring succumbed. Your father was instrumental in solving the crisis before it became an embarrassment."

"How exactly do you mean?" I asked, quaking.

"The village was disbanded, the groups broken up and sent to new settlements elsewhere." Gast shook his head and tutted. "Such unproductive types. Anyway, within a few years most of them had expired. The rest became drunks, I imagine."

"Did the children go back?"

Another sip of lemonade. "Herein lay your father's genius. Those still alive by graduation had nowhere to go that could be called home, so they moved to the cities and, I am certain, became fully productive members of society."

"My father eliminated the village?"

"In order to save its denizens," Gast clarified.

"And those children," I said. "Handled by you. And then … cast to the wind."

"It must be great fun hearing stories about your dad, eh! My condolences on his passing. I'll add him to my prayers this evening."

Gast leaned back and chuckled to himself at the flood of fond memories.

"I can't believe it," I stammered. With my shaking fingers, I wiped my eyes. I thought of Padre's story about the medieval village and the Inquisition.

"Oh, do not lose heart, my son. It's much easier here," said Gast. "We have far more goodwill with the police and the local community. Mexico is Catholic, truly. We are a small operation, but still in communion with Rome, though we are Tridentine and Vulgate through and through. We get our boys like Michael here from Catholic families who give them to us. We don't even need to ask."

"Let me talk with him," whispered Danny. "You're going the wrong way with this."

"I can't take this," I whispered back. "I want to pummel this old fucker."

"Go to that motel up the road, the pink one. I'll meet you there later."

I stood up.

"Surely you're not leaving?" asked Gast.

"Monsignor, he needs to rest," said Danny. "It was a long drive. We'll see him later."

"Michael," said Gast, "won't you see our guest out, please?"

Michael led me back to the first house, the way we came. We passed two other boys, walking with their hands held palm to palm before a black-cassocked priest.

"And here you are," said Michael once we reached the door. "Good day. And go with God."

I stooped to him. "It's Miguel, not Michael, isn't it?" I asked.

"I was," he said. "But now, I am Michael."

27

The evening sky ripened and before the sun set I had a warm tequila buzz.

Two doors from my new home, the Motel La Joya, was a bodega. After checking in, I bought a bottle. There had been no sign of Danny for hours, but I had no intention of returning to Gast's and fetching him. Instead, I figured no harm would come from wandering the barrio, taking discreet sips from a forty-pounder in a paper bag.

Under my breath, and bumbling over the lyrics, I sang Cat Stevens, singing about coming a long way, changing, asking where the children play. I was drunk.

Despondent to be spending any more time in Tijuana, after a couple of blocks of liberal sipping, I felt lost, stuck, and frustrated enough that I used my still-relatively-new Blackberry to do my first ever drunk dial.

"How nice to hear your voice, sugar. I was just thinking about you," said Melody.

"That's a nice thing to say. You're nice. You're a nice person, Melody."

"Thank you, but do I hear a little bit of alcohol in your voice?"

Oh my god. How did she know? And right off the bat, too. Experience, I realized.

"Maybe a little," I said. I was walking aimlessly, scuffing my feet as I went.

"Where are you?"

"Tijuana, Mexico. We met the monsignor. He is a disgusting old goblin, I tell you. Really, really, really grody guy."

"Hmm."

"But don't worry, we're working on it! We're working on the thing. You know. The *mission*."

I heard Melody sigh.

"Sugar, listen, I can't talk to you when you're like this."

"No, don't go, wait." My voice cracked with desperation. "Please."

"I've known too many people who get caught up in their own ropes," she said. "Let me give you some encouragement. And then I need to go. You are a good man. You're capable of doing good. And you are capable of fighting for good. But you gotta want to fight. Don't give up now. You are very, very close."

"I'm close?" I said. "To what?"

"Face it. I've seen this before. Keep it up. You are strong. You are almost there. It will be so good when you get there."

"Where am I going?"

"You know where you're going."

I did. "Who am I to say what's evil and good?"

"Mm. You feel like you're in the dark right now, sugar? I've heard the best way to help yourself is to help someone else. That's what I see you doing. And I am here cheering for you. I am clapping my hands hard as I can." Melody's voice was quiet, sincere, but clear as a trumpet.

"How?"

"Well," Melody said after a pause. "You can convince yourself of anything. Right now, you fight to relieve suffering. Yours and that poor boy's."

Ahead, I saw the edge of a small dirt-ground playground with some benches. A few adults smoked and chatted in the park. I made my way toward them.

"Melody, will you come here?"

"No," she said, but not in an unkind way. "I need to go. You sober up. Fight the good fight, sugar. Fight for the good win. Talk soon."

I stopped walking as Melody said goodbye and hung up.

I stood dumb on the sidewalk for an embarrassing amount of time, long enough for the people in the playground to notice me. I held the paper-bagged tequila bottle by the neck, just like a rubby. Finally, I crossed the street and sat down on a bench, facing the street with the playground to my back. A man in his thirties wearing a red bandana on his head, no shirt, and a pair of dirty, baggy jeans approached and slid in next to me on the bench.

"*Noches, güey*," he said.

"Hi."

"Ay! You American!"

"Sure."

"Hey, mang, welcome to Tijuana! You want to smoke?"

"No, thanks. Got a drink right here," I said, patting the paper bag.

"Ah! Finest Mexican liquors."

Suddenly, a contingent of four police cars arrived from two directions, stopping in front of a crumbling yellow bungalow. A dozen heavily armed men exited the cars and took up positions around the yellow house. Six entered the front door and then marched back outside escorting a man, no older than me, in handcuffs.

The man was in his underwear, with no shoes, and was bent forward by two cops who shoved him into the back of a car. My companion sucked air through his teeth. The other people in the playground silently and discreetly left the scene, but for a few of the youngest.

The man's family rushed outside. His wife banged on the roof of the police car and spoke rapidly to the commanding officer. I could not understand anything. An older daughter, or perhaps an aunt, had her arms around two children younger than ten. I could not tell if the kids were boys or girls, they were dressed in T-shirts and shorts, with trimmed hair. The children watched this lurid, dramatic scene with eyes so large I could see their whites from across the street illuminated by streetlamp only.

"Ay," said my friend. "So hard. Same thing happened to my papa when I was a kid."

"What happened?" I asked.

"Never saw him again."

The children stood in shock. They had no real expression on their faces except extreme alarm. They were neither speaking, nor crying.

"I wonder what the guy did? It's a good thing that girl is there to look after them," I said.

"Who?"

"The kids, man. Look at those poor kids."

"*Güey*, every kid in this barrio is a poor kid."

Two police cars left, taking the man away, and my companion chose that moment to leave, creeping away into the night.

While the wife cried and appealed to the remaining police officers, the "aunt" led the children back into the house. They were like zombies, not blinking, not turning their heads. Her care and serenity with the children, so gently talking and guiding them, moved me to the point I was blinking away tears.

"Antonio," I said. Out loud. Like a crazy drunk man sitting on a bench, drinking discount tequila from a bottle in a bag.

Back inside my motel room, I felt a seasickness I believed was coming from the neon green paint of the walls, lit by a fluorescent ceiling lamp. The room was hot, ugly, and smelled of mildew.

I dialed Jamie's phone number.

"Jamie," I said. "I need to talk with you."

"It's two in the morning," he said, croaky with sleep.

"It is? Oh shit. I'm sorry. I have no idea what, what the, you know. What the thing is. I've been travelling."

"You're drunk. Where are you?"

"Tijuana."

"Tijuana … bro, what the fuck? You're calling me soused at two in the morning from Mexico. You've been totally closed off from me the past couple weeks, I have no idea what's going on, and I'm going into the hospital in a couple days."

"I know, I'm sorry."

"You said you were going to get help, you said you were going to pull it together."

"I know, I know."

He told me to hang on a minute. I could tell he was getting out of bed and going someplace quiet in the house so he wouldn't wake Clare. The guilt rose up from my stomach like a mountain climber using my organs as holds. I regretted calling.

"You there?" he said. "What in great green fuck is going on?"

"I wanted to come back already and be there for your surgery," I said. "But I don't know now."

"Not only are you blitzed in Tijuana, you're off the wagon and partying too much to come back? This is not what I thought you had in mind when you said you were going to figure things out your way." Jamie moaned. "I'm disappointed in you, man."

"Jamie, listen."

"I expected more," he said. "You selfish prick."

"Listen, I'm sorry I've been drinking. I really am. I don't know when I can come back yet. But I feel like I'm close."

"Close?" His voice changed into a whisper-scream so he didn't wake the house. "What the fuck are you talking about? I'm going in for *brain* surgery in a couple days. It's not like having a tooth pulled! I may not wake up! Even if I do, I may not come back all the way! I'm scared shitless. I'm scared like you wouldn't believe."

"I want to come back right away. I don't want to be here," I said.

"Then come back. Now. Go get on a flight."

"I can do that, but then everything I'm working on will fail."

"What are you, a secret agent? I don't understand."

I made indeterminate noises, trying to find the first thread.

"I can't take this anymore," Jamie said. "What the fuck are you doing?"

So, here we are, I thought. *It's now or it won't be at all.*

I drank a slug of tequila. "I told you that I would give you the truth about Dad," I said. "I need to also tell you about me."

Over the next twenty minutes, I told Jamie about Dad's career at Indian Affairs, and as an Indian Agent, shipping thousands of children to schools around Canada where they were systematically abused by nuns and priests. Children died. Lives were destroyed. I told him about the deaths and broken families and ruined communities orchestrated by men like our father, who convinced us he was above reproach, who, along with Father Gast, posed as a saintly, ethical, perfect man and destroyed everything he touched.

Then I told him how betrayed I felt when our father and mother gave me to our parish priest like a toy to play with in the forest.

"You remember when they sent me on that camping trip with the priest?" I asked.

"Oh no," he said. I wondered if I could say more. Maybe this was the limit of what he could absorb. Maybe if I told him the rest things would change between us. I clammed up.

"Sorry," he said. "Keep going."

"Are you sure?"

"Absolutely. I'm ready for anything."

It was a relief to hear, but made it no easier to continue. "So, it ... he ... you know. Probably what you suspect."

"A pervert."

"Yes."

"Keep going," said Jamie. "I'm right here."

"So, I made a deal with him," I said. "He said something that terrified me. He said he would go after you, so we were out at this riverside, and he had a camera. I made a deal, and it was so he would leave you alone. I didn't know what was going on ... but I did it to protect you."

"Oh, man," said Jamie. "I'm so, so sorry."

"In a way, I'm glad because it kept him from you."

We let the quiet sit between us.

"You've been carrying this since we were kids," he said at last. "It's been killing you. I want to say I wish you'd told me earlier. But I don't want to say that because I'm worried it would make you feel guilty. I'm glad you finally told me, and it took the time it did. Everything I can think of saying to you makes me worry you'll feel guilty. You should not have any guilt. Goddamnit. I only wish you didn't feel like you had to deal with this alone."

"I'm just glad it worked."

The line was silent. I made use of the time to cry a little. Maybe Jamie was doing the same.

This was exhausting. After a few minutes, I had a few deep breaths and could speak. "You there?"

It was quiet.

"Say something," I said.

"I don't know what to say."

"I don't expect you to thank me or anything."

"Well, of course, thank you for telling me."

"No, I mean. You know … about the deal. To keep you out of it."

"Thank you?" His tone had an edge. "Why would I thank you?"

"I don't know. I just. I don't know."

"There's nothing to *thank* you for. Think about how fucked up that is. The abuse was out of your control. He created this situation. He manipulated you into thinking you were making some sort of sacrifice and saving me. You were a kid! It's completely his fault. And worse, it's still working — you feel like you made a deal with him, but you didn't get anything."

"I guess."

"If you think you did this to save me, it's just him deflecting more guilt onto me and responsibility onto you than either of us deserves. This is totally on him."

"I'd hate to think I did it without it having some sort of good coming out of it. And the good is that he didn't turn to you next."

"There's nothing good coming out of it. And it wasn't your choice. He manipulated you because that's what he did to get his way. He used everything at his disposal to make it seem like you had a choice. You had no choice."

"There are pictures. He had a camera. Those pictures are probably still being passed around."

"Did you hear what I said? He sacrificed you for his jollies. There's no justifying that after the fact. You didn't make a sacrifice for me. You were a kid. You had no choice."

I heard him blow his nose.

Finally, I told him about Melody. I said that she — without knowing much about me — seemed to understand me better than I did myself. I felt like I could be a better person when I was with her. And, I said, Melody believed in what I was doing.

So, what was it I was doing? What was this that was my way of "unblocking" myself? I explained to my brother I was trying to retrieve a boy who had been gifted to Father Sweet by his parents, and to give that boy a shot at life. A life unfettered by the grasping desires of unholy men.

At the end of our call, which ended after midnight my time, Jamie told me that it was worth my staying there as long as it took. He told me that somehow, he always knew, even though he said he didn't know. I promised him I would try to get back home in time for the surgery.

"Jamie, you there?"

"Yah. I'm just thinking … I finally … after what you told me … I think I finally know you. I just hope that when I wake up — after the operation — I recognize you."

I swallowed hard. "I love you," I whispered.

"Me, too."

28

I awoke at noon in my clothes. An empty bottle of tequila lay on the floor. I had been dreaming about digging with a pick-axe out of a culvert, under the silent, watchful gaze of the Green's Creek Hobo.

My head was pounding, but the dizziness was worse still.

There was a knock at the door. It occurred to me that I had heard it in my sleep. Someone had been knocking.

I lunged to the bathroom and threw up into the toilet. Judging by the mess, I had thrown up the night before, as well.

I wiped my face with a towel and staggered to the door. A figure darkened the doorway, backlit by sunlight. I didn't recognize him at first. It was Danny.

"You look terrible." Danny was clean-shaven, with a new haircut, and was wearing the black cassock of the priests in Gast's compound. He was back in the Roman collar.

"What happened?" I said, gesturing at his outfit and shading my eyes. "What the fuck?"

"Here," said Danny, handing me an envelope.

I took it and rubbed my forehead in confusion.

"It's details of when, where, and how Father Sweet will cross the border," Danny said, "and where they are now. He will bring Antony here. They are picking up a package for Gast on Thursday afternoon. It's all in there. They'll cross at Tecate because it's a minor border facility and the least likely to arouse suspicion. Gast's expecting him Thursday evening. He doesn't know I'm telling you."

"How — how did you ...?"

"You've got what you need now."

"But what — why are you dressed like that? How did you get this?"

"Thursday is the day they cross the border. You must confront Father Sweet before then."

"Thursday my brother's having surgery. No, no, no. Melody can do it with the police."

Danny frowned. "I guess. But I thought you wanted to see Antony personally. You've got to get him before they come to Mexico. Isn't that what you want?"

"Of course. But my brother is having brain surgery. Risky surgery."

"Let me in," Danny said, shaking his head. "I've done what you wanted. I held up my part of the bargain."

He entered.

"But I can't do it Thursday. I need to go back. This is no help."

"Father Sweet will be in Mexico by then. And you won't be able to do a thing. But suit yourself."

I squinted at him. "And what about you? What's all this?" I asked, gesturing at his getup.

He took a breath. "I'm staying here."

At first I thought he meant the motel room, then I realized he meant Mexico. His black cassock and refined appearance meant that he was going to stay here and hide with Gast.

"Don't do it," I said. "Bad choice."

"I need some sorting time for myself. I want to stay here."

I suggested he speak with Padre first. Someone to advise him.

Danny frowned. "Padre is not your friend," he said. "You think he's your friend?"

"I don't have friends," I said, steadying myself on the door frame.

Danny sat down and I lay on the bed in the fetal position.

"He's not my friend," said Danny. "He wants things from us, that's all. He wanted me and you to deliver Sweet to the authorities. After that I'm to return to the diocese, and then off I go to the Servants of the Paraclete."

"He wants justice for you-know-who," I suggested.

"Not the way you think. Sweet is outside the Catholic Church. They excommunicated him, and now they can say he's just one bad apple. He's the perfect, high-profile example for the Vatican. The Church doesn't want to say there's a problem with priests. They can say this isn't a priest problem. It's a Father Sweet problem."

"He wants my dad's boxes. The ones with all the details of your buddy Gast and the residential schools."

Danny nodded solemnly. "If you really want justice, don't give Padre those boxes. Just advice from a friend. Those boxes will wind up at the diocese and no one will ever see them again. He's an agent for the establishment, man."

"Aren't you?"

His face twisted into a mask of exasperation. "I know you don't buy it, but I take my vocation seriously. What matters is between me and God."

For the first time, I regarded him and he didn't revolt me. "Don't stay here, Danny. Look at these guys! Pull yourself together. I'll fly you home after Antonio is safe."

"Look," he said quietly. "I want you to know I appreciate that you've been paying for everything. Thank you. I mean that. I'm a bit of a refugee and that's why I'm going to stay here. The

Church is falling apart back home. I need to figure things out, and Gast has a good, disciplined compound here."

The light went on for me. "That's why it was important I take you here. You always planned to come here," I said.

He didn't reply.

"I am a fucking sucker," I said. "You *are* one of them, after all."

"Sorry."

"Maybe Melody can do it," I said. "Thursday, I mean."

Danny nodded. "Well, I'm sure she can. I think she's done this before. But I think it's a disservice to you."

"That's a cheap shot."

"Not if you think you're taking control of your life," Danny said. "You're saving yourself as much as Antony. It's obvious."

I felt sick. "What part of *my brother might die on the operating table* don't you understand? Get me some water," I said. "Besides. You're changing the subject. Why stay here?"

"It's not a parish. I can do some reflection and they'll leave me alone. I want to get back to the diocese eventually. My way."

Danny fetched a glass of water from the sink.

"Pff. Once you've gone rogue you think they'll let you back?"

"I do. Gast's well-connected."

I gave it a legitimate attempt. A good old varsity try to see things from his perspective. I found it sickening. Danny claimed to love his parish, but a parish is a fulcrum of community. People, fully integrated into other communities, perforate it with numerous checks, balances, and values. A parish interacts with the broader world. A church — a good church, or the kind of church I think my parents believed in — is porous. There are lawyers, teachers, adults, children, men, women, different ethnic groups, even varied languages. But what is a monastery or any strictly religious community? It is a closed society, a monoculture within a secure building. What makes people want to trade certainty and their lives for a blockaded institution in exchange for belonging?

"You're disgusting. All that bullshit. I should have called the cops on you as soon as you told me about Emily."

He smiled. "Then you wouldn't have gotten what you want."

"Just one man's opinion, but aren't you barricading yourself in?" I asked. "It's the opposite of what you've told me you believe in."

"I can tell you this now. You are patronizing. You've been that way with me from day one. You can't understand."

"If I didn't feel like I would puke, I would pop you right now."

"Let me tell you something. I used to own a Jetta. I used to think, whenever things got real bad, I would just take the passenger seat out and put a hammock in there. I'd live out of my car. I planned to drive out to Tofino. That was my escape plan. But now, I don't know. It's warm here. These guys will give me a home."

"This isn't the place. These guys are vampires. Don't be crazy. Get help."

"Like you?"

"I'm trying to do the right thing. I'm trying to confront everything that has fucked me up." I looked at him, he was smiling in a benign way that I had not seen in weeks. It was unsettling and made me think his mind was made up. "I'm trying to be a better person. Aren't you?"

"You look sort of crazy right now," he said.

"Oh, for fuck's sake," I said. "Do whatever you want. Molest more kids."

"These guys don't think there's anything wrong with me. Besides, you think I can just get a job and do something else?" Danny's voice shot up. "And go see a shrink?" He leaned forward and spread his hands. "Because I can't."

"If you stay with these people you will become just like them. Entirely. Shouldn't you be careful what you — *feed* yourself with?"

"I don't want to go into deprogramming with the Servants of the Paraclete. That's what's waiting for me if I go back. Paraclete cage. My life isn't mine. Besides, you're so clear on what to do — what about you? What are you going to do to get help for yourself if you're just going to throw everything over the fence to Melody? She can't save you. You've got to want it, man."

"What about your self-pitying speech about being bedevilled? Was that just lies? This is hiding."

"That's my choice to make. And, maybe it is," he said.

"You won't be able to come home. As soon as I'm back in Ottawa, I'm calling the police."

"Fine." A confident smile brushed his lips. "I'm not bothered. It's warm here. The tequila is cheap."

29

A couple of days later, I was back in Los Angeles, back in the Motel 6, engaged in a flurry of busy calls and emails to Ottawa and discussions with Melody.

I had spoken with Clare and told her to kiss Jamie for me as he went in, but neither Jamie nor I could bear to speak with the other. I didn't want to say the word *goodbye*. It would be a few hours now. Everything would be done.

Padre rang me again — I assume he kept trying because Danny had stopped answering — but I did not take the call. He sent me a text message instead. Padre was the oldest person from whom I had ever received a text message. And as it came in slowly, line by line, I was not sure what he thought was going on, but in the context, I found it kind of menacing.

> *I don't know what you are doing*
> *Danny says hes got a new plan*
> *You there?*
> *Are you trying to find peace?*

You won't talk
So I'll say it here
Finding spiritual solace is
Fighting medusa
You cannot look directly at what you fear
what repulses us
Faith, hope and charity
That's the mirror
Where you can view and fight the gorgon.
Via con dios.

I called Melody.

"You ready?" I asked.

"Pick you up in fifteen minutes."

I was clean-shaven and wearing conservative, nondescript clothing, as Melody had advised. For me, that meant dark clothing head to toe. Black golf shirt, black pants. Inadvertently, I had dressed like a priest. I went out onto the breezeway to wait and drank the rest of my Starbucks. The butterflies were alight in my gut. It was a warm, dry morning full of potential and possibility.

The housekeeping cart wheeled past, pushed by the woman who looked to me so much like Mrs. Paquime a few days ago. We exchanged smiles and said *buenas dias*.

Minutes later, I was in Melody's air-conditioned and fresh-scented Highlander. Clean and lightly floral. It smelled like her. We headed southeast.

The radio was tuned to an upbeat R&B station that inspired her to sing along from time to time. Especially when it was Whitney or Aretha. She sang those four songs beginning to end. As we got more into the desert, I felt relaxed, like we were heading off on a holiday. I smiled.

"I never thought I'd drive the California freeways this much in my life."

"I must say, you pulled it all together the past couple days," Melody said. "You thought of everything."

"Be prepared," I said, beaming.

30

Danny's note gave us the itinerary for Father Sweet and Antonio as provided to Monsignor Gast. The two had been driving around Arizona, Nevada, and California like Humbert and Lolita, but their last two days would be pre-ordained for a simple logistical reason.

Melody and her friends in the state police had worked out a good interception plan. Gast had asked Sweet to pick up a package in the eastern suburbs of San Diego on Thursday. We would wait until they arrived, and then it would be a good old-fashioned sting. Just like in *The Rockford Files*.

The house was on an average suburban row of bungalows. Cars had been placed strategically in four locations so that, once Sweet drove down the street toward the house, the street would be discreetly closed off behind them and ahead. It was a mousetrap.

Melody and I were around the corner from the street, in a small strip-mall plaza with a McDonald's, a Chevron, and a few shops, including a liquor store. By midafternoon, I had torn my nails so much that one of the undercover state troopers gave me four Band-Aids from his first aid kit without asking if I needed them. Melody and I sat drinking coffee at a window-side table in McDonald's. She texted back and forth with the stakeout on the street.

"You say you're doing this for Antonio," she said to me, without looking up from her phone, "but you really are doing this for yourself. You must realize."

"I've been hearing people say that a lot. I don't like it."

"Why not? It's okay for you to be selfish in this case. You've earned a little selfishness."

"I don't trust selfishness. Not even my own."

As I put on a Band-Aid, I said, "I really want to go over to that liquor store and buy some booze."

She did not look up from her phone. After a moment passed she asked, "How long has it been since you've had a drink?"

"Three days."

My words sat between us. She gave no impression that she would comment.

"You know, just to calm my nerves," I said. "But I won't."

"Good," she said, looking up and giving me a smile. "Because they're here, and we need to head over."

The time had come. It felt like sticking my finger in an electric socket.

Stepping outside was like stepping out of time. It did not seem like there was any wind. The sound vanished from the air but for our footfalls to the car and the sound of Melody turning the ignition switch. Melody may have talked, but whatever she said she had no audience. My heart thumped.

We rounded the corner and I saw four cars boxing in the driveway of a bungalow. We parked, and Melody waited for me to gather the courage to step out to approach the onlookers and the police. It all seemed kind of peaceful. No flashing lights or yellow tape.

Father Sweet stood there in a short-sleeved clerical shirt, smiling broadly, conversing with a uniformed San Diego police officer. He came up to the shoulder of the cop. His beard had become glittering white, but otherwise here was the unmistakable outline of the Pied Piper I remembered.

He gabbed chummily, as if it were a picnic.

Melody led me by the hand toward the senior detective, clearly a friend of hers. I don't recall what they said. Father Sweet's gravity pulled at my eyes. I was absorbed, transfixed, watching Father Sweet, who was not in handcuffs. From a distance you might even think it was merely a friendly discussion.

Father Sweet kept trying to stand to the side, rather than facing the police. It was a mug's trick he was using; a charm offensive. *I'm one of you,* he seemed to say. *Let's face this together.*

"Oh my! Piano is a wondrous, wondrous instrument," I heard him exclaim. I could just make out his words. He'd found his angle with the cop. Music. "How I would love to hear you play, my boy. I can see you have a sensitive, artful soul."

Charisma has gotten him out of this, I thought. *He's charmed his way out of this. We didn't get him. Of course, he's gotten out of this. He's convinced them it's a misunderstanding. He'll be giving that cop piano lessons before sundown.*

"Isn't he under arrest?" asked Melody, as if reading my mind.

"He is," said the detective. "We don't believe him to be a flight risk. The boy is with protective services over there."

I heard Father Sweet chuckle. "Oh, marvellous! How marvellous," he said.

I had the sense of dropping even more deeply out of time. A large bubble engulfed me, but for Father Sweet's murmuring words and his laughter it would have been silent. I could hear every ounce of breath as it passed in and out of his body. With dream-heavy, cautious steps, I drew closer.

He turned and saw me.

As though onstage, we stood opposite each other in a darkness that sucked away everything but us into dead air.

"You remember me?" I said, finding my mouth hard to work and my voice barely stronger than a whisper.

The light in his eyes dimmed as he examined me head to toe, searching for something recognizable. A parishioner? A colleague? A stagehand from the movie? Father Sweet's magnetism was still strong and he affected friendliness, but as he saw a stoniness in my face, he twitched with nervousness.

Finally, his eyes flashed with recognition. And then he frowned with disappointment. He shook his head slightly.

His lips curled into a smile. "Ah!" he said and brought his hands together, glancing at the police officer at his side, back to me, back to him. He looked like he'd just had a great idea. Obviously, he was concocting something.

"I'm so glad you are here," he said. "This happy coincidence of God's Own Doing! Perhaps, you can witness my character to these good people?"

His tone was that of a beggar on the street, asking for spare change. The circumstance seemed lost on him. I was astonished. He was asking if I could help him out of a jam.

"For old times!"

When I spoke, my tongue was fat and uncooperative. It took concentration to force my mouth into the words I wanted to say. Beads of sweat erupted at my hairline.

"To everything there is a season," I said slowly. "A time to keep silence, and a time to speak."

His head drew back and he chortled nervously.

"Do you know the movie *Scarface*?" I asked.

His smile died. He pointed his face up at me like an axe blade. It felt like the opprobrium of my own father. I straightened my spine so I could look down on him.

"Scarface says his motives were to get the money, then the power, then the women. Those were his priorities. The end goal was only to satisfy his sex drive. To get his rocks off. Is that all it is for you? All this charm, talent, and brains? All this theology? Just to blow your load on kids?"

He paused, and I saw a bit of the old parish priest. The kindly eyes that could comfort the bereaved, the eloquent baritone that assured children not to be frightened in the night.

"The holy man does not break his life into fragments," said Father Sweet. "But rather keeps it whole, so that all his thoughts, his actions are of one whole — the sole effort of praising God and building his kingdom."

"Right. So, the kids, then?"

"Anything else is sin," he said.

"And the kids?"

I expected him to become icy and haughty, but he kept up his beatific persona. "You know as well as any that I would never, *ever* hurt a child."

"It's not the same, is it?" I said. "They're the same words, but you mean something totally different."

He seemed confused.

"Anyone who brings down one of these little ones would be better drowned in the depth of the sea with a millstone around his neck," he said.

"We'll see what the judge says about your millstone."

"No, you don't understand. You see, I —"

"Words can't minimize what you do!" I shouted.

"Faith always is simple and outside of words," he replied, spreading his hands as if delivering a sermon on a divine truth. "In the end."

"For you — it's just a way to get your cock out. That's all it is. That's all any of this is."

He winced, and then looked at me with pity. "We ought to pray together."

"All right. I pray you get a judge who doesn't fall for your pious horseshit, and you do the same. Deal?"

"I need to give Antony a message," Sweet said. "Will you deliver it for me? Tell him to always to remember that no matter what anyone might —"

"No."

"Excuse me, my boy, I wasn't finished."

"Yes, you are."

He cocked his head at me.

"Nobody cares what you think," I said.

"Don't be rude. Please give him the message. The boy will be confused by all this," Sweet said, restarting. "It's important that he knows I am —"

"No, no message. He doesn't need to listen to you ever again."

He recoiled at my rudeness.

"Nobody will listen to you ever again. Good riddance to you."

My finger was dabbled with blood, and I reached forward to wipe some on his arm.

"Remember that," I said. "Remember."

He shook his head sadly. "I will pray for you," he said.

I felt a gentle hand touch my arm. It was Melody. The policeman remained at Father Sweet's side, holding him by the elbow. He led Father Sweet to a police car and placed him in the back.

"There's someone I'd like you to meet," Melody said, gently pulling me toward a minivan. "Before they go."

I felt an early morning disorientation, as if I had just woken up. "Where are they going?" I asked.

"Someplace safe. It's all right." Melody leaned into the minivan. Inside there were two women, and a thin boy of twelve or thirteen with dark hair. One could just make out the downy fuzz of a pre-pubescent moustache. He stared straight ahead through the windshield.

"Antonio," said Melody, "this is my friend. He wants to say hi."

I bent over, supporting myself by leaning on my knees. Between me and Antonio sat a child services agent with a ponytail.

"Antonio, my name is Jacob," I said, and smiled. "And I want to tell you you're not alone. I understand where you are. Because I was also a … an altar boy of … of Father Sweet."

The boy did not move, but slowly rolled his eyes toward me, not quite getting there.

"Antonio," I said. "Listen to what I'm going to say now. You don't need to say anything. Just listen."

The agent shifted uncomfortably in her seat. Melody was nearby, near enough to hear.

"You're going to get a lot of advice in the next few days," I said. "And you're going to have all sorts of questions of your own. I bet he gave you a lot of instruction about who you are and what you are. He said a lot of those things to me, and to other boys. When I was your age, I didn't know what was right and wrong. For me, I wanted someone to talk to me honestly." I took a breath. "So, I'm going to tell you what I wish someone had said to me, when I was your age and in your position."

Antonio looked down, gazing at my chest rather than looking me in the eye, but we seemed to be getting closer to connecting.

"It's going to be okay," I said. "None of what happened was your doing, even if you think it was. You had no control over it. Today's a new beginning. This is your life. *Your life*. Entirely yours. Not his. Not your parents'. Make your life what you want it to be. Your life is your own. You do not owe anybody anything. There's nothing stopping this from being the day you decide to be someone else. Nothing sticks to you. You are in control of your own life."

Antonio made eye contact with me. Emotionless, but he made eye contact. I smiled and nodded.

Almost imperceptibly, Antonio's head nodded the slightest amount.

"Antonio, kids can't sin. They can't. When I was in your place, I was terrified about good and evil and getting trapped by it. None of that is true. If you ever want to talk with someone else who's been on your road, I am one hundred percent in your corner, and I don't want anything from you in return," I said. The ponytailed agent winked at me and gave a confident nod.

"My name is Antony," he said in a faraway voice.

"Well, I'm very glad to meet you," I said.

I backed up. Melody and I stood side by side as the door closed and the minivan drove off.

Father Sweet — I nearly forgot — was still in the back of the police car, which had not yet left. I could see his tiny outline, gesturing and speaking and trying to persuade the cop in the front seat, who filled out paperwork. Father Sweet was performing a show for him. Trying to charm him. The cop seemed unmoved.

"So, you said your piece to that priest," said Melody. "How does it feel?"

"Not sure," I said. "I'm not sure it feels like anything. But I guess we did what I came for."

"Good," she replied. "I noticed something. He was telling you something I don't think you quite understood."

"Does it matter?"

"I think he was being honest, that he doesn't separate the different parts of his life. So what he does with children, which he doesn't see as wrong, is inseparable from his belief system."

"He's doing what he thinks is right?"

"That's what I'm saying. Some people believe they are on a mission to change things for the better by either restricting or loosening freedom, other people think only of helping themselves, and then there are some who manipulate only for the sake of manipulating. It's an unexamined instinct."

"Like a bear rummaging through garbage out of hunger or boredom."

"Or a bird knowing the time to crack through its shell."

I contemplated this. "Who cares?" I said, finally.

"Guys like him don't think they're hypocrites. He's convinced himself he's a good person, doing the work of the Lord. Even while he abuses kids."

With her warm hand on my back, she led me back toward the Highlander. "And I think it was good you didn't tell Antonio about what you're doing for his parents."

"I just didn't see how to say it without freaking him out."

"Let him find out later. It's enough to absorb for today." She smiled at me. "Now, let's go get a cheeseburger and a milkshake."

five months later

1

Spring came early after a warm February, and the sun baked the air perfectly for a walk. The ice was gone from the pavement, and snow had hardened into dirty moraines curbside. We had just returned from circling the block around the residence. But Mother had grown fussy and angry, and although we had had a positive visit, she needed a nap. Like a toddler.

"Here, Mother," I said. "Take my arm, just like we're walking the red carpet together."

This made her smile and I guided her back to her room. Clare had given me the new school pictures of Kitty and Harry to update the frames and I almost forgot. Mother sat on the edge of her bed and wheezed a bit as she removed her cream-coloured cardigan. I fetched the pictures as I hung my jacket.

"I nearly forgot about Kitty and Harry's new pictures. They're absolutely adorable." I showed her each picture one by one.

Each photo held as much interest to her as a label on a can of soup.

"That's Kitty, Jamie's daughter. Your granddaughter. Look at that huge smile. And here's Harry, Jamie's son. Your grandson. The twins are in grade one."

She moved to the window, staring with her mouth slightly agape, as if she might say something, but there was nothing. I watched her curved shoulders at the window, then put the photos into their frames, updating Mother's decor with a new look at the best parts of her life.

Jamie entered the room, eating one of the donuts we'd brought for the nurses. His hair was growing in well. It had lengthened to the point now as if he'd had a trim, professional haircut. He had lost fifteen pounds, but otherwise looked healthy as a wolf.

"Now, Mum," said Jamie. "Lie down, and we'll tuck you in for a nap."

She lay back, and Jamie helped settle her with the afghan. She stared up at us as we tucked her in.

Jamie leaned in to kiss her cheek and she recoiled from him. He kissed her anyway.

"I love you, Mum," Jamie said.

Without saying goodbye, I moved to the hallway. It was not my idea to come back, but Jamie wanted to see her. And there wasn't anything I would not do if he asked me. Jamie's decency flattered her, and I admired him for it in spite of myself. She was not really there. Only the shadow of her resentments and frustration lay in that bed, I figured.

"Why do you bother?" I asked. "There's a point where you've got to get real, no?"

"She's my mother. I just hope a little tiny part of her recognizes she still has family, and that we love her. If not, then it's a part of me and you that we're looking after."

As we walked to the elevator, Jamie asked, "What's wrong? Are you crying?"

"No," I said. "I think I'm just happy you're here."

2

Once Father Sweet was charged with five counts, the PR and tabloid gossip machine rumbled awake. Griff Kelsey was embroiled in a new scandal, thanks to his pastor. Not only was he accused of being an anti-Semite, a racist, an out-of-control addict, and a violent bully, he now was the sponsor of — allegedly — a pedophile. Father Sweet himself was unable to post bail for his kidnapping charge and all the other charges, yet Kelsey left him rotting in jail. Moreover, once he was in the news, seven other survivors came forward with stories about him.

But not Father Danny Lemieux. Danny had all but dissolved into Tijuana.

Melody encouraged me to testify, even though no charges could be laid in my case; it would help the overall process against Father Sweet. I agreed.

I agreed excitedly, because it was another excuse to visit Melody in Los Angeles. She had taken a new job within the National Center for Missing and Exploited Children, but I still checked in with her from time to time via text. She had a positive effect on me. Each time we connected, whether by text or the odd phone call, I felt like I was getting closer to hope, farther from the trainwreck.

We spoke by phone.

"Did you get everything set for the Paquimes?" asked Melody.

"I did."

"You don't sound convinced."

"It's not that," I replied. "Firstly, I think it was a good idea you had, Melody. A great solution. Again, thank you. I wouldn't have come up with it. And it's not like I don't appreciate or respect the solution."

"But," she drawled.

"Well, I feel like I'm displacing them. Like I'm taking them from their lands someplace else. 'For their own good.'"

"But, they didn't want to go back to Mexico."

"I know that, but they were being forced into that choice. And I feel like I'm doing, not the same, but … manipulating … I mean, who am I?"

"What does that mean?"

"Am I no better than my dad?"

Melody breathed deeply in contemplation.

"Some folks may say you're just another privileged white boy who got what he wanted in the end. Is that it?"

"I guess. Yah."

"Privilege is wrong when you don't share it. You needed to share your privilege. That's why I made the suggestion. You understand?"

"Yes."

"It's because you could offer help. You needed to help. The difference is the operation of free will. Options for how the Paquime family could live their lives the way they wanted to. You offered help, with an option. You shared your privilege. You're not forcing them to do anything."

If there was a moment I could point to, a moment when I felt set free, it was then.

I started attending AA meetings some time after New Year's, around the same time I got a walking-distance part-time job logging inventory at an industrial battery warehouse near Carleton. It was a client of our old friend David, who worked as a partner at Jamie's law firm. And, just before Christmas, I got into a regular schedule with one of Clare's suggested therapists, a woman on Somerset Street. I rode my bike to my appointments when it wasn't slushy and walked when it was. And, for a couple glorious weeks last month, the canal was frozen, and I skated to my shrink's office.

Physically, I had not been in such good shape in years. Jamie suggested we join a beer league hockey team, and I said the beer part didn't work for me. So, we joined an adult ringette team. We were the only men on the team, but I felt better about no pressure to drink, and Jamie enjoyed not being jostled and bumped as much. But yes, we were mocked unmercifully at the rink for playing on a women's team. I did not care.

In a few days, I would see the Paquimes again and I was very excited.

One thing remained to deal with — the boxes in the basement of the house. Dad's boxes.

In my apartment, I sat down at the window, near my new peperomia plant. My first plant. I tested the moisture of the soil with my forefinger. Out my window was the bright day and I could just make out the Rideau River, which had broken up early after the unseasonable warm late winter we were in.

Of all the things in our Blackburn Hamlet house that were left after Clare, Jamie, and I had gone through everything, there remained only one object I wanted to keep. It was the *dewe'igan*, the hand drum Dad was gifted by Indian Affairs when he retired.

It was a mystery to me why I kept it, but the look of it comforted me. I hung it out of the sunlight on the wall of my flat. The hand drum was about a cubit in diameter and adorned with a painted turtle, in a Cree woodland style. I admired it while I sat.

I sucked air and looked at the phone number I had written on the well-worn piece of paper in my palm. I had been carrying this paper for months. This was the afternoon, I had decided, to finally make the call.

I dialed and waited for the pickup, then a familiar, warm voice came on the line.

I identified myself to him. To Mike Racine.

"I don't know if you remember me, but you had a big impact on my life.... I wish I had gotten to know you better when I had the chance."

"I remember you," he said. "I know who you are."

"I wish I had come back to Scouts when you led the troop. Somehow, I think things might have gone differently for me."

"Mm-hm?"

"I saw you at my dad's funeral. I wanted to talk with you."

"Your dad and I had our differences," Mike said.

"You and me both."

"Big believer in rules," he said, "your dad."

"I think so." I cleared my throat. "I've learned a lot about my father recently. I never really knew anything about him and what he did for a living, until after he died. You see, he kept a lot of records and hid them in the basement. Records from Indian Affairs. Boxes and boxes of files."

Mike took a few moments. "What kind of files?"

My mouth suddenly went dry. "Well, um. Letters and ledgers. It is an ugly story. Sterilization, beatings, runaways. Deaths. Of children. From schools."

"How many boxes?"

"Maybe twenty or thirty."

"Files like that were usually destroyed. Sounds like your dad hung on to them for some reason."

"Maybe he wanted to save them to do the right thing."

"I doubt it," said Mike. "But I understand that kids need to believe what they need to about their parents."

"My dad used to tell me I had to do what he said because he was my father. That never seemed like enough of a reason to me."

"One time, me and George Erasmus talked about that. It's hard to change minds. People get locked in ways of doing things that don't make sense. I came to work at Indian Affairs to make change. Your dad did not like change."

"Why do you think he kept the documents?"

"I don't want to guess."

"I do," I said. "Maybe he planned to do something. He must have known what he was doing was wrong. Maybe he wanted to fix the mistake, but he didn't know how." I was surprised to hear myself trying to make excuses for my dad.

I watched my little corner of the river, nervously waiting for Mike to respond.

"I don't know about that," Mike said at last. "Harry LaForme, and a group of other people, survivors from the residential schools, are getting ready to do something big. Like what they did in South Africa. After Apartheid."

"Planning to do what?"

"Shining a big light on what was done at these schools. Canada is like South Africa, but most people don't know. Or maybe they do know, and they don't care, eh."

"I care."

"If you want to help," Mike said, "you can start by loading those boxes of yours into my truck."

Tectonically, the weight shifted from that grotesque paper mountain I inherited — a chronicle of hurt, ignorance, and malpractice — and it shifted to the sky. We would literally exhume those fungous, sinful deeds to killing light. And I could help with my small part.

Conversation shifted gears.

"A group of us are going hunting in a few weeks," said Mike. "You want to come, Jake? Might be good for you."

"I don't know if I can."

"Up to you. You won't have to do any of the cleaning or gutting. We'll do that. It's mostly camping. But we'll bring something home."

"I've fished before, but … hunting and killing something, I don't know. It's a generous offer. Don't get me wrong. I guess I'm just scared."

"You learn respect hunting. People spend too much of their time in life floating downstream like a leaf."

For a while he said nothing.

Then he said, "The Creator made a big world. We share it. When you die, you'll go back to it. Spirit comes in and out of us, and everything else."

"That makes sense to me," I said.

"Doesn't matter what you call it. Nothing ever begins or ends."

3

Jamie still wasn't cleared to drive, so Clare and I took their cars to the airport. I drove Jamie's Mercedes and Clare drove her Grand Caravan. With all that, we had room for the luggage and for all five passengers.

Jamie was great unpacking everything once we arrived at the house. The Paquimes had eight huge suitcases, and apparently there was more coming, being shipped later.

"Welcome to your new home," I said to the four of them. To Jamie and I our house seemed average, but Matias and Antonio called it a castle.

"You boys each get your own room," I said to them.

Nothing had ever felt as clear and right as Melody's suggestion to sponsor the Paquimes and have them live for a year — rent-free — in our parents' house.

"Save up a bit from your job at the Blackburn Arms," I said to Mr. Paquime. "I'm looking forward to the new menu items."

The plan had saved them from being deported to Mexico. My old friend Paul Lozinski — the baby from that memorable *bris* we attended — was an immigration lawyer now, and we managed to fast-track the Paquimes. Everything fell into place.

The only question Mrs. Paquime had asked was whether there was a Catholic church nearby.

Mr. Paquime shook all our hands vigorously.

It was too cool for a picnic outside, but we had a happy, loud feast in the dining room. Afterward, Jamie and I told the boys we wanted to show them something.

In the garage, there were four bikes. Two junior Nakamura mountain bikes with training wheels, which we gave to Kitty and Harry. And for the Paquime boys, our two vintage Mustang CCMs, which I had restored to pristine, gleaming condition. We told the boys that, when they outgrew the Mustangs, they needed to pass them along to Kitty and Harry so they could have a turn.

"Matias and Antonio," I said. "Jamie and I want to show you the best thing about your new home."

As Clare gave Mrs. Paquime a tour of the house, which Clare and I had revamped to her specifications, Jamie and I set off on foot with the kids. We helped Kitty and Harry with their bikes while Matias and Antonio zipped along toward the greenbelt. We wanted to show them the forest, which was smaller now as the city had grown in all around Blackburn, but wonderous still.

It swung out before us, the woods. To the left, one of the Capital Commission's working arboretums and glass houses. To the right, our old stomping grounds, which twenty-five more years of children and shenanigans charged with an even more exciting vibe.

"Is this another country?" asked Matias.

"It's a preserved natural space called a greenbelt," I said. "People use it like a wild park. Jamie and I used to play here when we were young."

We headed into the forest together along the Tauvette Trail, with the Paquime boys.

"Stop and listen," I said to Antonio after five minutes of tramping into the sticks. The trails were pounded down solid, but it was too early yet for any carpet of the first springtime shoots and florets. "Hear how quiet it is? You'd never think the suburbs are that way and the city is that way. You get to touch nature. Just wait until the leaves are on the trees."

"That way is Hornet's Nest," said Jamie. A bunch of soccer pitches — footie fields. "Let's go this way toward Green's Creek."

I said to Antonio, "You can learn more about people and yourself than you think out here. You just need to listen."

Kitty and Harry hollered as their bikes sunk and rose over the trail.

"Here it is," Jamie said.

I failed to see it at first. The tree, at one time looking like God's hand reaching upward to pluck an apple from the clouds, had metastasized and thickened. God's forearm seemed too weak a description. It had become a monument, devouring and clearing competing growth around its trunk. The packed trails encircled it as a plaza. We may have started it, but two more generations of kids had built forward on our start.

All my lashings were gone, but I recognized a couple of braces which, twenty-five years later, still supported the platform, which had acted a shelter and kept the rot out.

"Can we go up?" asked Kitty. Jamie gave her a boost so she could be first. The boys followed.

The main platform in the crook of the hand was large, and a secondary one had been added on the thumb, braced against a sixth finger that had come in since our day. There were two roofs. It had become a version of the very temple I hoped it might become.

"There's ABCs here!" cried Harry.

"Initials," said Antonio. "There are a bunch of initials here."

Jamie and I eyeballed each other with glad respect. "Read them out, Antonio," Jamie said.

"KB. TB. DS. DS. JS. RS. ES. SN. BN. BF. JS. PR. JR. DS. JC. CL. SM. SM. BJM. SM. GC. OO. JM. JM."

"There we are. Don't get smug, buddy," Jamie said to me. "But that sounds like a legacy."

The kids scrambled back down.

"When we were kids like you, Jamie and I started building this treehouse," I said to their awed faces. "And those other initials are probably the other kids who looked after it once we started."

"Did you live here?" asked Matias.

We laughed.

"We wanted to!" Jamie said.

"Whenever someone tells you they think they know better," I said to Antonio, "you can come here and get the truth. Everything you need to know about anything is here. You just need to watch and listen. And learn from it."

I wasn't sure he heard me, but I wasn't concerned. He would discover what was here whether someone told him to look for it, or not. You can't hide natural truth.

"Let's head back now," said Jamie. "Lunch at the house."

Kitty and Harry were tired, but too thrilled with their mountain bikes to stop now. *Those bikes are freedom*, I thought. *Jamie and I gave them freedom. And a place to explore it in peace. The best gift one generation can give the next.*

Antonio and Matias raced ahead, pointing and marvelling. So different from the Los Angeles concrete. Spring will get in full gear, the first tender leaves will sprout and the ground will be blanketed with blue flowers and trilliums. What magic awaits these boys.

Antonio could now do the good work of saving himself, maybe by also saving someone else. In saving another you can save yourself. Repossess yourself.

As we walked through the white, shadowy light of the afternoon forest, I felt like the grand old place was asleep. But it would soon awaken, and when it did it could finally see and recognize me again. I loved these four kids deeply. May they find the truth and build the lives they want in the way they want.

I slapped Jamie's back.

All the weight of the past thirty years now felt to me as light as the sky over our heads.

At one time Jamie and I felt this land belonged to us. But you don't have to own it for it to be home. Moving freely, being what you want and feeling what you want and finding inspiration by what captivates you is what makes a place feel like home. There's no better salvation than finding your way home. Home should feel like the truth. And the truth had set me free.

Acknowledgements

Two influential writers, neither of whom I met in person, had a big impact on my writing and died during the creation of this book: Richard Wagamese, the Anishinaabe journalist and novelist; and Richard Sipe, the psychologist, activist, and former Benedictine friar. Both promoted decency and justice. Please read their important work.

Several editors and advisers were indispensable working on cultural sensitivity and readability. I appreciate your guidance, Adrienne Kerr, Scott Fraser, Shannon Whibbs, Sean Costello, Nancy and Sam Ifergan, Mike Aron, Dominic Farrell, Danielle Sinclair, and Herbie Barnes.

The commissioners of the *Final Report of the Truth and Reconciliation Commission* have created an invaluable resource that I hope will prevent history from repeating. Their work, especially *Canada's Residential Schools: The History, Part Two, 1939–2000*, inspired the Indian Agent–Gast communication found in this story. I encourage all Canadians to read the *Summary Report* of the TRC.

Kendra Martin, Randall Howard, Carl Brand, and Kirk Howard were instrumental, helpful, and patient with me on this project. Kathryn Lane's support was invaluable.

Special thanks to Alex Janvier, AOE, for speaking with me about his experiences and in allowing his quote to open the story.

While I wrote this book, Barbara Blaine, the founder of SNAP, the Survivors Network for those Abused by Priests, passed away. Her work carries on and SNAP continues to have a powerful impact. Thank you, Tim Lennon and assorted members of SNAP, for sharing with me and listening to me, and thank you to SNAP.

My parents were not like the parents in this story, and for that, I'm grateful.

I'm thankful to several priests who followed vocations beyond the Church and had a positive impact on my life, and on those I care about.

My old writing buddies continue to inspire me, even thirty years later. They are Tom Abray, Timothy S. Johnston, Rev. L. Smith, R. Morrow, and Paul Maurice.

My wife, Susan, is my first and best reader.